"The
Leah

She knew by the gleam in Mike's eyes and the hint of a smile on his lips that he was remembering their parting the night before. "Don't look at me that way. I know what you're thinking, but one kiss, particularly a stolen one, doesn't constitute a romance. Or even an attraction."

"True," he conceded. "And I'd even agree with that in this case, except for one thing." He paused and grinned, and she knew she was in trouble. "Last night when I kissed you, you kissed me back."

She opened her mouth to argue, but he was right. She had admitted weeks ago that she was attracted to him, but she had deluded herself into believing that it was nothing more than an impersonal physical attraction.

But it was more than that. Much more. That terrified her. Dear heaven, she couldn't have those kinds of feelings for Mike McCall.

But she did.

Dear Reader,

Special Edition welcomes you to a brand-new year of romance! As always, we are committed to providing you with captivating love stories that will take your breath away.

This January, Lisa Jackson wraps up her engrossing FOREVER FAMILY miniseries with *A Family Kind of Wedding*. THAT SPECIAL WOMAN! Katie Kinkaid has her hands full being an ace reporter—and a full-time mom. But when a sexy, mysterious Texas rancher crosses her path, her life changes forever!

In these next three stories, love conquers all. First, a twist of fate brings an adorably insecure heroine face-to-face with the reclusive millionaire of her dreams in bestselling author Susan Mallery's emotional love story, *The Millionaire Bachelor*. Next, Ginna Gray continues her popular series, THE BLAINES AND THE McCALLS OF CROCKETT, TEXAS, with *Meant for Each Other*. In this poignant story, Dr. Mike McCall heroically saves a life and wins the heart of an alluring colleague in the process. And onetime teenage sweethearts march down the wedding aisle in *I Take This Man—Again!* by Carole Halston.

Also this month, acclaimed historical author Leigh Greenwood debuts in Special Edition with *Just What the Doctor Ordered*— a heartwarming tale about a brooding doctor finding his heart in a remote mountain community. Finally, in *Prenuptial Agreement* by Doris Rangel, a rugged rancher marries for his son's sake, but he's about to fall in love for real....

I hope you enjoy January's selections. We wish you all the best for a happy new year!

Sincerely,
Karen Taylor Richman
Senior Editor

Please address questions and book requests to:
Silhouette Reader Service
U.S.: 3010 Walden Ave., P.O. Box 1325, Buffalo, NY 14269
Canadian: P.O. Box 609, Fort Erie, Ont. L2A 5X3

GINNA GRAY
MEANT FOR EACH OTHER

Silhouette®

SPECIAL EDITION®

Published by Silhouette Books

America's Publisher of Contemporary Romance

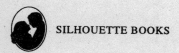 SILHOUETTE BOOKS

ISBN 0-373-24221-2

MEANT FOR EACH OTHER

Printed in U.S.A.

Books by Ginna Gray

Silhouette Special Edition

Golden Illusion #171
The Heart's Yearning #265
Sweet Promise #320
Cristen's Choice #373
*Fools Rush In #416
*Where Angels Fear #468
If There Be Love #528
*Once in a Lifetime #661
*A Good Man Walks In #722
*Building Dreams #792
*Forever #854
*Always #891
The Bride Price #973
Alissa's Miracle #1117
*Meant for Each Other #1221

Silhouette Romance

The Gentling #285
The Perfect Match #311
Heart of the Hurricane #338
Images #352
First Love, Last Love #374
The Courtship of Dani #417
Sting of the Scorpion #826

Silhouette Books

Silhouette Christmas Stories 1987
"Season of Miracles"

*The Blaines and the McCalls of Crockett, Texas

GINNA GRAY

A native Houstonian, Ginna Gray admits that, since childhood, she has been a compulsive reader as well as a head-in-the-clouds dreamer. Long accustomed to expressing her creativity in tangible ways—Ginna also enjoys painting and needlework—she finally decided to try putting her fantasies and wild imaginations down on paper. The result? The mother of two now spends eight hours a day as a full-time writer.

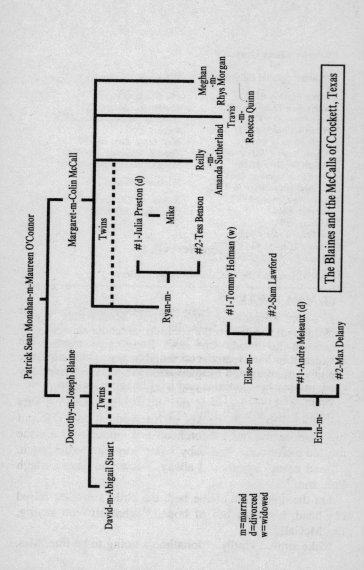

The Blaines and the McCalls of Crockett, Texas

Patrick Sean Monahan-m-Maureen O'Connor

Dorothy-m-Joseph Blaine   Margaret-m-Colin McCall

David-m-Abigail Stuart   Twins

Twins

Meghan
-m-
Rhys Morgan

Travis
-m-
Rebecca Quinn

Reilly
-m-
Amanda Sutherland

#1-Julia Preston (d)

Mike

#2-Tess Benson

Ryan-m-

Elise-m-

#1-Tommy Holman (w)

#2-Sam Lawford

Erin-m-

#1-Andre Meleaux (d)

#2-Max Delany

m=married d=divorced w=widowed

Chapter One

The crisis had passed.

The peaceful way the baby slept confirmed that, but for his own peace of mind Mike had to check. He pressed the stethoscope to the infant's back, moving the chest piece an inch or so every few seconds, listening. Gradually, the sound of the baby's unimpeded breathing and the steady beat of the tiny heart brought a smile to his mouth.

Sighing, Mike removed the stethoscope from his ears and stuck it into the pocket of his medical coat. He put his hand on the child's forehead and smoothed back the tousled blond curls. The baby's skin was cool to the touch. "Good going, Jonathon. I always knew you were a tough little nut."

On the other side of the bed, the child's mother raised her head, her eyes full of hope. "What are you saying, Dr. McCall?"

Mike smiled kindly. "Jonathon's going to be fine, Mrs.

Cunningham. The worst is over. Barring further complications, which I don't anticipate, in another few days you can probably take him home.''

"Oh, thank God. Thank *God!*" Mrs. Cunningham covered her face with her hands and burst into tears.

Giving comfort was second nature to Mike. Without a thought, he skirted the end of the bed and patted the woman's shoulder. Immediately, she turned and grabbed his hand, holding it between hers, and looked up at him with abject gratitude.

"Thank you, Dr. McCall. Thank you, thank you, thank you. You saved our baby's life.''

"Mrs. Cunningham, you don't have to thank me. This is why I became a pediatrician—to help kids like Jonathon. Trust me, seeing your baby on the road to recovery is as much a thrill for me as it is for you.''

Nearly hysterical with relief and fatigue, Mrs. Cunningham continued to babble her thanks. It took another five minutes for Mike to calm the woman and persuade her to get some rest on the rollaway bed beside her son's crib.

When he finally left the hospital room he paused in the hallway outside the door and leaned against the wall. Now that the crisis had passed, weariness overwhelmed him. Closing his eyes, he rubbed the back of his neck and rolled his shoulders, groaning as the taut muscles and joints relaxed.

"Dr. McCall, may I have a word with you, please?''

Mike recognized the voice instantly. At first, though, he thought that exhaustion had caused him to hallucinate. Surprise shot through him when he opened his eyes and saw Dr. Leah Albright hurrying toward him.

It was the first time since he had joined the staff at St. Francis Hospital that she had sought him out. On a few rare occasions, when she had delivered a baby who was in trouble and no other pediatrician was available, she'd been forced to consult with him, but at those times she'd had him paged or had her nurse call him, and their meetings invariably had been short and to the point. The rest of the time she seemed to go out of her way to avoid him.

Even as tired as Mike was, he noted her graceful carriage and the way her lab coat fluttered around her fantastic legs. A smile tugged at his mouth. Dr. Leah Albright was one gorgeous woman.

As she drew near he straightened away from the wall and ran his hand through his hair. "Sure thing. What's up, Doctor?"

She stopped in front of him, and at once Mike felt that zing of electricity he always experienced whenever she was near. If she felt it, too, she didn't show it. Her manner was as crisp and reserved as always.

"Dr. McCall, are you aware that my half brother is here in the hospital, critically ill with leukemia? That he needs a bone marrow transplant?"

If Mike hadn't been so tired he might have chuckled. As usual, she came straight to the point—no shilly-shallying, no polite small talk, no pretense of friendship. "Yeah. I'd heard that from one of the nurses. How's he doing?"

"His condition is deteriorating daily."

"I'm sorry to hear that. So, who's his doctor?" It was a common enough question, especially among the medical community, but it seemed to irritate her.

"Dr. Sweeney."

Mike nodded. "Good, good. He's a fine man. The best."

"Yes, I know. That's why I took Quinton to him," she said impatiently. "Are you also aware of the plea Henry Scarborough issued on Quinton's behalf, asking all the doctors and nurses and the rest of the hospital staff to be tested as possible bone marrow donors?"

"Yes, I am." He'd read the hospital administrator's memo almost a week ago, but he'd been so busy trying to save baby Jonathon he'd barely given it a thought since then.

"I see. Do you have some sort of objection to being tested? Or to the procedure?"

He blinked, taken aback. "No, of course not."

"Then why haven't you done so? Practically everyone else on the hospital staff has been tested. Even the cafeteria personnel and the janitorial crew."

Anger vibrated in her voice, which surprised him. Leah Albright was known for her reserve and control. Mike ran his hand through his hair again. "Look, I'm sorry about that. It wasn't deliberate. I just haven't had the time."

"Haven't had the time? My brother's life is at stake, Doctor."

"So was my patient's," he retorted with the first hint of annoyance. Mike was normally good-natured and slow to anger, but he was bone weary and in no mood to defend himself from unwarranted accusations, even if they did come from the most attractive woman he'd ever met. "I've spent the last five days trying to save a ten-month-old baby. In that time I haven't slept more than two hours at a stretch or sat down to a decent meal. You'll have to excuse me if I didn't take time out, but as a doctor you must know that my patient had to come first."

Her aggression evaporated. She even had the grace to look embarrassed.

"I see. I'm sorry, Doctor. I didn't realize."

Mike waved aside her apology, already regretting the flare of temper. "That's okay. I shouldn't have snapped at you. I'm just tired. Look, I know you're concerned about your brother. I've got a brother myself. And two sisters. If their lives were threatened I'd be just as upset."

"Does that mean you'll be tested?" she pressed.

He sighed. "Sure."

She seemed to sag with relief. "Oh, thank you. Thank you so much. If you hurry you can make it to the lab before it closes for the day."

"What? You expect me to do it *now*? This *minute*? Look, I'm sorry, but I'm dead on my feet. Right now all I want is a quick shower and about twelve straight hours of uninterrupted sleep. I'll be happy to cooperate and do whatever I can, but it'll have to be tomorrow."

"Please, Doctor, wait!" Leah grabbed his arm when he started to walk away. "I know we're not exactly friends and I have no right to pressure you, but this is so important. Every minute is critical for Quinton. Please. Won't you do it today?"

"Look, Dr. Albright—"

"Please. I'm begging you. Please."

Her fingers tightened on Mike's arm until her fingernails dug into his flesh through his shirt and lab coat, but he barely noticed. He was too stunned to see her eyes fill with tears. Never in a million years had he expected to see Dr. Leah Albright all emotional and weepy.

Of course the reaction was his undoing. As it did his father and all the other men in his family, the sight of a woman's tears turned him to mush. He tried, but with her staring at him that way, her blue eyes shimmering through that watery wall banked against her lower eyelids, how could he refuse?

He exhaled a long sigh. "All right, Doctor, you win. I'll go today, since it's so important to you."

"Oh, thank you. Thank you so much. I can't tell you how grateful I am. I'll be forever in your debt. And if I can ever be of help to you with one of your patients, just let me know."

A wry grimace lifted one corner of Mike's mouth. This seemed to be his day for receiving gushing thanks from overwrought women. Though gratitude wasn't exactly what he wanted from Leah Albright, he supposed it was an improvement over the cool indifference he'd been getting from her for the past two years.

"Hey, no problem. I'll go right now."

He took a step, then hesitated and turned back. She watched him with such anxious hope that he almost flinched. "Look" he said softly. "I know this is none of my business, but I'd advise you not to get your hopes up too high. As a doctor you have to know the chances are astronomical that you'll find a donor among the hospital staff." Which was precisely why he hadn't been too concerned about failing to get himself tested before now. "It would be a miracle if you found someone from such a small sample of people who came even remotely close to matching your brother's human leukocyte antigens. If I were you, I'd try the National Donor Registry. They're your best hope."

"Yes, I know. We already have, but so far with no luck."

"I see. Well, I wouldn't give up," Mike said kindly. "New people register with them every day. There's always a chance that a match for your brother will eventually turn up."

"I know. But Quinton doesn't have all that long to wait." Leah sniffed and wiped the tears from her eyes with her fingertips. "So in the meantime I'm going to continue to beat the bushes and recruit help from everyone I know. I love my brother very much, and I'm going to do everything in my power to keep him alive."

"I understand. In your place I'd probably do the same."

A strange look came over Leah's face. Then she backed away a step and gave a fluttery gesture not at all typical of her. "Yes, well, uh, thank you again, Dr. McCall. I, uh, I'd better get back to my brother now."

Mike watched her walk away and shook his head. That was one beautiful, complicated lady.

He turned and headed for the lab with a feeling of sadness and futility. This was a waste of time.

But what the hell. If it made her feel better, why not?

Leah felt awful. Inside her, duty and love warred with guilt, and the turmoil was eating her alive.

The battle had been going on without letup all afternoon, ever since she had gotten Mike McCall to agree to her request. Not even when she had stood beside Quinton's bed and gazed at his pale face had she been able to completely shake off the pangs of conscience.

What she was doing was wrong, ethically and morally. No matter how she tried to rationalize, she couldn't escape that truth.

She turned into her driveway and brought her car to a stop behind her father's rented Mercedes. But what choice did she have? Quinton's life was at stake. She couldn't—*wouldn't*—let him die. Gritting her teeth, she climbed from the car and headed up the brick walkway. If she had to lie, cheat and steal to save her brother she would.

The aroma of one of Cleo's delicious meals greeted Leah the moment she stepped through the front door. An instant later the motherly woman bustled through the swinging kitchen door at the back of the central hallway, wiping her hands on her apron.

"Ah, Miss Leah, I thought I heard you come in."

Leah gave her a tired smile. "Good evening, Cleo." She laid her medical bag on the seat of the hall tree and started to shrug out of her coat.

"Here now, let me take your things for you," Cleo said. "I swear, the hours you keep it's a wonder you've got the energy left to stand."

Leah surrendered to the elderly housekeeper's fussing

with a tolerant smile. When Leah had come to live with her father after her mother's death, Cleo had taken the grieving fifteen-year-old under her wing. In the past eighteen years Leah had received more attention and affection from the elderly housekeeper than she ever had from her father and stepmother.

When Leah had completed her medical training and taken Quinton and moved to Houston, it had seemed only natural that Cleo go with them. Not even Julia had objected. They had agreed that Cleo would continue to work for Julia and Peter whenever they were in Dallas, but since that occurred so seldom, she spent far more time with Leah and Quinton than she did with the elder Albrights.

Leah sniffed the air appreciatively. "Mmm, something smells heavenly. I hope I haven't ruined dinner by being so late."

"No. It's nothing that won't keep for a bit while you put your feet up and unwind. If the missus says anything I'll tell her that dinner isn't ready yet. Not much she can do about that." Cleo leaned close and lowered her voice to barely above a whisper. "But if I were you, I'd get myself in there right away. She's been in a snit that you weren't here for cocktails."

"Thanks, Cleo."

Leah patted the woman's shoulder and headed for the living room, shaking her head. Nothing, not even a family crisis, was allowed to disrupt Julia's lifestyle.

She put up with Cleo's occasional insubordination only because the housekeeper had been with the family so long—and because she knew what a jewel she had. Not only did the woman work magic in a kitchen, but she knew, down to the last calorie, what it took to maintain Julia's size-six figure.

Leah's mouth twisted. At least her father and step-mother cared enough about their son to drop everything and hurry home when she had called and told them of Quinton's condition. Considering how much they enjoyed their jet-setting lifestyle, that was saying a lot, she supposed.

Julia looked up when Leah walked into the room. "Darling. Thank goodness you're home at last. Did you speak to Mike?"

As always, her stepmother was a picture of elegance. This evening she was attired in a mauve silk dress that, for all its simplicity, probably cost the earth; her blond tinted hair was perfectly coiffed and her nails and makeup were impeccable. Yet there was a hint of fear in her eyes, and for once an anxious furrow had been allowed to crease her brow.

Immediately, Leah felt a pang of remorse for her less-than-kind thoughts. Julia was self-absorbed and thoroughly spoiled, but in her own way, she did love her son.

"Yes, I talked to him." With a sigh, Leah sank onto a chair.

"What did he say?"

"Julia, love, let the child catch her breath," Peter Albright admonished gently, which earned him a pout from his wife. He turned to Leah with a fond smile. "May I get you a drink, my dear? A sherry, perhaps?"

"Thank you, Dad. That would be lovely. All in all, it's been a rough day."

Though she had never felt close to her father, Leah nevertheless experienced a surge of pride as she watched him stroll to the antique buffet that served as a bar.

Peter Albright was one of those men who would always turn female heads. Still slender in his early sixties, he had the elegant carriage of a much younger man, a thick head of silver hair, classic features and a perpetual tan that set off his startling blue eyes.

Those eyes were the only feature that she had inherited

from him. In every other way she looked exactly like her mother. Though her father had been kind and generous with her, Leah often wondered if that resemblance was why there was this distance between them. He adored Quinton, and even though he and Julia spent far more time abroad than at home, the relationship between father and son was warm and loving.

Sighing, Leah dismissed the futile thoughts. They inevitably led nowhere, and she was feeling awful enough without going down that road. Leaning her head against the high chair back, she closed her eyes.

She should have known that Julia would not allow her a respite.

"Honestly, Leah, I'll never understand why you insist on having a career. Especially one as grueling and, well, as messy and inconvenient as medicine."

There was a pause, and even with her eyes closed Leah could picture her stepmother's little shudder of distaste.

"The demands on your time are simply outrageous. Your patients call at all hours of the day or night and off you go. Why, you're at their beck and call like some servant."

Leah opened one eye and gave her stepmother a droll look. "I'm an obstetrician, Julia. I can't very well tell a mother in labor to wait until office hours to deliver, now can I?"

Julia firmed her mouth and sniffed. "That's another thing. I don't know how you can bear to do what you do. Delivering babies is so…so earthy. And it isn't as though you need to work. You have the money from your mother's estate and the trust fund your father set up for you. And if you hadn't been so stubborn you could have had a wonderful marriage."

"Julia, please. Let's not get into that again."

"Well, I'm sorry, but I think it's such a terrible waste.

Lyle was a wonderful young man and suitable in every way. I'll never understand why you broke off your engagement to him.''

Leah grimaced. ''Suitable'' to Julia meant he came from a wealthy, socially prominent family. ''I told you, Lyle decided he didn't want to be married to a doctor.''

Actually, that wasn't the entire truth. Lyle had been fine with the idea at first.

They had met in med school, and she had been bowled over by his good looks and charm. Within three months they had become engaged. Leah had thought she'd found the perfect mate and dreamed of them opening a practice together. However, within a year things had begun to sour.

She had excelled academically and been at the top of her class, whereas Lyle had barely squeaked by. In the past, family influence had opened doors for him, and everything he wanted had come easily. He had not been prepared for the grind of medical school. When he flunked out halfway through their second year, he had angrily demanded that she drop out, as well. Unable to abide the idea of her succeeding where he had failed, he had given her an ultimatum: she could have him, or she could become a doctor, but not both.

Though heartbroken, Leah had returned his ring.

Since then she had discovered that most men, no matter how successful, were threatened by her intelligence and competence. As a result she had kept an emotional distance between her and the few men she had dated. Until she met one who was secure enough within himself to accept a woman as an equal she would remain single.

''Can you blame him?'' Julia retorted. ''Just look at the impossible hours you keep. No man wants to be married to a woman who is never there.''

''Then breaking off the engagement was the right decision, wasn't it? In any case, I really don't want to discuss the matter any more, so could we please drop it?''

"Leah is right, darling," Peter said, handing his daughter a small cut-crystal glass. "She made her choice years ago, and no matter how we feel, we must accept it. And to be perfectly honest, given the state of our son's health, I, for one, have found having a doctor in the family to be something of a blessing."

"Well, I suppose that is true," Julia conceded grudgingly. "At least she understands all that medical mumbo jumbo. And she can deal with Mike for us." She arched an elegant eyebrow at Leah. "So, tell us. What happened with him today?"

"When I brought the matter to his attention he was quite willing to help. I checked with the lab before I left the hospital. He was tested this afternoon."

"Thank God for that."

"Do you think he suspects anything?" Peter asked.

Julia gave a little moan, and her hand fluttered to her throat. "Don't even *say* that."

"No, I don't think so." Leah ignored her stepmother's outburst. "At first I was afraid that maybe he did and that was why he hadn't been tested, but it turns out that he was working around the clock the last five days, trying to save an infant, and he simply didn't have time."

"Yes, well, the important thing is, it's done. Now we just have to wait and see if his HAJs or whatever you call them are compatible with Quinton's."

"Julia, I told you, the term is 'HLAs.' Human leukocyte antigens. They're the proteins in the immune system that recognize and reject foreign tissue."

"Whatever. As long as Mike's match Quinton's I don't care what you call them."

Frowning, Leah looked down at her glass and ran her finger around the rim. "About that—I still don't feel right about this. Maybe, well, maybe we should tell Mike the truth.''

"*What?* Have you lost your *mind?* Oh, my Lord. I don't *believe* this!'' Julia sent her husband a desperate look. "Talk to her, Peter.''

"Leah, we've been all through this and you agreed. This is how it must be.''

"I know, I know. But it just doesn't seem right.''

"Right? I don't *care* if it's *right* or not,'' Julia insisted. "All I care about is saving Quinton's life. I should think that would be *your* main concern, too.''

"It is. Of course it is. But...'' Leah set her empty glass on the end table beside her chair and rose and walked to the window. She crossed her arms over her midriff and absently rubbed her elbows as she stared out through gathering dusk at the rose garden that occupied the side yard. It was late winter, and the scene was barren and forlorn, the pruned bushes bare and sticklike. Somehow the sight suited her mood.

"But what?'' her stepmother demanded impatiently.

Leah looked over her shoulder, her glance sliding from her father to Julia. "I just think that Dr. McCall has a right to know that Quinton is his half brother.''

Chapter Two

"*No!*" Julia shot up off the sofa and glared at Leah. "No! We are not going to tell him. Absolutely not! I won't hear of it. Anyway, why should we? You said yourself that most donors never know who received their bone marrow. Why should this case be any different?"

"Because it is. To start with, Mike didn't volunteer to be a donor. We sought out him precisely because he is related to Quinton. If we're lucky and he is a match, we're asking him to save the life of his half brother—a brother he doesn't even know exists. It's deceitful to keep that information from him."

"I don't care! What Mike doesn't know won't hurt him."

"What about Quinton? Don't you think he'll be curious about the person who saved his life? How do you suppose he'll feel if he ever learns that it was his half brother? How will he feel even to learn that he *has* a half brother?"

"He won't find out. You swore you'd never tell him, and your father and I certainly won't. Isn't that right, darling?" Julia said, turning to her husband for support.

"If that's what you want, dearest," Peter soothed. "Although Leah does have a point. You know how inquisitive Quinton is. If he ever finds out that he has an older brother and we've been keeping it from him all these years, there's no telling how he will react."

"He won't find out," Julia insisted. "We'll simply let him think his benefactor is a stranger who listed with the National Donor Registry. He knows the identity of those people is confidential."

Leah ground her teeth. "Julia, the more lies you tell the worse things get. The truth always seems to come out eventually. Even if it doesn't, I'm just not comfortable with this. I think we should tell Mike and Quinton the truth."

"And what if Mike refuses to help just to strike out at me for leaving him and his father?"

"You don't know that will happen."

"Oh, I know, all right. Believe me, I know." Julia began to pace, twisting her hands together. "My first husband was a hard man. I wounded his precious male ego when I left him. To a man like Ryan McCall, that's unforgivable. There's no knowing what kind of lies he's told Mike about me. Ryan is sure to have poisoned his mind against me by now."

If he has, who could blame him? Leah thought. Not only had Julia walked out on her first husband when he was struggling to keep his business afloat, but she had gone straight into the arms of another man—a much older, wealthy man. Three years later, when she had met Leah's father, Julia had been a rich widow.

At first Leah had thought that Julia married her father for his money, as well, but gradually she realized that the two were devoted to each other. In Peter Albright, Julia had apparently found her true love—a handsome, wealthy man who adored her and found her self-centered nature utterly captivating. He not only indulged, but shared her passion for, the jet-setting lifestyle.

"Julia, I'll admit that I don't know Mike McCall very well, but he doesn't seem like the vindictive type to me."

"That shows how little you know. I'm telling you, the boy always was just like his father." Julia sniffed and assumed a wounded look. "Neither Ryan nor Mike ever cared two cents about me, about what *I* wanted. If Mike thought he could hurt me through Quinton, I'm positive he would."

The whine in her stepmother's voice set Leah's teeth on edge, but she managed to keep her voice calm. "Julia, you haven't even seen your elder son in twenty-five years. You can't possibly know how he will react to this situation. Dr. McCall has a sterling reputation. Everyone at the hospital admires and respects him, and his patients adore him. I don't think he'll refuse to help his own half brother, no matter how he feels about you."

"And what if you're wrong?" Julia challenged. "Are you willing to risk it? Do you want to take that kind of chance with Quinton's life?"

Leah opened her mouth, hesitated, then closed it again. Frustration consumed her—her conscience pulling her one way; fear for her brother, another.

She turned back to the window and hugged herself tightly. Quinton was the most important person in her world. She might have been sixteen when he was born, but from the beginning she had been more of a mother to him than Julia.

Her stepmother couldn't be right about Mike. He was a doctor, for heaven's sake. A man dedicated to saving lives. Surely he wouldn't let a boy die to spite his mother. Would he?

"Well?" Julia prodded. "Do you want to take that risk?"

Leah closed her eyes. Finally she released a long sigh. "No. No, I suppose not."

A few days later Mike stormed into Henry Scarborough's office. He marched across the carpet to the desk, slapped his hands on the top and glared. "Your secretary said this was urgent. I'm telling you right now, Henry, it had better be. I left a waiting room full of sick kids to come running over here." Though easygoing, Mike had a temper that, when roused, was formidable. Interrupting him when he was with a patient was guaranteed to get explosive results.

"I assure you, this matter is extremely urgent. Otherwise, I wouldn't have summoned you in the middle of the afternoon." With one finger Henry pushed a folder across the desk toward Mike. "The blood workups are in."

"What blood workups? What the hell are you talking about?"

"He's talking about the test I persuaded you to take."

Mike snapped his head around toward the voice, and for the first time he saw the two people sitting on the sofa on the other side of the office.

"Dr. Albright. Dr. Sweeney. I'm sorry. I didn't see you there." Which said a lot about the state of his temper, he thought with a flash of wry humor. Normally, he could sense Leah's presence if she got within a hundred yards of him.

"That's all right. You were rather distracted," Dr. Sweeney said, fighting back a grin.

"Yes, well…" As Mike straightened, Leah's comment registered. Only then did he notice that she was sitting forward on the edge of the sofa, twisting her hands together in her lap. "Is something wrong? Oh, no, don't tell me there was some foul-up with the test I took. Is that what this is about?"

"No. No, it's nothing like that," Leah insisted.

"Hardly."

Henry chuckled, and Mike looked back at the hospital administrator.

"Actually, I have good news. It turns out that you are a perfect donor match for Dr. Albright's brother."

"*What?* Are you serious?"

Henry Scarborough smiled at Mike's astonishment, looking as smug as though he himself had performed a miracle. "Completely serious. Your HLAs are a perfect match for Quinton Albright's."

Mike sank onto one of the chairs in front of the desk. Too stunned to speak, he looked from Henry to Dr. Sweeney to Leah.

She watched him, chewing at her lower lip, her fingers still twisting and untwisting in her lap. Raw hope glittered in her eyes.

The sight touched Mike, but when he saw the flicker of fear there, too, he felt as though someone had punched him in the gut. Dear Lord. Was she really worried that he might refuse to help her brother—provided he really *was* a viable donor?

His gaze switched to Dr. Sweeney again. "Are you sure there hasn't been some mistake? It just doesn't seem possible."

"There's no mistake. I'll admit, serendipitous matches such as this are rare, but they do happen now and then. Once, after checking all his relatives and every registry in the country, a man's fiancée turned out to be his perfect match." Dr. Sweeney spread his hands wide. "These things happen. When they do, I've found it best to not question good fortune.''

"Yeah, I suppose you're right.'' Mike looked at Leah and managed a shaken smile. "Seems your determination paid off.''

"Then you will be a donor?''

"Of course. I didn't think there was a prayer I'd turn out to be a match, but I'm happy I did, for your sake. And your brother's, of course.''

The older doctor rubbed his hands together. "Good, good. Now then, when can we schedule the transplant?''

"Well, I'll have to have my receptionist clear my calendar and find someone to cover for me, but I'd say in…oh, three or four days.''

"Three or four days! But—''

"Calm down, Leah,'' Dr. Sweeney soothed, putting a hand on her arm. "There are some procedures I must perform to get Quinton ready for the surgery. Three or four days will do fine. Shall we tentatively plan on Friday morning at eight?''

"Suits me.''

Dr. Sweeney excused himself to make rounds, and Leah and Mike followed him out of the administrator's office. In the hall she hesitated, then turned to him and touched his hand. Her vivid blue eyes shimmered with unshed tears as they looked into his. "Thank you, Doctor, for wh—''

"'Mike.''"

"Wh-what?''

"Call me 'Mike.''"

"Oh. Well, uh, all right…Mike. I can't tell you how grateful I am, how grateful my whole family will be when I tell them what you're doing.''

"I'm happy to help, Leah.'' Her eyes widened slightly at his use of her first name, but she didn't object.

"Please know, Doc—uh, Mike, that if I can ever do anything for you—anything at all—you only have to ask."

"Well, now that you mention it, there is one thing."

"Just name it."

Smiling, Mike leaned in closer and murmured, "Have dinner with me tonight."

"D-dinner? Oh! I...I, uh, I'm sorry, I can't."

"Other plans?"

"No. Yes! That is, I need to stay with Quinton."

"How about tomorrow night?"

"Well, you see, my parents have just flown in to be with Quinton and, well..."

She looked so flustered Mike would have laughed if it hadn't been so obvious that she was horrified at the thought of going out with him. So much for his fatal charm with the ladies. He knew he should let it go, but he wasn't quite willing to do that. He might never get another chance like this one. "I see. Then how about a rain check? I tell you what, when the transplant is complete and your brother is out of the woods, we'll go out and celebrate. How about that?"

"I, uh, I suppose that would be all right."

"Good. Then it's a date."

She gave him a reluctant nod and backed away a step. "I really do have to go now. I need to tell Quinton the good news."

"Yeah, and I'd better get back to my patients before my receptionist quits," Mike agreed, but when she turned to leave he remained where he was and watched her hurry away, his expression thoughtful.

Well. That was a first. He'd never had to coerce a woman into going out with him before. He'd backed her into a corner and made it damn near impossible for her to say no. Not without appearing to be one colossal ingrate.

It hadn't been fair of him, he supposed. Probably he

oúght to call her and let her off the hook. The woman obviously didn't want to have anything to do with him.

Shrugging, Mike turned and headed back to his office. What the hell. The least she could do was share a meal with him. Surely a little bone marrow rated that much.

Once she was out of Mike's sight, Leah ducked into the first ladies' room she found. She went straight to the line of washbasins, ran cold water over her wrists and splashed some on her face. Patting her cheeks with a paper towel, she stared at her reflection in the mirror above the sinks. She was flushed and her heart was racing and her eyes were overly bright. Mike had caught her completely by surprise. Never in her wildest dreams had she expected him to ask her out.

The mere thought made her heart skip a beat. Mike McCall and her? Impossible.

She shuddered to think what he would say if he ever learned of her connection to his mother.

She could only hope that by the time Quinton recovered Mike would have forgotten about calling in that rain check. If not, she would just have to makes excuses until he gave up. She couldn't go out with Julia's son.

Impatiently, she told herself to stop worrying. The invitation had probably just been an impulse. She would deal with the problem when and if it came up, which it probably wouldn't. Right now she had to get a grip on herself and go tell Quinton the good news.

Pressing the damp towel to her throat, she closed her eyes, drew several deep breaths and willed her racing pulse to calm.

Ten minutes later when she entered her brother's room, Leah was once again in control of her emotions.

Mike eased opened the back door of his parents' house and stuck his head inside the kitchen. Spotting Tess standing at the stove, he grinned and gave a low wolf whistle. "Hiya, gorgeous."

His stepmother whirled around, holding a wooden spoon in one hand. Her eyes lit up when she spied him. "Mike!" Opening her arms wide, she rushed across the room and, spoon and all, enveloped him in a hug the instant he stepped inside. "Sweetheart, it's so good to see you. It's been weeks. We were beginning to think you had forgotten us."

"I know, and I'm sorry, but I've been snowed under lately. Half my patients have the flu, and it seems that all those who don't have come down with chicken pox."

"Oh, the poor darlings. And you, you must have been worked to death."

"It was hectic for a while, but nothing I couldn't handle. Really," he added, seeing her worried expression.

Not convinced, Tess searched his face, her eyes full of motherly concern. Mike pretended to scowl. "Hey, don't fret, Tess. I'm fine. Couldn't be better. Okay?"

Despite his protest, her concern warmed him. It was typical of Tess. She was a gentle, loving, nurturing woman, and he blessed the day that she had come into their lives.

Though his father adored Tess, at first, out of bitterness, he had tried like hell to resist her charms. Not Mike. From the time he had met her as a thirteen-year-old kid, he'd been drawn to her softness and her giving nature. He and his dad had been on their own for eight years, and he had been starved for feminine attention and a mother's love, and Tess, bless her, had taken him into her heart without reservation. She might not have borne him, as she had his two sisters and brother, but in his heart she was his mother—the only one he had ever known, or at least the only one he could remember.

After an inspection satisfied her that he wasn't about to keel over from exhaustion, Tess smiled tenderly and patted his cheek. "If you say so. Anyway, I'm glad you came by. We don't see nearly enough of you these days."

"Yeah, well, the feeling is mutual." Mike raised his head and sniffed. "Something sure smells good. I hope there's enough for one more."

"There's always enough for you. You know that." She put the spoon down on the counter and linked her arm through his. "Now, come on, let's go into the den. Your dad will be so pleased to see you. So will the kids."

Mike's father sat in his favorite chair reading the newspaper. Eight-year-old Katy lay sprawled on her belly on the floor in front of him, her gaze glued to the television.

"Look who's here," Tess said.

Mike's baby sister tossed an indifferent glance over her shoulder, did a double take and shot up like an uncoiling spring. "Mike!" she squealed, and launched herself into his arms.

"Hey, Katydid! How's it going?" He whirled around with the child, and she squealed again with delight.

Mike's father lowered his newspaper and got to his feet, a smile softening his harshly handsome face.

"When did you get here? Are you staying for dinner? Will you play checkers with me after?" Katy asked.

"Katy, let your brother catch his breath before you start bombarding him with questions," their father ordered.

Ryan clapped a hand on his son's shoulder, and when Mike turned his head and met his gaze he felt that old familiar tug of love and admiration for this strong, good man who was both his father and his best friend. A few wrinkles lined his father's face these days and his hair was going gray, but at fifty-five, Ryan McCall was still lean and fit and ruggedly handsome.

"Hi, Dad."

"'Evening, Son. It's good to see you. You are staying for dinner, I hope.''

"You bet. I wouldn't miss a chance at Tess's cooking. Just the smell is driving me nuts."

"Mmm, you and me both."

Ryan glanced at his wife, and they exchanged a look so full of love and unspoken communion that Mike felt a twinge of envy. His father and stepmother had a special relationship, a sort of bonding of souls that you rarely saw. Even after sixteen years of marriage the sexual tension between them was so strong the air practically crackled with it when they were in the same room.

"Well, you're going to have to wait a bit," she informed them. "Dinner won't be ready for another half hour."

Ryan gave Mike's shoulder another pat and nodded toward the bar in the corner. "If you want something to tide you over, there are beer and soft drinks in the fridge and the usual assortment of hard stuff. Help yourself."

Mike was behind the bar, bending to inspect the contents of the small refrigerator, when a commotion erupted in the hallway just outside the room. Seconds later the elder of Mike's sisters, sixteen-year-old Molly, burst into the den. Dogging her heels and making sappy faces at the back of her head came their brother.

"Stop it, you little dweeb, or I'm going to slap you silly."

Thirteen-year-old Ethan was not in the least intimidated. He danced around her, weaving and bobbing, thumbs stuck in his ears, fingers wagging, a taunting expression on his face.

"'Molly and Steven, sittin' in a tree, K-I-S-S-I-N-G,'" he chanted in a tormenting singsong.

"Oh, that is *so* immature."

"'First came love, then came marriage, then came—'"

"Moth-er! Will you *please* make this brat *shut up?*"

"Ethan, behave yourself."

"'A baby in a baby carriage.'"

"All right, Ethan, that's enough," Ryan ordered in the quiet but firm voice that all the McCall children, Mike included, knew meant business. "Leave your sister alone."

"I was just singing a song. I wasn't doing nothing," the gangly boy insisted, giving his father a wounded look.

"You weren't doing *anything,*" the former schoolteacher in Tess corrected automatically. "And I want you to stop it right now."

"Aw, Mom—"

"You heard your mother."

"Shoot. A guy can't have any fun around here," Ethan groused, and flopped on the sofa in a sulk, his arms crossed over his scrawny chest.

"Ah, yes, the plaintive call of adolescence." Mike popped the tab on a soft drink. "I remember it well."

Molly swiveled her head around. "Mike! I didn't know you were here."

For a second Ethan jerked to attention, his eyes widening with excitement. Just as quickly he subdued the reaction, slumped back on his spine and strove to appear cool. Rolling his head on the sofa back he smiled lazily. "Yo, Mike. How's it going, man?"

"Great. Just great. So how's school?"

Ethan groaned.

Grinning, Mike tipped up the can of soft drink and took a long pull as he came out from behind the bar. He paused beside the sofa long enough to ruffle the boy's red hair, then he went to his sister and gave her a hug. "Hiya, beautiful. I swear, you're getting prettier by the day."

"Really? Do you mean that, or are you just teasing?"

Molly cast a baleful glance at her younger brother. "Like someone else I know."

"Sweetie, I'm dead serious. One of these days you're going to be as gorgeous as your mother."

Molly blushed, but it was easy to see that she was pleased.

"Hey, Mike, got any new jokes?"

"Oh, please. Does a goose go barefoot?" Tess said, chuckling.

"Honestly, Ethan, you are such a baby." Molly gave a sniff of pure disgust. "You know that Mike just makes up those corny jokes to entertain his sick patients."

"Yeah, right. Then why have I been listening to them ever since he was four years old?" Ryan muttered, but one corner of his mouth twitched.

"Sure I've got a joke. Knock, knock," Mike started.

"Who's there?"

"Cash."

"Cash who?"

"Gee, Ethan, I didn't realize you were some kind of nut."

The boy fell over on the sofa in a fit of giggles, while Molly rolled her eyes. Mike grinned at his groaning parents.

"Tell me one! Tell me one, Mike!" Katy jumped up and down, clapping her hands.

"Okay, munchkin. Here's yours. Knock, knock."

"Who's there?"

"Snow."

"Snow who?"

"Snow use asking me. I don't know."

The giggles from Katy and Ethan and his parents' groans all increased in volume, and Mike's grin widened.

"Mothhh-er, make them stop!" Molly wailed. "Steven

will be here any minute. I'll just die if they tell any of those awful jokes in front of him.''

''Steven?'' Mike looked at his sister, then his parents. ''Who's Steven?''

''Aw, he's just some geeky guy Molly's all goo-goo eyed over. She's always talking to him on the phone and mooning over his picture.''

''I don't do any such thing! And Steven is *not* a geek! And if you say anything to embarrass me when he comes to pick me up for our date, I swear I'll make you sorry, Ethan McCall.''

''Date? What do you mean, *date?* You're going out with a *boy?* All by *yourself?*''

''Of course with a boy. You don't have to make such a big deal of it. This is my first single date, but I've been double-dating for the past six months.''

''What! Why didn't anybody tell me?'' Mike felt as though he'd been punched in the gut. His little sister, out with some hormone-crazed adolescent? Not if he could help it.

''Maybe because we knew you'd go ballistic.''

''With good cause,'' Mike fired back. ''You're too young to be dating.''

Molly rolled her eyes. ''You see what I mean. You're as bad as Daddy.''

Mike turned an accusing look on his father. ''I can't believe you're allowing this.''

''Hey, I don't like it any more than you do, but I got outvoted. Her mother thinks it's okay.''

''It most certainly is *not* okay! Tess, what were you thinking? Why, she's just a baby.''

''I am *not* a baby. I'm almost seventeen!''

Mike snorted. ''Yeah, in another seven months. I don't like this. I don't like it one bit. Just what do you know about this young punk?''

"Mom!"

"Calm down, Molly. Everything will be fine." Tess sent her stepson a reproving look. "Mike, I know this is difficult for you and your father to accept, but Molly is growing up, and sixteen *is* old enough to date. I seem to recall that you dated at sixteen, just as soon as you got your driver's license."

"Yeah, well, that was different."

"No, dearest, it wasn't. I know you don't believe it, but you're just going to have to trust me on this." Smiling, Tess patted Mike's cheek. "Now, wipe that frown off your face, and when Steven comes to pick Molly up you be nice to him."

It wasn't easy. When the introductions were made Mike had to grit his teeth and force a smile as he shook the seventeen-year-old's hand. The kid was painfully shy—gangly and awkward, all hands and feet and bobbing Adam's apple. Mike might have felt sorry for him if he had been dating anyone else's sister. Before he could ask the kid any questions, Molly hustled him out the door.

"Don't worry. She'll be fine." Taking both Mike and his father by the arm, Tess steered them away from the window and toward the dinning room as Steven's battered pickup roared down the street. "Stop worrying. Molly is a sensible girl with a level head on her shoulders and a strong sense of right and wrong."

"It's not *her* behavior I'm worried about," Mike grumbled.

He was so unsettled he contributed little to the conversation over dinner beyond an occasional grunt or nod. He barely even tasted the delicious roast chicken and dressing that Tess had made. He couldn't help it. Anyway, it was a big-brother's prerogative to worry about his sister.

Mike supposed, technically speaking, he wasn't really Molly's brother. They weren't blood kin, anyway.

Molly was Tess's daughter from her first marriage, but her husband had died before she had even known she was expecting his child. Molly had been only a few months old when Tess and his father had married, and from that day forward, as far as Mike was concerned, Molly had been his baby sister. In his heart, she was as much his sister as Kate.

Mike spent so much time fretting over Molly he almost forgot the reason he had come over. Halfway through coffee and dessert, he made the announcement as casually as possible.

"By the way, just so you'll know, I'm taking a few days off this coming week."

"Good. You need a vacation."

"Tess is right. You work too hard. It'll do you good to get away for a while. Where are you going?"

"Well, actually, I'm not going anywhere.... I'm going to donate bone marrow on Friday."

Tess's fork stopped halfway to her mouth. "What did you say?"

"I'm donating bone marrow," he repeated, keeping his gaze on his food and his voice matter-of-fact. "Dr. Albright's younger brother has leukemia. He's critical. His only chance is a transplant. It's the darnedest thing—a million-to-one miracle, really—but my HLAs match his perfectly."

"Dr. Albright," Tess said tentatively. "That's the young woman doctor you told us about, isn't it?"

"Yes."

"The one who won't give you the time of day, right?"

His father's bluntness came as no surprise to Mike. Nor did the slight edge to his voice. Ryan McCall loved Tess more than life itself. She had made him happy beyond his wildest dreams. Still, every now and then traces of the old bitterness toward Mike's mother, and women as a whole, surfaced.

"Yeah, well, there's no accounting for taste," Mike replied with a grin. "The point is, her brother needs my help."

"Is this procedure dangerous?" Tess tried to appear calm, but her hand shook as she reached for her coffee cup.

"Nah, not really. Not for me, at any rate. From my side, it's fairly simple. After the doctors harvest my marrow I'll have to stay in the hospital for a few days while my body recovers and regenerates marrow. That's all. It'll be touch-and-go for Dr. Albright's brother, though."

"Are you sure you want to do this?" Ryan watched his son, his face harsh with concern.

"A seventeen-year-old kid will die if I don't, Dad."

"Can't they get anyone else?"

"Apparently not. They've been trying to find someone for weeks with no luck. I'm the boy's only hope."

"I see." Ryan thought for a moment, then said decisively, "Reilly and I were going to the Dallas Home Show tomorrow, but I'll have my secretary cancel my reservations so Tess and I can be there."

"Whoa, wait a minute. That's not necessary. There's no need for either of you to be there. Look, I know how important the Dallas Home Show is to your business. I don't want you to miss that. Besides, I swear to you, the risks for me are minimal."

A frown creased Ryan's brow. "You're sure about that?"

"Hey, I'm a doctor. Remember? You just go on to Dallas. I'll be fine."

Tess reached across the table and put her hand on her husband's arm. "Do as Mike says, darling. And don't worry. I'll be there with him."

"What? No, really, Tess. That's not necessary."

She gave him a level look, one he knew brooked no argument.

"Nevertheless, Michael, I *will* be there."

Chapter Three

Friday morning, Leah entered her brother's hospital room before daylight. They wouldn't be taking him to surgery for another hour and a half, but she had spent a restless night, tossing and turning, too keyed up to sleep, and she hadn't been able to bear waiting at home a moment longer.

Leah stood at Quinton's side and gazed down at him through the plastic bubble that surrounded his bed. It hurt her to see him so isolated, but it was vital for his protection.

Over the past few days, in preparation for surgery, he had been given massive and aggressive immunosuppression therapy. The process would help to reduce the possibility of his body rejecting the donor tissue, but at the same time it left him vulnerable to every disease that came down the pike. The plastic bubble provided the sterile environment that would be necessary until the doctors were sure his body had accepted the new marrow and his immune system had begun functioning again.

A painful tightness squeezed Leah's chest. Quinton looked terrible. Chemotherapy had robbed him of all his beautiful blond hair, and he was pitifully thin and pale. The dark circles under his eyes and his gaunt cheekbones made him look like a concentration camp victim.

He was sleeping soundly—so soundly Leah experienced a moment's panic. She put her hand into the glove that was molded into the side of the plastic bubble and pressed her fingertips to his neck. She closed her eyes as relief washed over her. His pulse was weak, but it was there.

The plastic crackled as she withdrew her hand from the glove, and Quinton's eyes fluttered open. The instant they focused on her, hope lit his face.

"Hi, Sis. Is it time?"

"No, it'll be a while yet before they come for you. I got here early to keep you company."

"Where are Mom and Dad?"

"When I left, they were drinking coffee and trying to focus their eyes. You know your mother. Julia considers ten o'clock the crack of dawn. But don't worry, they'll be here."

"Yeah. I know. Is the guy here? The donor?"

The fear in his voice almost made her wince, but she forced a reassuring smile. "Yes. One of the nurses told me they put him in a room right down the hall last night."

"Are you sure? What if he changed his mind?"

"He won't. Don't worry."

"But what if he did?"

"Quinton—"

"Would you go see? Please. Just so I'll know for sure."

Leah sighed, but she inserted her hand into glove again and gave his arm a squeeze. "All right. It's a waste of time, but if it'll make you feel better I'll go check."

Mike McCall's room was about fifty feet away at the

end of the hall. As Leah hurried down the carpeted corridor she experienced a renewed stab of guilt. How strange and sad it was that two brothers who had never met—who were not even aware of each other's existence—were here on the same floor, separated by only a few feet.

She had tried again only the night before to persuade Julia to tell Quinton and Mike the truth, but with no success. She'd had her father halfway convinced that it was the right thing to do, but as usual, Julia had reacted with anger. When that had not worked, she had resorted to pitiful weeping, and Peter had caved in like a sand castle at high tide.

Leah shook her head. In most ways her father was a strong man, but he dissolved into mush when Julia turned on the tears.

At that hour of the morning, Leah had not expected to find anyone, with the possible exception of a nurse, in Mike's room. When she pushed open the door and stepped inside she pulled up short. Mike appeared to be asleep, but a woman stood beside his bed, holding his hand and bending solicitously over him.

"I'm sorry. I didn't realize Dr. McCall had a visitor."

The woman looked up and smiled, and Leah experienced a strange sensation in her chest—like a small kick in her heart.

It took a moment for her to realize that the woman was older than she had at first thought—somewhere in her mid to late forties—but she had a kind of wholesome beauty that was ageless. She was slender and shapely, with red hair and whiskey-brown eyes, but she exuded gentle serenity that seemed at odds with her flamboyant coloring. Leah hadn't thought that Mike McCall was the type to fall for an older woman, but it was easy to see why he had chosen this one.

Leah started to back away, but the woman stopped her.

"Oh, please don't leave on my account."

"No, really. I don't want to intrude."

"You're not intruding. I'm just keeping Mike company while he waits to be taken to surgery."

Mike's eyelids fluttered open and his bleary gaze found Leah. He gave her a lopsided grin. "Well, well, look who's here. Hiya, gorgeous."

"Hello, Dr. McCall."

"'Mike.' Told you. Call me 'Mike.'" He lifted his hand and gestured weakly toward the other woman. "You met Tess yet? Tess, this...this is Dr. Leah Albright. Best-looking doctor in the whole damned hospital. Shoot, in the whole damned state." He squinted and tried to focus, but his eyes refused to work and finally he gave up. "What're you doing here, pretty lady?" He had a dopey look on his face and his speech was so slurred he sounded drunk.

Leah smiled. "I just came to see if you were prepped for surgery," she replied, but Mike had drifted off to sleep again.

"He's been given a sedative," the redhead confided in a whisper.

She gave Leah a once-over. "The moment I saw you I was certain you were Dr. Albright. You look exactly as Mike described you."

"I do?" Surprised fluttered through Leah. Why on earth had Mike described her to one of his women?

"Oh, my, yes. It's very nice to meet you, at last. I've been looking forward to doing so for years."

She had? Leah cleared her throat. "I see. And you are?"

"Oh, my, how silly of me." Smiling, the redhead came around the end of the bed with her hand outstretched. "I'm Tess McCall—Mike's stepmother."

His stepmother? This beautiful woman was Mike's

stepmother? It didn't seem possible. At first Leah experienced an odd sense of relief, but the feeling was instantly replaced by panic.

"Oh, I…I see." She was barely aware of shaking hands with Tess McCall as her mind raced frantically for a way to deal with this unwelcome complication.

Why on earth hadn't it occurred to her that Mike's parents might be there for the surgery? Especially given what a close-knit family his was purported to be. She had been so wrapped up in her own problems that she had forgotten that Mike, too, had loved ones and family who would be as concerned about him as she was about Quinton.

Dear heaven, if Mike's father ran into Julia, this whole thing could blow up in their faces.

"I'm pleased to meet you, Mrs. McCall. Is, uh, is your husband here?" she asked, darting a look around.

"No, Ryan had to go out of town on business. Actually, Mike claimed it wasn't necessary for me to be here, either, but we wouldn't hear of him undergoing this procedure alone, no matter how risk free he claims it is."

"Yes, of course. I understand." Leah felt almost weak with relief. Thank heaven.

For the first time since she'd entered the room, a genuine smile curved her lips. "Mrs. McCall, I can't tell you how grateful my parents and I are for what Mike is doing for my brother."

Turning back to the bed, Tess gazed down at Mike with a tender smile and smoothed his dark hair off his forehead. "I'm sure he's quite happy to do what he can. That's the kind of man Mike is."

"Yes, I had heard that about him." Leah shifted from one foot to the other. "Well, I, uh, I'd better be getting back to my brother. It was nice meeting you, Mrs. McCall."

She slipped out the door before Tess could reply and

hurried back down the corridor, her mind still racing madly. How was she going to keep Julia and Tess McCall from meeting? With a groan, Leah realized that probably wasn't going to be possible—not unless Tess remained in Mike's hospital room all day, which seemed highly unlikely.

Leah chewed on her bottom lip. This could develop into a sticky situation. Julia's last name was different now, and she was here as Quinton's mother. Leah didn't think that Tess would put two and two together and realize that Julia was Mike's mother, as well. However, it wasn't Tess's reaction that concerned her. It was Julia's.

No doubt, Tess knew all about Julia from her husband and Mike, but Leah's stepmother knew nothing of Tess. Julia had no inkling that Ryan had remarried. She had often said that she had broken his heart. Leah had gotten the impression that Julia preferred to think that Ryan McCall was pining away for her. She doubted that her stepmother would be pleased to discover that for years her ex-husband had been happily married to someone else.

Dr. Sweeney and Dr. Brennan, the anesthetist, were talking to Quinton when Leah entered his room. The sight of them instantly wiped every other concern right out of her mind.

For the next several minutes, she listened as the doctors went over the procedure and the hoped-for results and possible complications with Quinton one last time. All the while the two doctors subtly performed a pre-op exam of their patient, checking his eyes, ears and throat, gently probing other areas of his body and asking questions.

Dr. Sweeney had no sooner finished and pronounced Quinton fit for the transplant than Julia and Peter arrived.

Julia swept into the room all misty eyed and fluttery. Leah had the cynical thought that the dramatic show was mostly to impress the doctors.

To Leah's relief, Julia had only a few minutes to play the role of distraught mother before a pair of orderlies whisked Quinton away.

Then the interminable waiting began.

In the lounge set aside for family members, Leah at first tried to keep an upbeat attitude and engage her parents in conversation, but that proved to be a wasted effort. After a while, she fell silent, but no one seemed to notice.

Leah wondered why she had bothered. She had never been close to her father. As for Julia, even in the best of situations, she had never been able to carry on any sort of meaningful conversation with her for long. They were too different. Other than Leah's father and Quinton, they simply had nothing in common.

Time crept by. Peter drank one cup of coffee after another and stared at the floor, while Julia leafed through a fashion magazine. Leah was too wired to sit still. She paced back and forth the length of the room, glancing at the clock or her watch every minute or so.

They'd had the lounge to themselves for over an hour when Mike's stepmother suddenly walked in. Leah's heart gave a leap, and she barely suppressed a gasp. She had forgotten all about Tess McCall.

Tess paused just inside the doorway and cast a sympathetic glance her way. Then her gaze slid to Julia and Peter. "I do hope I'm not intruding, Dr. Albright, but I thought you'd like to know that Mike is back in his room and resting comfortably."

Leah looked nervously at Julia. At the mention of Mike her head came up like an animal who had caught a scent. She tossed the fashion magazine aside and studied Tess.

"Oh, good. I'm glad."

"Apparently, everything went well. He's still groggy, but he insisted that there was no reason for me to stay. Since he's sleeping mostly, I agreed, but I wanted to come by and tell you and your family that I'll be praying for all of you.''

''Thank you. That's very kind. We appreciate it.''

Leah was touched by her concern, but at the same time she wanted her to leave before Julia got even more curious. It was a futile hope.

Her heart sank as her stepmother stood and came over to join them. ''I couldn't help but overhear. Do I understand correctly? Are you talking about Mike McCall? The man who is donating bone marrow to Quinton?''

''Yes, I am. And you must be Quinton's mother.''

''That's right. And you are...?''

''I'm Mike's mother.''

''His *mother?*''

''Well, his stepmother, actually, but I think of him as my son. His father and I have been married for sixteen years now, and I love Mike as much as I do my own children.''

Julia looked as though she'd been slapped. Leah held her breath. Julia eyed Tess from head to toe with eyes as cold as a glacier. At the very least, Leah expected an insult, perhaps even a full-blown tantrum, but her stepmother surprised her.

''I see.''

Tess blinked. She obviously sensed the antagonism in Julia's tone but was mystified by it. She glanced at Leah, then at Julia again, before taking a half step back. ''Well, I, uh, I guess I'd better be going. Good luck.''

''Thank you, Mrs. McCall.''

The minute Tess was out of sight Julia turned on Leah. ''You knew! You knew that Ryan had remarried, didn't you?''

''Yes, but I found out only last week.''

''Why didn't you tell me?''

Because I didn't want to initiate a scene like this one,

Leah thought, but she knew saying that would only exacerbate the situation. "It...it didn't occur to me that you would be interested."

"Not *interested?* I was married to Ryan!"

"That was twenty-five years ago, Julia. Since then you've remarried twice and had another child. So has he. What's the difference?"

"But *I* left him!" she wailed like a petulant child.

"Ah, I see."

Julia stiffened. Though she was shorter than Leah by two inches, she drew herself up to her full height and managed to look down her nose at her stepdaughter. "And just what do you mean by that? I don't think I like your tone, young lady."

"Now, now, dearest. Don't upset yourself. I'm sure Leah didn't mean any disrespect. Besides," Peter added gently, "it's not as though you still care for the man, now is it?"

"No. No, of course I don't. You know that I love only you, my darling. It's just that it burns me up for that woman to come in here and call herself Mike's mother. No matter what has happened, *I* am Mike's mother. *I'm* the one who carried him, the one who suffered through that hideous labor to give birth to him."

"Of course you are, dearest. I understand completely. You're on edge and worried about Quinton. Your nerves are raw, and that woman's sudden appearance was more than you could take at the moment. That's the real reason you're so upset."

Julia raised a fluttery hand to her forehead and sighed. "You're right, of course, my darling. You know me so well. I'm just so overwrought is all."

"Of course you are. Why don't you come over here and sit down, and I'll get you a cup of coffee."

Leah wanted to say that there was more to being a

mother than giving birth, but she knew it would only lead to another irate outburst. Julia was a master at overlooking her own shortcomings and mistakes and blaming everything on others.

Gritting her teeth, Leah gazed out the window and said nothing as her father soothed Julia's ruffled feathers.

A part of Leah wished that her father and stepmother had not bothered to return from Europe to be with Quinton for the surgery. She understood that he needed their support, but having them in her home was wearing. Julia's ceaseless laments about the parties and social events they were missing with their friends in Europe, her complaints about Leah's career and what she considered the inadequacies of Leah's home, of her lifestyle and social life—rather her lack of social life—were becoming unbearable.

That morning when they had struggled out of bed, Julia had immediately began to moan and complain about the early hour, and Leah's father hadn't been much better. It had been almost more than Leah's stretched nerves could take.

She had wanted to scream at them ''For pity's sake! Your son is dying of cancer and is about to undergo a serious operation that is his last hope. Can't you stop thinking of yourselves for one day?''

Instead, as always, she bit back the angry words, announced that she had early-morning rounds to make and rushed out. And, as usual, she wanted to kick herself for taking the coward's way out.

But what choice did she have? In the past, whenever she had crossed Julia, her stepmother had countered with veiled threats to remove Quinton from Leah's care.

Leah didn't really believe she would do it. Julia was well pleased with their arrangement. Knowing that Leah could be counted on to look after Quinton in every situation eased her conscience and left her free to gallivant wherever she pleased when she pleased. Certainly, Julia wasn't about to stay home and look after her son.

In all honesty, Leah had to admit that the arrangement suited her, as well. From the moment Quinton was born, she had always been more of a mother to him than Julia.

If Julia had been upset to find herself pregnant in her midthirties, Leah had been overjoyed at the prospect of having a brother or sister.

Losing her mother at fifteen had been a crushing blow. Leah had barely known her father, and her loneliness and feelings of abandonment and loss had only increased when she had moved in with him and his bride. She'd felt like an outsider, and she'd felt unwanted. The birth of a baby brother had been like a gift from heaven for the lost, grieving teenager she had been, giving her someone to love and a sense of purpose.

Her devotion to her baby brother had also helped cement her relationship with her father and Julia. They had been delighted that she was so attached to the baby, and they had felt confident about leaving their son in Leah's capable hands. Within months of Quinton's birth, they had resumed their carefree lifestyle.

In the early years Leah had had the help of a full-time nanny and Cleo, but they all knew that the real responsibility had been hers. When she had moved to Houston and taken Quinton with her, Julia and Peter had accepted the change in living arrangements without a word of protest. If anything, they had seemed to take it for granted that Quinton would reside with his sister, wherever that happened to be.

The arrangement worked to everyone's advantage, but it also gave Julia the leverage she needed to have her way. Leah didn't think she would actually remove Quinton from her care, but she didn't dare call her bluff. In ten months Quinton would turn eighteen, and would no longer be under his parents' authority. Until then, she would have to keep on biting her tongue.

The arrival of Dr. Sweeney pushed the gloomy thoughts right out of her mind. Leah turned away from the window, her heart pounding. "Is it over? Is Quinton all right?"

Dr. Sweeney took her hands and patted them. Fear tightened her chest when she noticed how weary and serious he looked. "Oh, Lord, is something wrong?"

"Now, now, Leah. Don't upset yourself." He smiled kindly and squeezed her hands. "The procedure went off perfectly, and your brother is doing as well as can be expected at this point."

"What does that mean?" Peter asked.

"Your son is a very sick young man. Going into the procedure he was as weak and as near death as anyone comes, and he survived. We can't expect him to rebound instantly. It could take days, possibly even weeks, before we know for certain that his body has accepted the foreign marrow. Even if the transplant is successful, it will take a long time for him to recover, and spontaneous rejection sometimes occurs without warning weeks down the road."

"But I thought this would be a cure. Now you're saying he could still die, even with the transplant?"

"There's always that chance in these cases, Mrs. Albright. I explained that to you. However, at this point, your son is holding his own. What I'm telling you now is, he has a long and difficult recovery ahead of him, but with the proper care and a little luck I think he will make it."

"I hope you're right, Doctor." Peter put his arm around his wife's shoulders and drew her to him as she began to weep. "Dear God, I hope you're right."

Blindly, Leah reached for her father's free hand and squeezed it. "Don't worry, Dad. He'll make it.

"He has to make it," Leah insisted to herself.

Chapter Four

"Dr. McCall! Just where do you think you're going?"

Mike grimaced and stopped in his tracks. Damn. Did the woman have eyes in the back of her head? Gertrude Zankowski was a superb head nurse, and in a crisis there was no one he would rather have on his team. However, she ran her floor with an iron hand and a bark that would put a marine drill instructor to shame.

Mike turned and gave her his most charming smile. "I'm just getting some air."

She arched on eyebrow. "At six-thirty in the morning? Dr. Sweeney's instructions were for you to have forty-eight hours of bed rest. It's been only twenty-three by my count."

"Ah, c'mon, Gert, have a heart. I'm sick of that bed. Besides, I feel fine. My part in the procedure was minor. So where's the harm in going for a little stroll? Hmm? It's not as though I'm going back to work."

"Humph. I wouldn't put it past you to make your rounds in your pajamas and robe, even though two perfectly good doctors are covering for you." She shook an admonishing finger at him. "I know you, Dr. McCall. You're so involved with your patients you don't trust anyone else to look after them."

"Hey, it's not a crime to care about your patients, you know."

"No, it isn't. Actually, caring is an admirable quality. One of many that I admire about you."

Mike's grin returned. "Why, Gert, I didn't know you cared."

"However," she continued, ignoring the comment, "at the moment you are a patient on my floor, and as long as you are, you will follow your doctor's orders. So don't think you can pull a fast one on me."

"Me? Now, would I do that to my favorite nurse?"

"In a New York second. And you can knock off the Irish charm, Doctor. It won't work on me."

Giving in, Mike sighed and ran his hand through his rumpled hair. "Look, to tell you the truth, I was just going to peek in on Dr. Albright's brother. See how he's coming along. I've sorta got a vested interest in the kid, you know."

"Is that wise, Doctor? It's usually best to maintain donor anonymity."

"Hey, I just want to check on the kid is all. I'm not going to tell him I'm his donor. C'mon, Gert, give me a break."

Arms crossed under her ample bosom, Nurse Zankowski pursed her lips and studied him through narrowed eyes. "I suppose if I don't, you'll just sneak out when I'm not looking, won't you?"

Mike grinned. "You got it."

She shook her head and scowled, but he could tell she

was weakening. "Oh, very well. I'll let you go on one condition.

"What's that?"

"You have to use a wheelchair."

"Ah, Gert, I don't need—"

"You either use a chair or I'll call the orderlies and have them stuff you back in that bed. Those are your only choices, Doctor."

Mike muttered about dictatorial women, but when Gert had one of her nurses bring a wheelchair over he complied. "Satisfied?" he demanded, shooting her a sulky look when he was seated.

"Yes. And be back here in twenty minutes."

"Tyrant." Giving her one last annoyed look, he jabbed the controls and sent the wheelchair whirring down the hall at top speed.

Like his uncle Reilly, his father's twin, Mike could never stay angry for long. By the time he reached the glass-walled ICU cubicle where Quinton was being monitored, his annoyance had faded. When he looked through the glass at the youth in the plastic bubble, it disappeared completely. He felt like a jerk for complaining at all, when this boy was the one who had it rough.

"Well, well, if it isn't my favorite kiddie doctor."

Mike turned the wheelchair and winked at the ICU nurse. "'Morning, Alice. How's it going?"

Alice Perkins was an attractive brunette in her early thirties. They had gone out a few times, shortly after Mike had come to St. Francis Hospital. She was funny and sweet and they'd had a good time together, but it hadn't taken long for them both to realize that the spark just wasn't there. They had, however, remained good friends.

"Aside from my aching feet, not bad. How about you? You feeling okay after getting your bones sucked out?"

"Jeez, Alice, your bedside manner could use some work. But to answer your question, I feel fine."

"Good. So, did you come to see the kid?"

"Yeah, I thought I'd find out how he was doing."

"So far he's holding his own." Alice shook her head. "I'm worried about Dr. Albright, though. She hasn't left his side since the surgery. Look at her. She's wiped out."

Mike maneuvered the wheelchair closer to the glass wall. The boy was sleeping. Curled up in a chair next to the bed, so was Leah.

Alice was right; she looked exhausted.

The nurse came to stand beside Mike. "If she wasn't a doctor on staff she wouldn't have been allowed to stay in there all night. You ask me, it was a mistake."

"Someone ought to persuade her to go home and get some rest," Mike murmured.

"You want to give it a shot?"

"Me? Oh, no. I don't think so. I doubt she'd listen to me."

"Well, it's going to take someone with more clout than I have. Lord knows, I've tried."

"Hmm. Maybe I'll give Dr. Sweeney a call when I get back to my room."

"Thanks, Mike. I was hoping you'd say that. I didn't feel it was my place."

Another nurse walked into ICU, and Alice gave Mike's shoulder a pat. "Look, my shift is over in a few minutes and I have to go brief Susan on the patients before I leave, but if you want to go in and get a closer look at the boy, feel free."

"No, I don't want to disturb them. Anyway, I just came by to see how the kid was doing."

That had truly been Mike's intention, but for the rest of the day he couldn't stop thinking about Leah and her brother. He kept picturing her curled up in that chair beside the boy's bed, her clothes rumpled, her hair mussed. Her mouth had been bare of lipstick, the rest of her makeup had all but faded away, and her face had been etched with fatigue. Still, she had looked beautiful.

Finally, Mike couldn't stand it any longer. Curiosity about this younger brother who elicited so much devotion from the reserved and seemingly unemotional Dr. Leah Albright drew him back to ICU that evening.

Nurse Zankowski had completed her shift and gone, but she had left instructions, and despite his protests, Mike once again found himself in a wheelchair.

A self-satisfied smile curved his mouth when he arrived in ICU and found Leah gone. Apparently, his call to Dr. Sweeney had produced results.

The boy was still sleeping. Wanting a closer look, Mike eased the wheelchair inside the cubicle and stopped beside the end of the bed.

Poor kid. He looked like hell. Chemo had left him bald, and he was too thin. Even so, it was easy to see that in good health he would be a big, strapping teenager. His skin was so pale it was almost translucent, and the dark circles around his sunken eyes and the sharpness of his nose and cheekbones gave him the look of a cadaver.

Of course, his condition was not surprising. Cancer was not Mike's field of expertise, but he knew the drill with transplant patients. Before the procedure, the doctors had deliberately destroyed what little was left of the boy's poorly functioning immune system with immunosuppression therapy in order to reduce the risk of his body rejecting the new marrow. Unavoidably, the aggressive treatment brought the already ailing patient almost to the point of death. It was a closer brush than most would ever know, one Mike was not sure that he himself would have the courage to face.

Mike studied the boy for some resemblance to his sister,

but he could find none. Leah had finely molded features that gave her a delicate appearance. Her brother's were sharply etched and strong, almost craggy. He would be a handsome kid if he was healthy, Mike thought.

The muted beeps drew Mike's attention to the monitors above the bed, to which the boy was connected by a mass of wires. At least his vital signs were stable, Mike mused. Unable to resist, he took the chart from the pocket in side of the plastic bubble and studied the notations made by the doctors and nurses.

So far, so good. Despite the kid's appearance, he was progressing as well as anyone could expect at this point. No sign of rejection. No fever. Even a slight reduction in white cells. "Way to go, champ," Mike murmured. "Keep it up, and you'll be kicking butt on the football field this time next year."

"Who...who are you?"

Mike looked up and found himself the focus of a pair of eyes so blue that not even illness or the distortion of the plastic bubble could dim their vividness. Instantly, he revised his earlier opinion; those eyes were exactly like Leah's.

"Sorry. I didn't mean to wake you." Mike hooked the chart back in place. Leaning into the chair, he smiled at the boy. "I'm Dr. Mike McCall. I'm on staff here."

"Yeah? Why haven't I seen you before?"

"Actually, I'm not on your case. I'm a pediatrician. But I know your sister, and since I had some time on my hands, I thought I'd stop in and see how you were doing."

Quinton looked him over. "You been sick or something?"

"Who me? Nah, I'm as healthy as a horse."

"Then why're you in pajamas? Why do you need a wheelchair?"

"Ah, I see. I've, uh, I've just gone through a minor

surgical procedure, that's all. Actually, I would have gone home yesterday if not for a head nurse who's descended from Attila the Hun.''

Quinton's mouth twitched. ''Yeah, I've had a couple like that.''

''You mean Nurse Perkins and Nurse Stafford. Trust me, kid, together they couldn't hold a candle to Top Sergeant Zankowski. The woman's a dictator.''

Quinton stared at Mike. ''This surgical procedure you had—it wouldn't happen to have been a bone marrow harvest, would it?''

The question caught Mike by surprise. All he could do for a moment was gape. ''I, uh…''

''You were my donor, weren't you?''

''What makes you think that?'' Mike asked, stalling.

''You're here in the hospital. In a wheelchair. You've just had a procedure done, but you're healthy, so it must not have been for you. Even though you're not one of my doctors you were curious about my condition. It all fits.''

The kid was bright; he'd give him that. Mike considered lying, but only for a moment. He believed in being honest with kids. If you wanted someone to trust you, you had to be straight with them.

For several moments he met Quinton's probing gaze while he mulled over the situation. He couldn't think of any valid reason to withhold the information from the boy. Usually, both the donor's and the patient's identity were kept confidential to protect the privacy of both parties. But what the heck. From the beginning Mike had known who would be getting his marrow. It seemed only fair that Quinton know who had given it to him, particularly since it was obvious that the boy wanted to.

As for himself, Mike had no problem with that. If knowing made the kid feel they were somehow connected, even if he wanted to pursue a friendship, where was the harm? Actually, he kinda liked the kid. He was courageous and tenacious—a real fighter.

But it was more than that, Mike realized. He couldn't pinpoint why, but he felt strangely drawn to Quinton.

Probably because he's Leah's brother, he decided finally.

"Yeah, well, I guess you got me, pal. It was my marrow."

"I thought so. Look, I, uh…I wanta thank you. I really appreciate what you did."

"Hey, kid, no problem. It wasn't a big thing for me. It wasn't particularly painful or even complicated. They harvested a little marrow and now all I have to do is rest for a couple of days while my body replaces it, and I'll be as good as new. You're the one who's got a long fight ahead."

"Maybe. Still, you didn't have to do it."

Mike shrugged. "We were a damned near perfect match and it was no hardship for me. I figured, why not? Besides, I'm a doctor. It's my job to save lives if I can."

"Yeah. My sister is like that." Though his voice was weak, there was a smile in it, and a touch of pride. "She'll work herself into the ground and do whatever it takes to save one of her patients."

"Yes, I know. Dr. Albright is an excellent doctor. I often refer patients to her."

"No kidding? Hey, that's great."

A huge yawn overtook the boy, and his eyes begin to droop. Mike smiled and started backing the wheelchair away from the bed. "Look, I'd better go and let you rest."

"Okay. Will you come back again sometime?"

"Sure. I'll stop by after my rounds tomorrow. How's that?"

"That'll be…neat," Quinton mumbled as his eyes fluttered shut.

Mike guided the wheelchair out the door, but in the corridor he stopped and poked his head back inside. "Hey, kid!"

Quinton blinked and tried to focus. "Y-yeah?"

"Remember. That's my marrow you've got. You take good care of it, you hear?"

A ghost of a smile twitched Quinton's mouth. "Sure thing, Doc."

During the following week, each evening after his rounds, Mike dropped by Quinton's room for a short visit. As luck would have it, after nearly six weeks of dealing with major illnesses and crisis situations, suddenly his practice consisted of nothing more serious than routine checkups and a few normal childhood maladies such as head colds or cuts. All week, the only patients Mike had in the hospital were a tonsillectomy and a three-year-old scheduled for X rays to check out a chronic bladder problem. By five or so each evening he was finished and free to stop by Quinton's room.

During those visits, Mike learned a lot about the boy. Quinton liked baseball and football, card games, video and board games, cars and girls, not necessarily in that order. That the boy and his sister were close came as no surprise to Mike. What did surprise him was learning that Quinton lived with Leah.

In one conversation, the boy had casually mentioned that his parents traveled so much they spent more time away than at home. Apparently, Leah had always been the one to look after him.

Mike thought it a bit strange, even sad. When you were a teenager, sometimes you thought your parents were a royal pain, but he couldn't imagine not having them around when you were growing up. His dad had always been there for him, and, for the past sixteen years, so had Tess.

Another thing he discovered about Quinton, which was a big plus in the kid's favor, was that he thought Mike's jokes were hilarious. Every evening he had two or three new ones for the boy.

"Knock, knock."

A grin split Quinton's face when he looked and saw Mike standing in the doorway a week after their first meeting. "Who's there?"

"Goose."

"Goose who?"

"Goose who's knocking at your door."

Quinton groaned and rolled his eyes.

"Knock, knock."

"Who's there?" the boy asked again in a long-suffering voice that didn't fool Mike for a minute.

"Jewel."

"Jewel who?"

"Jewel remember me when you see my face."

Smothering a giggle, Quinton shook his head. "Aw, Mike, how do you come up with those corny things?"

"Wait, there's more. Knock, knock."

"Who's there?"

"Sam."

"Sam who?"

"Sam person who knocked last time."

This time Quinton gave up and laughed. "Man, I'll bet the little kids you treat think you're a riot."

"Whaddaya mean, *think?* My kids *know* I'm funny. I'll have you know I've been called the Jeff Foxworthy of the pediatrics floor."

"I'll bet. What's that you got under your arm?"

Mike set the box on the bedside table. "Checkers. I figured since you've improved so much during the past

week, you'd probably be up to a game. I'm sure you're
getting bored with nothing to do but watch TV.''

"Yeah, kinda. But how're we gonna manage it with me
in here and you out there?''

"Easy. I'll push the table close to the bed so you can
reach the board using the glove in the side of your bubble."

"I don't know. It'll be hard to handle those little checkers with that glove on.''

"What's the matter? Afraid you'll get beat?"

Quinton responded to the challenge instantly. Rolling
onto his side, he fumbled for the glove. "No way, man.
Set 'em up. And prepare to get whupped.''

"Ho, ho. Big talk comes cheap. Let's see some action,
chump.''

An hour and a half later, Leah checked her watch as
she hurried down the hospital corridor. Six-thirty. Not as
early as she had planned, but at least it was better than
she'd managed to do all week.

She had hoped to knock off early today so that she
could spend more time with Quinton. Every evening since
she'd returned to work her waiting room had been packed.
By the time she had finished and reached Quinton's room
he'd been so drowsy and tired they'd barely had a chance
to talk before he'd drifted off to sleep. Today, just as she
was leaving her office, one of her expectant mothers had
called to say she was on the way to the hospital. Merci-
fully, the labor had been short and the delivery normal.

Leah was optimistic about Quinton's chances. He had
a long way to go, but already he had made marvelous
progress, and according to his doctors, his mood was upbeat and cheery, which always helped.

She breezed into ICU a moment later, prepared to apologize once again for being late, but the words were never

poken. When she glanced inside Quinton's cubicle she erked to a halt. "What the devil—"

The sight of Mike McCall sitting beside Quinton's bed nearly stopped her heart.

Lying on his side with his right hand stuck in the plastic glove, Quinton studied the checkerboard on the table beside the bed. After a moment he picked up a black checker and jumped three red ones on the board, then hooted when Mike groaned. "Gotcha!"

"Hey, don't get cocky, kid. This game's not over yet."

Leah stared, horror-struck. The two of them were laughing and razzing each other like old friends!

Or brothers.

The thought sent her charging into the room.

"Dr. McCall, what're you doing here?"

"Oh, hi, Sis. I didn't see you come in."

Mike looked up from the checkerboard. "Hiya, Doc. I'm just keeping Quinton company."

"Oh, really? How long has this been going on?" Her voice came out harsher than she had intended, but she couldn't help it. Fear had her nerves jumping like a drop of water on a hot griddle.

"Sis? What's wrong? You're acting like you don't want Mike to visit me."

Her gaze switched to Quinton, and she experienced a pang when she saw the look of puzzlement and hurt on his face.

She forced the harshness from her voice and managed a weak smile. "Don't be silly, Quinton. It's not that. It's just that, well, I was surprised to see Dr. McCall here. He isn't one of your physicians, after all."

"I'm not here as a doctor, Leah," Mike said quietly, watching her. "I'm here as a friend. I stopped by the day after Quinton's transplant and we had a nice chat. I've dropped by every day since then."

"Every day?" she repeated weakly, feeling sick

"Quinton, I'm surprised at you. Why didn't you tell me?"

"I guess I was so tired by the time you got here that
forgot. Anyway, why didn't you tell me that Mike wa
my donor?"

Shock slammed into Leah like an iron fist, nearl
knocking the breath out of her. She whirled on Mike
"You *told* him? Without consulting me? How coul
you?"

"Actually—"

"Why shouldn't I know?" Quinton demanded, befor
Mike could finish.

It was the first time Leah had heard that belligerent ton
in her brother's voice, and she deeply regretted it, but a
the moment, she had a more pressing problem to dea
with. She gritted her teeth and forced a calmer tone
"Quinton, I told you donors' names are kept confidentia
to preserve their privacy."

"I don't have any objection to Quinton knowing that i
was me who donated the marrow." Mike shrugged. "Af
ter all, I knew who he was beforehand, so it seems only
fair. But to set the record straight, I didn't tell him. H
guessed." He winked at Quinton. "The kid's a smar
cookie."

"Yes, he is, but—"

"Gee, what's the big deal anyway?" Quinton de
manded. "Mike doesn't mind. And I like having him vis
me."

"Quinton, dearest, Dr. McCall is a busy doctor with a
heavy workload. I understand that you enjoy his company
but you can't take up all his free time. Not when he'
done so much for you already."

Quinton looked crestfallen. "Oh. I didn't think of that."

"Hey, buddy, don't worry about it," Mike said quickly
before turning to Leah. "Look, I'm not that busy righ

now. I wouldn't be spending time with Quinton if I didn't want to. Unless you have some objection to us being friends, I'd like to continue.''

"Shoot, why would she mind? You don't, do you, Sis?"

Leah's heart sank. "I...no. No, of course not."

What else could she say? After what Mike had done for them, she would look like a rude ingrate if she was truthful. Quinton was obviously struck with a giant case of hero worship, and who could blame him? Mike had saved his life.

"Good." Mike turned his attention back to the checkerboard. "Now then, where were we?"

"About half a minute away from me winning," Quinton taunted with a grin.

"Yeah, well, like I said, the game's not over yet, chump," Mike drawled, and jumped two of Mike's checkers and swept them off the board.

Mike won the game—barely. Over the next hour, they played two more, teasing each other mercilessly the whole while. Quinton won both times by a narrow margin. Whether Mike had deliberately let him win Leah didn't know, but she suspected as much.

As she sat by and watched the brothers and listened to their banter, it struck her that she had never met anyone as open and friendly as Mike, or anyone who had such a good rapport with young people. After watching him in action, it was not surprising that he had gone into pediatrics.

By the end of the last game Quinton was visibly tired, and Mike stood up. "I'd better go and let you get some rest, tiger. I'll stop by tomorrow after rounds and we'll have a rematch."

"I'll just whup you again, but if you're into humiliation, I'm game."

The boast ended with a huge yawn, and Mike grinned.

"Big talk. We'll see if you can back it up." As he headed for the door he looked at Leah and said, "Can I speak to you outside for a minute, Leah?"

For some reason, Leah's heart gave a little leap, but she nodded and followed him out. What could he want to talk to her about? Immediately her guilty conscience took over, arousing her worst fear. Oh, Lord, had he somehow discovered that Quinton was his brother? Was he about to tear into her for tricking him?

In the hall she braced herself and faced him with her arms crossed over her midriff. "Yes?"

"Regardless of what you said in there, I get the feeling that you're opposed to me visiting Quinton. Is there a problem I'm not aware of?"

Oh, yes, there was a problem, all right. A huge one. She was terrified that if they spent much time together Mike might somehow discover the truth. But of course she couldn't tell him that.

The simple question put her on the spot, and for a moment she was so flustered all she could do was stare at him while she groped for an excuse.

"I'm just not comfortable with him knowing you were his donor, that's all," she finally blurted out.

"Look, I wouldn't have told him if he hadn't guessed. As I said before, the kid's smart."

"True. However, I doubt that he would have figured it out if you had stayed away."

Mike shrugged. "Maybe. But what harm does it do? He obviously wanted to know who had given him a chance at life."

"Of course he wanted to know. He's an impressionable seventeen-year-old. You're a hero to him."

"Look, I can deal with a little hero worship, if that's

what's bothering you. Besides, I like the kid. If he wants us to be buddies, that's fine with me.''

Leah nearly groaned. How could she fight that kind of generosity? To make matters worse, she knew that Quinton was starved for male attention. Mike was a strong, intelligent, caring and decent man. He would provide exactly the sort of masculine influence Quinton needed in his life.

How ironic.

"Is it really the ethics that are troubling you?" Mike asked softly, watching her. "Or is it me you object to?"

"No, of course not," she said too quickly.

His wry look reeked with disbelief, and Leah felt heat flood her face and neck. He gave her a coaxing smile. "I'm really a nice guy, you know. Just ask anyone."

"I know that."

"Do you? Then why do you go out of your way to avoid me?"

"I—I don't."

"Sure you do. You've done it for years, ever since I joined the staff here. And the minute I walk into a room you're in, you leave."

"You're imagining things."

"Am I? Okay, fine. Have dinner with me."

The invitation caught her off guard and set her heart to racing. "D-dinner? You mean tonight?"

"Yeah. You haven't eaten, have you?"

"No," she admitted before she thought, then could have kicked herself.

"Neither have I. So why don't we go to a quiet restaurant where we can unwind over a nice meal and talk, maybe get to know each other."

"I, uh...I—"

"You have to eat sometime." He edged closer.

Leah found it suddenly difficult to breathe and retreated

a step, only to bump into the wall at her back. Mike's smile was knowing, and she felt her color rise. He braced his arm against the wall beside her head and lowered his voice to a coaxing murmur.

"And remember, you owe me a rain check."

He was so close she could smell his scent, dark and masculine and uniquely his. Mixed with it was the smell of antiseptic soap—the doctors' cologne—and the combination was surprisingly heady.

Leah couldn't remember when she had been so aware of a man. Mike was well over six feet tall and broad shouldered. She had to tip her head back at a sharp angle to look up at him. When she did she experienced another little jolt as her gaze ran over chiseled features, raven black hair and eyes the pale, cool blue of the ocean in winter. Dear Lord, why hadn't she noticed before how good-looking he was? No wonder the nurses and other females on staff turned to putty whenever he was around.

Suddenly realizing that he was waiting for her answer, Leah blinked twice and gave her head a tiny shake. "I remember. But it can't be tonight. My dad and stepmother are expecting me home."

"That's right. You did mention they were here. I'm surprised I haven't run into them."

Leah made a fluttery gesture with her hands. "Oh. Well, that's, uh, that's because they both came down with the flu just after Quinton's transplant. Then they both had a relapse. They, uh, they're still recovering."

"Ah, I see. Too bad. Well, Quinton will be here for a while. I'm sure I'll get the chance to meet them before long."

Leah fervently hoped not, but she gave him a weak smile. "Yes, I imagine so. But you can see that tonight I need to get home and check on them."

He studied her for an interminable time, his gaze probing. Leah fought the urge to squirm and prayed the lie didn't show on her face. Finally he pushed away from the wall.

"Okay, Doc. You're off the hook for now, but that makes two you owe me."

He winked and touched her cheek with the tip of his forefinger, making her jolt again. Electricity streaked through her body from the point of contact all the way to her toes.

"Good night, gorgeous. I'll see you tomorrow."

Still leaning against the wall, Leah watched him stride away down the hall. An odd tightness squeezed her chest and her heart seemed to be doing an erratic dance against her rib cage. Until now, she had always thought of Mike as—not an enemy, exactly—but a danger, someone to be avoided. The very thought of him visiting her brother daily, perhaps discovering the truth, filled her with alarm and dread, but she was also aware that a part of her—the foolish, female part of her—experienced a little thrill at the idea of seeing him every day.

When she realized the drift her thoughts were taking she snorted and straightened away from the wall. Heaven help her, where had that come from? What nonsense. Of course she didn't want Mike hanging around her brother's room. Or around her. The stray thought must have been brought on by exhaustion.

Like it or not, however, it looked as though she had no choice but to resign herself to Mike's presence in the sick-room.

Which meant that somehow she would also have to come up with a way to keep him and Julia from running into each other.

Chapter Five

Leaving her patient to get dressed, Leah stepped out of the examination room and closed the door behind her. She paused in the hallway to rub the back of her neck and flex her taut shoulders. Across the hall in another examination room, her nurse, Sandy Johnson, was straightening up and readying the examining table for tomorrow morning.

At least, Leah hoped it was for tomorrow morning.

"Please tell me that was the last patient," she pleaded as Sandy finished and joined her in the hallway, pulling the door shut on the spotless room.

Sandy chuckled. "It was."

"Good. I'm about to drop."

As they talked, the two women walked toward the front office, where Leah's receptionist, Mary Ann Trent, was filing away the day's patient charts.

"You do look a little peaked, Doctor," Sandy remarked. "What's the matter? Have a late night? Maybe with a certain yummy pediatrician? Hmm?"

"Don't be ridiculous. I told you, there is nothing going on between Dr. McCall and me."

"Uh-huh. If you say so."

"It's true. He visits Quinton, not me. They have formed a bond, which is only natural under the circumstances."

"Uh-huh. That gorgeous hunk drops by every evening just to see a seventeen-year-old kid. We believe that, don't we, Mary Ann?"

"Oh, yes, definitely." The receptionist exchanged a look with Sandy. "We're just wondering what sort of bond he's formed with you. From the look of you, it's pretty intense."

"All right, you two. Knock it off. You both know perfectly well that I was rousted out of bed at 2:00 a.m. to deliver a baby. I've been up ever since, so naturally I'm tired. I'm going to stop by Quinton's room for a short visit, then head home, take a relaxing hot bath and go to bed. With any luck, none of my mothers-to-be will call and I'll get a decent night's rest."

"Humph. If you want to relax I can think of a much more enjoyable way to do it than taking a hot bath," Sandy drawled. "Unless, of course, you take it with a tall, dark, handsome man."

"Yeah. Preferably one who's a doctor," Mary Ann tacked on with an innocent look.

"For the last time, get it through your heads—I am not interested in Dr. McCall."

Sandy snorted. "Not interested? Doctor, a woman would have to be dead, blind or comatose not to be interested in a man like that."

She shook her head woefully. "If you ask me, it's a shame—a crime, really—that he's a pediatrician. Imagine, those good looks and all that delicious masculinity wasted on a bunch of rug-rats. If he were almost any other kind of doctor and I were ten or fifteen years younger, I guarantee you—I'd be his patient. And you can bet the farm that I'd have a chronic ailment that required frequent attention.''

Mary Ann sighed. "I know what you mean. Just the thought of him examining me makes me weak.'' She fanned her hand in front of her face. "Be still my heart.''

"Honestly, you two are pathetic. Mike is just a man. A very nice man, it's true, but still just a man like any other.''

Which was a whopping lie. Even as Leah spoke the words she half expected lightning to strike her down. As she was learning nightly, Mike McCall was anything but ordinary.

"*Just* a man! Like any *other!*" Mary Ann squeaked. "Doctor, you'd better run a test on your hormones. And get your eyes checked while you're at it. The man is a hunk—six feet two, black hair, sea-blue eyes, rugged good looks and a killer smile. And as if all that weren't enough, he's a *doctor,* for heaven's sake. A doctor who loves kids, no less. What more could a woman want?''

"That's right,'' Sandy agreed. "If Dr. McCall is *just* a man, then King Kong was just an ape. Moby Dick was just a fish. The Rocky Mountains are just a pile of dirt and rocks. The South Pole is—''

Chuckling, Leah held up both hands. "Okay, okay. You've made your point. Dr. McCall is a prize. A prince among men. I'll concede that. I just don't happen to be interested.''

Liar, her conscience jabbed. *You know you could be, under the right circumstances.*

Which was a complication she had not anticipated. In the past she had been so concerned with avoiding Mike, she had never thought of him in that way. Also, what little she had known of him beyond his reputation as an excel-

lent doctor had been based on information received from
Julia, none of which had been very complimentary.

"He was always such a difficult child. From the time
he was born he was just like his father," her stepmother
had complained. "Ryan is a hard man and as cold as steel.
And he's selfish. He was totally indifferent to *my* feelings,
my needs. A wife is entitled to her husband's affections.
Not that Ryan was a particularly loving man," she had
said, sniffing. "What few tender feelings he did have were
always for that family of his. They always came first. I'm
quite sure that as Mike has matured he has become just
as bad."

Knowing Julia, Leah had listened with a grain of salt
to her complaints about the husband and son she had abandoned. Even so, she had not expected to actually like
Mike.

These past few weeks, however, she had gotten to know
him, not as Julia's son but as a person.

To Leah's surprise, she had discovered that Mike was
a warm, intelligent, caring, man with a devilish sense of
humor and an innate sex appeal that took her breath away.

Of course that was all there was to it, Leah assured
herself. A little unexpected chemistry. Mike was a good-
looking man and she was a normal, healthy woman in her
prime. These last few years she had been so wrapped up
in her busy practice she had almost forgotten that, but it
was nevertheless true.

Leah shrugged out of her lab coat and retrieved her
purse and coat from the closet. "If you ladies are finished
teasing, I'm going to see my brother."

Sandy sobered. "How is Quinton doing?"

"Actually, he's progressing quite well. They moved
him into a private room today. He's still in a bubble, but
at least this one is big enough for him to get out of bed
and walk around a bit. He has a long recovery ahead, but

the prognosis is excellent and his spirits are high." Thanks in no small part to his new best friend and hero, Leah silently acknowledged.

"That's great," Mary Ann said. "Be sure and tell him hi for us and give him our love."

"I will. See you both tomorrow."

"And give our love to Dr. McCall," Sandy called after her.

Shaking her head, Leah headed down the hallway. She couldn't get angry with Sandy and Mary Ann. The two women were her friends and the closest thing she had to sisters.

In all fairness, she couldn't really blame them for speculating about her and Mike. He had visited Quinton every evening for the past four weeks, and the hospital grapevine was buzzing.

Leah didn't like it, but there was nothing she could do to stop the gossip. St. Francis Hospital was like a small town. News spread among the staff before you could take the elevator from the top floor to the lobby.

At least she had managed to keep Julia in the dark about Mike's nightly visits—so far, at any rate.

Leah was not normally a devious person, but she thought that withholding that bit of information seemed wise in this instance. In many ways, her stepmother was like a spoiled child—self-centered, volatile and unpredictable. Julia had a convoluted manner of looking at things. There was no way of knowing how she would react to the news of her two sons meeting, much less forming a friendship.

After encountering Tess McCall the morning of Quinton's transplant, Julia had raged and carried on for days, as though she, not Ryan, had been the wronged party in their marriage. She had wanted to march over to her ex-husband's home and vent her spleen on him and his wife.

It had taken the combined efforts of Leah and her father to dissuade her.

A casual mention to Quinton that Julia might disapprove of him getting to know his donor and might even go so far as to have Mike barred from the room had been all the incentive that her brother had needed to keep quiet about Mike's visits.

For all Julia's neglect and indifferent mothering, Quinton loved her and was touchingly loyal. He accepted his parents' frequent and prolonged absences with forbearance and always made excuses for Julia's shortcomings and self-indulgences, but he knew as well as Leah the unpredictability of his mother's temper and behavior.

Luckily, Leah had also managed to persuade Julia to stay away from the hospital in the evenings, although her stepmother had not made it easy.

"I think it's an outrage that a mother can't see her son whenever she wants," she had argued.

"Julia, I told you, if you confine your visits to the early afternoons, Mike will most likely be with his patients, and your risk of running into him in the hospital will be much less."

"So? I don't see why we're going to so much trouble, anyway," Julia had groused. "I mean, at this point, what difference does it make if I do happen to run into Mike? I doubt that he'll recognize me. It's been twenty-five years, for heaven's sake. And even if by some chance he does, so what? What's he going to do? Demand his bone marrow back?"

Leah did not even try to point out the colossal callousness of that statement. With Julia, what was the point? In her mind, right and wrong were determined by what she wanted.

Instead, Leah gritted her teeth and strove for patience. "Julia, don't you see? We're doing this to protect Quinton. Imagine how upset he would be to learn the truth at this point. He isn't nearly strong enough to handle that news. A patient's mental and emotional state have a direct bearing on his recovery. That sort of shock could set him back weeks, maybe even reverse all the progress he's made. We can't take that chance.''

''Leah's right, my darling,'' her father had gently urged. ''We must think of what's best for our son.''

''Oh, I suppose you're right. I hadn't thought of it that way. Very well. I don't like it, but I guess, for Quinton's sake, we can confine our visits to the afternoon hours.''

Despite her grousing, Leah suspected that Julia was secretly pleased with the arrangement. She knew her stepmother; Julia rarely rose before noon, so skipping morning visits was no hardship, and she liked to keep her evenings free for social engagements. Already, she and Peter had hooked up with old friends who lived in the River Oaks section of Houston. Most nights, Leah returned home after a long day of working and visiting with Quinton afterward to find them out.

Oh, yes, Leah thought, afternoon visits with Quinton suited Julia just fine.

Now, if they could just get through the next few months without her stepmother learning about Mike's visits, they would be home free. If Quinton continued to improve at his current rate, by summer he would be discharged from the hospital. Already, Julia was making plans to return to the south of France as soon as Quinton was strong enough to come home.

Personally, Leah couldn't wait. Quinton's usual reaction to his parents' departure was a mixture of disappointment and acceptance, but this time, thanks to the attention he was receiving from Mike, she didn't think he would mind that much—at least, not until he realized that Mike's daily visits would probably end once he left the hospital.

It seemed that possibility had not occurred to Quinton.

Leah had been trying to come up with a tactful way of preparing him, but she knew that no matter what she said, he would be crushed, so she had held her tongue.

Leah herself viewed the prospect with mixed emotions. Common sense told her the best thing, certainly the safest thing, would be for her brother and Mike to part company. On the other hand, ethically and emotionally, that seemed wrong. They were brothers and as such had a right to a relationship. Plus, there was no denying that being around Mike was good for Quinton.

Leah walked into her brother's new room expecting to find him and Mike wrangling good-naturedly over some game or watching sports on television, as they had been every evening when she arrived, but Quinton was alone. Looking dejected, he lay propped up in the bed inside the isolation chamber that reminded her of a huge plastic wind sock.

Leah was disconcerted at how deflated she herself felt. She quickly brushed the reaction aside, telling herself that it wasn't because she had been looking forward to seeing Mike. She had simply grown accustomed to him being there each evening.

"Well, hi there, sweetie," she greeted Quinton, forcing a bright note into her voice. "How does it feel to get out of ICU and into your own room?"

Quinton shrugged his thin shoulders and grimaced, but he didn't bother to look at her. "Okay, I guess," he said in a woebegone voice.

"Hey, what's this? What's wrong? I thought you'd be happy they moved you? You've been saying for days that you wanted out of that glass box."

"I did. I do." Quinton plucked at the sheet that lay across his chest. "I just wish Mike were here is all."

"Well, perhaps he's busy."

"Yeah, he sent word that he had an emergency."

Relief poured through Leah. She had been afraid that Mike had simply grown bored with the nightly visits. Quinton would be devastated if his hero suddenly dropped him.

"Ah, well, that explains it." She lifted his chart from the pocket in the side of the bubble to scan the latest entries. "I did warn you that Mike is a busy doctor with a large practice. You have to expect these sort of things. After living with me all these years you should know that."

"I guess. It's just that tonight was kinda special. You know? And I wanted him to be here."

Satisfied with what she'd read, Leah replaced the chart. "I'm sure he would have been if he could. But look on the bright side—you still have me."

Quinton had the grace to give her an apologetic half smile. "Yeah. Thanks, Sis. I really appreciate you spending every evening with me."

"Hey, sweetie, no problem." She stuck her hand inside the plastic glove and gave his cheek a pat, the way she had done all his life. "Now then, what would you like to do? Play cards? Watch television? Or how about a game of Monopoly?"

He shrugged. "Whatever."

Two hours later, Quinton was still glum. Like most teenage boys, he tended to be a competitive game player, but not even losing five games of gin rummy in a row to his sister sparked enough interest to rouse him out of his funk.

Throughout the evening Leah remained determinedly cheerful, laughing and teasing, doing her best to coax him into a better mood, but it grew more and more difficult. Especially since she was feeling a bit down, too.

As much as she hated to admit it, the evening visit just wasn't the same without Mike.

At first she had been edgy and uncomfortable in his presence. She had tried to remain a little apart from him and Quinton, to sit back quietly and observe their interaction without participating, but somehow that plan had gone awry. Without her quite knowing how it happened, she and Mike had become friends.

There was something about Mike that drew you, a sort of effortless charm that beguiled and beckoned like the warmth of a cheery fire on a cold night. And it was just as irresistible.

Before Leah had realized what was happening, she found herself joining in lively discussions about everything from the Dallas Cowboys' chances of making it to the Super Bowl the next year to the possible existence of life on other planets. The three of them regularly played spirited games of Trivial Pursuit, Pictionary and Aggravation that often as not resulted in good-natured insults and bantering. Though that sort of teasing was new to Leah, she was soon enjoying it and giving as good as she got. At other times, if Quinton had had a bad day and was fatigued, they watched television together.

Oddly, even that was more enjoyable when Mike was there.

Gradually, as Leah had let down her guard and they'd gotten better acquainted, she'd realized that he was not at all the way Julia had painted him. She was impressed by Mike's good nature and unaffected manner, by his genuine friendliness. Most of all, she was impressed by his compassion and caring.

Seeing the way Quinton responded to Mike's attention, Leah realized sadly just how much her brother had missed having a strong male presence in his life. Though it wasn't an easy admission to make, she also realized that she could not have asked for a better role model for Quinton than Mike McCall.

After a couple of hours of trying to cheer up Quinton, Leah felt her cheeks begin to hurt from smiling, and she was getting so put out she wanted to shake him. She had to keep biting her tongue and reminding herself that he was just a boy and he was still in serious condition, for all that the transplant appeared to be a success.

Finally, however, when Quinton answered yet another of her questions with a grunt, Leah lost patience. "All right, that's it." She slapped her cards down. "I'm not going to sit here any longer and watch you mope. I'm tired, and I haven't had any dinner, so I'm leaving. Maybe you'll be in a better mood tomorrow."

"Ah, Sis, I didn't mean—"

"Knock, knock."

Quinton's gaze whipped to the doorway, and his face lit up like the Las Vegas Strip. "Mike!"

Leah's heart gave a little skip at the sound of Mike's voice, but when she turned toward the door her expression was calm.

He was dressed in green scrubs. The short sleeves of the loose garment revealed broad shoulders and muscular arms, the latter covered with silky dark hair. The wide vee neck also revealed the first few inches of the dark thatch that covered his chest.

Leah's breathing became shallow. She caught herself staring at those shadowy curls just below his collarbone and quickly looked away, but as he strolled past her into the room her gaze was drawn to his backside. She stared, experiencing a funny feeling in the pit of her stomach at the way the green cotton clung to taut buttocks, at the flexing movements of the firm flesh. She had been around men in scrubs for almost half her life. Why hadn't she noticed before what a sexy garment they were?

Mike's hair stuck up in tufts where he'd run his fingers through it and whisker stubble shadowed his jaw. Fatigue had etched lines around his eyes and he looked exhausted, but that didn't prevent him from teasing Quinton.

"Hey, that's not what you're supposed to answer."

"Sorry," Quinton apologized, grinning. "Start over."

"Okay. But get it right this time. Knock, knock."

"Who's there?"

"Wah."

"Wah who?"

"Hey, you don't have to get excited just because I'm here!"

"Arrrrghhh." Quinton clutched his throat as though he were choking. "Ah, man, every night you come up with a cornier one."

"Every night?" Leah echoed, looking stupefied. "Are you telling me that the two of you go through this routine every night?"

"Yeah, Mike's got a million knock-knock jokes."

"That's right. I even have one for you, Doc."

"Oh, boy, this oughta be good," Quinton said with relish.

"Knock, knock."

Leah glanced uncomfortably at her brother and then Mike. "I really don't think—"

"Ah c'mon, Sis."

"Quinton—"

"It's just a joke. Be a sport."

"But it's so silly."

"What's the matter, Doc?" Mike drawled. "Afraid word will get out and shatter that dignified image of yours? Don't you know that being silly now and then is good for the soul? Keeps us medical types from taking ourselves too seriously and developing God complexes.

C'mon, loosen up a little. For once, do something just for the fun of it.''

Leah hesitated, biting the inside of her lip, but when she glanced at Quinton and saw the pleading look in his eyes she gave in. ''Oh, all right.''

Mike grinned. ''Knock, knock.''

''Who's there?'' she asked in a bored voice.

''Sara.''

''Sara who?''

''Sara doctor in the house?''

''Heaven help me,'' Leah muttered, but Quinton's laughter was contagious, and she found herself fighting back a smile. ''Mike, that was awful.''

''Thanks.''

Her confusion seemed to amuse Quinton even more. ''Don't you get it, Sis? That's what make knock-knocks so funny. The cornier they are, the better.''

''I see.'' She cast another look at Mike. ''In that case, you must be a riot during rounds.''

''I do my best,'' he replied with such obvious cockiness she had to laugh.

''Look, kid, I just dropped by to see how you liked your new digs, but I can't stay. I have been dealing with an emergency and haven't eaten all day. If I don't throw some chow down my throat soon *I'm* going to wind up in emergency.''

''That's okay. I understand.''

Leah's jaw dropped. She couldn't believe it! For two hours he had been feeling sorry for himself because Mike wasn't there, while she had done everything but stand on her head to cheer him up. She opened her mouth to remind him of that, but before she could speak he went on in the same genial tone.

''Hey, I know. Leah hasn't eaten, either. Why don't you take her with you.''

"Quinton!"

"Good idea, kid." Mike's eyes twinkled at her. "How about it, Doc? You game?"

"Oh, uh, thank you, but no. I really couldn't."

"Why not?" Quinton demanded. "You just said you were hungry."

Leah aimed a strained smile at her brother. "Quinton, I'd like to have dinner with Mike, but I'm sure that Cleo already has dinner waiting for me."

"Nuh-uh. This is her bingo night, remember? And Mom and Dad were going to that party at the Mathesons'. If you go home you'll just have to scrounge up something and nuke it in the microwave." Grinning, he looked at Mike and confided, "Leah's a terrible cook. We'd starve without Cleo."

"Is that right? Well, we don't want that to happen, so I guess you'd better come along with me, Doc."

"No, really, I can't. I...I'm exhausted. What I really need is an early night."

"So do I. But that's no problem. I know this great little restaurant not far from here. We can have a nice meal and relax and I'll bring you back to pick up your car all within an hour. Hour and a half, tops."

"You mean you're going dressed like that?" Her eyes ran over his scrubs, and he grinned and shrugged.

"Sure. It's an informal place. Besides, they're used to people coming in like this. A lot of hospital people eat there."

"You see? That'll work out perfect," Quinton insisted. "You have to eat. You might as well do it with Mike."

Leah bit her lower lip.

Mike eyes danced and his smile oozed male triumph. "Gotcha," he mouthed at her, and she felt her face heat up.

Chuckling, he grasped her elbow. "Say good-night to your brother, Doc."

"No, wait. I…"

Mike ignored her stammering. "See ya, sport."

Leah cast a helpless look over her shoulder at Quinton. "I'll be by tomorrow evening as usual."

"Sure." Grinning from ear to ear, he waved. "You two have a good time, now."

The restaurant Mike took her to was a little family-owned place about a half mile from the hospital. Red-and-white checked cloths covered the tables, and in the center of each sat a small vase of daisies and a votive candle.

Winter had given way to spring. The night was cool but pleasantly so; still, a small fire danced in the fireplace, its cheery glow reflecting in the polished wood floor. Baskets dripping with ivy and ferns hung from the wooden beams spanning the ceiling, and the lush potted palms, ficus trees and scheffleras scattered around the room screened the tables from one another, creating cozy little nooks and the illusion of privacy.

Though Leah appeared calm, her nerves were still humming when she and Mike sat down at a secluded table in a window alcove. News of this little tête-à-tête would be all over the hospital by morning, she thought as she shook out her napkin and spread it over her lap.

Mike had not helped. She could still see the avid interest in the faces of the nurses as he had called good-night to them and led her past the floor station with his hand resting at the small of her back.

In the car on the way to the restaurant she had been quiet, and even now she could not quite bring herself to speak or look directly at him. She had no idea what to say. It was one thing to banter with him when Quinton was there as a buffer, and quite another to make small talk across a candlelit table when it was just the two of them in a secluded corner of a romantic restaurant.

For something to do, Leah reached for her water glass, but her hand trembled so, the edge clacked against her teeth when she took a sip.

"Don't tell me you're nervous."

Over the rim of the glass she looked into Mike's twinkling eyes. Feeling hot color rise in her neck, she quickly set the glass back on the table. "No, of course not," she lied.

"Uh-huh." His smile was gently mocking.

He placed his hand over hers where it lay curled in a fist on top of the checked tablecloth. His touch sent a little jolt up her arm, and she jerked back reflexively, but his big hand engulfed her smaller one, holding tight. His skin felt incredibly warm against her icy fingers.

"Relax. We're just two friends having dinner together. Nothing to be nervous about."

She stared at him across the table, struck by the truth of his words. Yes, as strange as that was, they were friends. Although, throughout the past weeks, the gleam in Mike's eyes, the way he touched her, the intimate tone of his voice, all made it clear that he would like them to be more. If she was honest, she would like that, too, but it wasn't possible. Of all the men in the world, he was the last one she could ever have.

She had gained his friendship under false pretenses and had no right even to that. If he knew the truth he would probably despise her. And she wouldn't blame him.

How had she gotten herself into this mess? When she had set the wheels in motion for Mike to be tested she had known there would be risks, but she hadn't anticipated things would get so complicated. Naively, she had assumed that Mike's part in the whole affair would be quick and impersonal; he would donate a little marrow, then go on about his business, none the wiser, and with any luck, Quinton would recover. She should have realized that nothing was that simple.

She gave him a wan smile. "Really, I'm not nervous. Just tired and a little wobbly. One of my patients got me out of bed around two this morning. She delivered at 7:48 so there wasn't much point in going home."

"Aw, a new baby. That's great." Mike's whole face softened and his voice grew warm. "Boy or girl?"

"Girl. Seven pounds ten ounces, healthy and vigorous. She was screaming her head off the minute she made her entrance."

"That's nice. It must be rewarding to help bring little ones into the world."

"It is. I love it."

"Yeah," he murmured, smiling warmly into her eyes. "You know, back when I was deciding on a specialty I was torn between pediatrics and obstetrics. I love babies, but in your job you have to let them go as soon as they're born. I decided I'd rather be around while they're growing up."

Leah gazed at him across the flickering candle and felt a strange tightness in her chest. She had never known a man who so obviously and openly loved children.

In any other man this degree of emotional attachment might be thought of as effeminate, but no one could doubt Mike's masculinity. He was, in fact, the most masculine man she had ever met, which made his devotion all the more touching. If she ever had children of her own, he was exactly the kind of man she would want to look after them, as a doctor and as a father.

Her long-standing policy had been to avoid even the most remote contact with Mike, and when asked by new parents to recommend a baby doctor she had always suggested someone else. In the future, however, no matter how things turned out, she knew that he would top her list of preferred pediatricians.

For the next hour they talked shop over an excellent dinner of chicken Parmesan and salad. They discussed particularly difficult cases each had encountered; the advantages and disadvantages of practicing medicine in a big hospital like St. Francis, of living in a city the size of Houston; the rumor that was going around that Henry Scarborough was leaving his post as hospital administrator; and they speculated on who would replace him if he did. They told each other stories of the crazy things that had happened during their med school and intern days and the antics of the inevitable class clown each had known.

Mike was a wonderful storyteller. In addition to warmth and a devilish sense of humor, he also had a great sense of drama and timing. Soon Leah forgot about all the reasons she shouldn't be there with him and began to relax. Before long she was laughing and enjoying herself.

After coffee, when Mike announced it was time to keep his promise and take her back to her car, she was surprised at how let down she felt. She couldn't remember the last time she had enjoyed herself so much.

On the drive back they continued their conversation, but now there was a subdued quality to their talk. Awareness and a hum of tension ran just below the surface.

When Mike drove into the dimly lit doctors' parking lot Leah's chest grew inexplicably tight. He pulled the Cadillac into the closest free slot to her sporty little Lexus, about thirty feet down the row, and killed the engine.

"Here we are, back in an hour and twenty-eight minutes. Just like I promised." His smile was a flash of white in the dark car.

"Yes, so we are." Her gaze flickered away for a moment, sweeping over the shadowy forms of the other cars, before returning to his face. "Thank you for the dinner, Mike. I enjoyed it."

He didn't move except to hook his arm over the back of the seat, but somehow he seemed nearer, his eyes searching hers through the dim glow given off by the orange halogen lamps in the parking lot. "Good, I'm glad. So did I."

He fingered the edge of her coat collar, and Leah sat perfectly still. For an instant she thought she felt his fingers toying with the ends of her hair, but she couldn't be certain. A little shiver ran down her spine.

She swallowed hard and twisted her fingers together, her gaze still locked with his. Remotely, she could hear the traffic going by on Fannin Street and the distant *whop-whop-whop-whop* of a medical helicopter taking off from the helipad on top of the hospital.

Another car drove into the parking lot, breaking the spell. Leah pulled her gaze from Mike and reached for the door handle. "Well, I guess I'll see you tomorrow. Good night."

"Wait, I'll walk you to your car."

"Oh, no, please, that's not necessary. Really," she protested, but she could have saved her breath. He was out of the car and skirting the rear before she stepped out.

Side by side, they walked in silence without touching. Now and then the sleeve of his scrubs brushed the sleeve of her spring coat. She felt that gossamer contact as surely as though he'd clamped his hand around her arm.

"Well, here we are," she said inanely when they reached her car. The vehicle made a little *chirp* when she touched the electronic opener. She started to climb in, then paused to look back at him, standing in the wedge between the car and the open door. "Good night, Mike."

He stepped closer, bracing one hand on the top edge of the door, the other on the roof, trapping her. In the burnt-orange glow from a nearby halogen lamp his pale eyes glittered. His gaze dropped to her mouth, then to the pulse beating at the base of her throat, and his eyes grew heavy lidded. Leah's chest squeezed so tight she couldn't breathe.

"Good night, Leah," he said softly, and with a nod, he turned and walked back toward his car.

Holding on to the door for support, Leah watched him go, relief and disappointment warring within her.

Ten feet or so away, Mike suddenly stopped. For a few seconds he stood perfectly still. "Ah, what the hell."

He spun around and marched back toward her with a long, deliberate stride. Confused, Leah watched him, wondering what he'd forgotten. By the time he was close enough for her to see his expression it was too late.

He did not slow his pace but came to an abrupt halt in front of her, and without a word, he dragged her against his chest and crushed his mouth to hers.

The kiss was electrifying. Stunning.

Every cell in Leah's body hummed; every nerve ending crackled and sparked. For a moment, all she could do was cling to Mike, while her heart boomed and her mind went blank and her body reacted helplessly to the bombardment of her senses, going warm and weak and tingly.

She felt as though her insides were melting, and she sagged against him. Had her very life depended on it, she could not have resisted. Of their own volition, her arms slipped around his waist and she clutched his back. Helplessly, her mouth responded to his like a flower opening to the sun, and as their tongues entwined in a sensual dance she pressed against him.

Leah was acutely aware of several things at once—the firmness of his lips rocking over hers; his taste and the pleasant roughness of his tongue against hers; his scent, mixed with a faint antiseptic smell; the coarseness of the cotton scrub against her palms; the heavy pounding of his heart beneath; his heat and hardness pressing against her. The thundering beat of her own heart. Beyond those tactile sensations, nothing else existed for her—no traffic going by, no buzzing street lamp, no cool night breeze whipping her hair around their faces. There was just the two of them...and the hot, thrilling kiss.

Though masterful and thorough, it was over quickly. Releasing her, Mike drew back only inches and clasped her face between his palms, looking deep into her eyes. Leah's heart caromed around her chest like a smacked billiard ball as she saw the intense look on his face.

"I've been wanting to do that for years."

Surprise shot through her, widening her eyes, but he gave her no chance to speak.

"That and more," he continued with unabashed frankness. "Ever since I first met you. And you might as well know, I mean to go on doing it."

He released her so suddenly she would have fallen had she not grasped the top of the car door with both hands. She stood there in the small wedge of space, clinging to the vehicle, her face slack with shock as she watched him stalk away through the darkness.

Slowly, still not taking her eyes from him, she raised her trembling hand and pressed her fingertips to her lips. They were still wet from his kiss and slightly swollen. The cool night breeze feathered over the damp flesh, sending a shiver through her, but she didn't move.

Down the row, Mike got into his car, and a second later she heard the engine start. The sound made her jump and jerked her out of her stupor. Still unable to move, she watched his taillights until he turned right at the end of the row.

Several more seconds ticked by, but finally her legs threatened to give way beneath her. Releasing a long breath, Leah climbed into her own car, but for a long time she merely sat there, gripping the steering wheel with both hands, her gaze still fixed on the point where Mike's car had disappeared from sight.

Mike wanted her—had wanted her for years. Her heart skipped a beat at the thought. Not in all that time had she guessed. The possibility had never even occurred to her.

But then, Mike did not know what she knew.

Slowly, she touched her trembling fingertips to her mouth again and closed her eyes. Dear Lord. What was she going to do?

Chapter Six

The next day after office hours Leah made her rounds to check on her new mothers, then headed for Quinton's room with a determined stride.

She had given the matter a lot of thought and had reached the decision that this attraction between Mike and her would never do. The only sensible choice she had was to call a halt before things went any further. That he had taken a shine to Quinton was enough of a complication without a romance between the two of them compounding matters.

That she was attracted to him was irrelevant and pointless. She and Mike could never have a future together. Any sort of relationship between them, even a lasting friendship, given the circumstances, was impossible, and to let this…this flirtation go on would only spell disaster and hurt for both of them. And for Quinton.

Besides, she couldn't go through another twenty-four hours like the ones that had just passed.

All night she had been restless and had gotten little sleep, and today she'd been so preoccupied she'd barely been able to concentrate.

Sandy had noticed. Several times she had given Leah curious looks. Once, after an examination, when her patient Kim Dayton had begun a litany of the discomforts she was suffering, Leah's mind had wandered, as it had been prone to do all day. While Mrs. Dayton droned on about her aching back and swollen feet, three-an-hour trips to the bathroom and endless heartburn, Leah had silently grappled with the new and unexpected development with Mike.

She had been so lost in thought several seconds of silence had ticked by before she realized that her patient had stopped talking and, along with Sandy, was looking at her curiously.

Leah had saved face by claiming that she had merely been trying to think of a way to ease Kim's discomfort. That had satisfied her patient but not Sandy.

"Would you mind telling me what's going on?" her nurse had demanded the instant they were alone.

"Going on? I don't know what you mean."

"Don't give me that innocent look. You've got something on your mind. All day you've been walking around in a daze, as though someone had smacked you a good one upside the head. You haven't heard half of what's been said. So c'mon. Tell me what's up."

"You're imagining things," Leah had insisted, and plucked the medical file from its holder by the door and entered the next treatment room. Sandy had had no choice but to follow her inside, but it had been clear from her expression that she had not believed her.

Leah grimaced. She knew Sandy's feelings were hurt, but it couldn't be helped. Normally, she confided in her friend, but this time she could not. To do so would have meant explaining Mike's true relationship to Quinton, and that she could not do. Not only had she given her word to her father and Julia, but she was not anxious to reveal her part in the deception.

Pausing outside Quinton's room, Leah sighed and tossed her hair back over her shoulders. She should never have listened to Julia. If Quinton's condition had not been so critical she wouldn't have.

From the beginning she had told her stepmother that they were going about this the wrong way, but as usual, Julia wouldn't listen. Now every day Leah felt as though she were getting mired deeper and deeper in deceit. Short of confessing the truth and risking Mike's anger, perhaps even Quinton's health, there wasn't a thing she could do to change the situation.

As usual, Mike was already there, slouched in a chair beside the bed. Tonight he was dressed in a beautifully cut charcoal suit, crisp white shirt and charcoal-and-rust tie, and he looked even sexier than he had the night before in the green scrubs.

As though drawn by a magnet, the instant Leah stepped into the room her gaze sought him out, but when she found him watching her she quickly glanced away again.

A sudden, vivid memory of that shattering kiss in the parking lot sent heat rushing to her face, and she felt awkward and embarrassed. Her only defense was to ignore the seductive look in Mike's eyes and concentrate on her brother.

"Hi there, sweetie," she said brightly, half turning her back on Mike. "How do you feel tonight?" She took his chart out of the pocket in the side of the bubble and began to scan it, as much for something to do that would keep her gaze from Mike's as out of habit.

"Great. Mike was just telling me all about last night."

"What?" She swung around. "You did *what?*"

"He told me what a good time you two had," Quinton answered before Mike had a chance, drawing his sister's gaze again. His grin stretched from ear to ear.

Leah bristled like a cornered cat. "Oh, he did, did he?"

"Yeah. Sounds like you guys really hit it off." Quinton reined in his smile and tried his best to act casual. "You know, I've been thinking. Since I'm so much better, you two don't have to sit around here with me every evening. I think you should get out and enjoy yourselves more, like you did last night. Maybe take in a movie or something."

Surprise and dismay rippled through Leah. Dear heaven. Quinton was shamelessly playing matchmaker. Until that moment she had not realized that he had so much as given a thought to the possibility of a romance between her and Mike. Last night she had assumed his suggestion that she have dinner with him had merely been an awkward impulse. Now she realized how wrong she had been. Her brother's willingness to forgo his hero's company, even for an evening now and then, spoke volumes about how much he wanted them to get together.

Then again, perhaps the idea hadn't originated with Quinton at all. Perhaps someone had planted the seed in his mind.

"I see." Leah stuffed the patient chart back into the pocket and shot Mike a lethal look. "May I speak to you outside for a moment?"

"Sure." He rolled to his feet, giving Quinton a wink. "Be right back, sport."

The instant they stepped into the hall and the door closed behind them, Leah spun around. "I can't believe you did that."

"Did what?"

"Oh, don't you put on that innocent act with me, Mike McCall. You know exactly what I'm talking about. You—"

Two nurses walking by slanted curious glances their way, and Leah clamped her mouth shut. She gave the women a tight smile and waited until they had passed before hissing, "You had no business telling Quinton about last night."

"Is that all?"

"Is that *all!* Listen, you—"

Another nurse stepped out of a room across the hall and an orderly got off the elevator and headed toward them.

"We can't discuss this here." Mike looked around, then grasped her elbow. "Come with me."

"Wait! What do you think you're doing?" Leah tried to pry his fingers from her arm, but they wouldn't budge. He ignored her protests and her feeble attempt to hold back and hauled her down the corridor. She almost had to trot to keep up with his long stride.

"We can have a little privacy in here." He opened a door at the end of the hall and hustled her into a small supply room filled with linens and soaps and patient hygiene kits.

The instant he closed the door Leah pulled her arm free and renewed her attack. "You had no right to tell my brother about last night. No right at all. Not only was it tacky and ungentlemanly, it was downright underhanded. If you think that you can—"

"Whoa, whoa. Let's set the record straight here. The only thing I told Quinton about last night was that we had a nice dinner and a pleasant evening of conversation."

Leah stared at him. "Th-that's all?"

"That's all." He held up three fingers on his right hand. "Scout's honor."

"Oh, I see. Then why on earth was he..." She paused and slanted him an embarrassed look, her neck and face heating up again.

"Matchmaking?" Mike finished for her, and grinned

when her color deepened. "Maybe because he's a smart kid. He probably picked up the vibes."

"What vibes? What're you talking about?"

"I'm talking about the attraction between us."

That gave her a start. As she met his warm gaze her nerves began to twang. Suddenly, she became aware of several things she hadn't noticed before: how small the storage room was and how Mike's broad-shouldered frame seemed to dominate the tiny space; how close together they were. How isolated.

"Don't be absurd. There's nothing between us."

She knew by the gleam in his eyes and the hint of a smile on his lips that he was remembering their parting the night before. Her blush deepened, but she refused to back down. "Don't look at me that way. I know what you're thinking. But one kiss, particularly a stolen one, doesn't constitute a romance. Or even an attraction."

"True," he conceded. "And I'd even agree with that in this case, except for one thing." He paused and grinned, and she knew she was in trouble. "Last night when I kissed you, you kissed me back."

"I did no such—"

"C'mon, Leah, don't bother to deny it. I was there, remember. I know when a woman responds to my kisses. If that wasn't passion, lady, you've got a funny way of showing indifference."

"Well, you're wrong. Although, given your reputation, it's hardly surprising that you'd think so," she snapped, using disdain to hide her panic. "From what I hear, you've dated every single female on the hospital staff."

Mike grinned. "Not *every* single female. Just the good-looking ones. Hey, just kidding," he added with a chuckle when she shot him a disgusted look. "Anyway, what did you expect? I had to do something while I was waiting for you to notice I was alive. C'mon, Leah, why don't you just admit it? You're as attracted to me as I am to you."

She could never lie worth a fig, but she decided to give it her best shot anyway. "That's not true. I...I...that is...

He ignored her sputtering. "Anyway, you know as well as I do that this thing between us didn't just start last night. For weeks we've spent almost every evening together—"

"Visiting Quinton!"

"That's right. Nevertheless, we were together. We've gotten to know each other during those visits, grown comfortable with each other, laughed together, argued, learned that we have a lot in common and that we really like each other. And every night the sexual tension in that room has been thick enough to cut with a knife. I'm not surprised that Quinton sensed it."

She opened her mouth to argue, but there was nothing she could say. He was right. She had been lying to herself, pretending that being with her brother was the only reason she looked forward to those nightly visits, telling herself that the odd, fizzy feeling she experienced in Mike's presence was merely nerves and that the camaraderie that had developed between them meant nothing. She had admitted weeks ago that she was attracted to him, but she had deluded herself into believing that it was nothing more than an impersonal physical attraction, much like what she would experience toward a movie star or any other attractive man. But it was more than that. Much more.

That terrified her. Dear heaven, she couldn't have those kind of feelings for Julia's son. She simply couldn't.

But she did.

Her shoulders sagged. "All right, I admit it. I do find you attractive. But that doesn't mean I want to get involved with you."

Mike cocked his head to one side and studied her. "Why not?"

The blunt question caught her off guard. She could not tell him the truth, and she found herself groping for an answer. "There are several reasons."

"Name one."

"Well, for one thing, I don't have time."

"C'mon, you have to do better than that. I'm a doctor, too, remember. Which makes it perfect. Who better to know and understand the kind of demands that are made on your time? Sweetheart, even doctors have to have a social life. Most of us manage to fall in love and get married and have families just like everybody else. So what are your other reasons?"

Married? Leah stared at him, a frisson of alarm and excitement zinging through her. Surely he was just speaking in generalities. The chance of a marriage between her and Mike was nil. Still, she couldn't deny that the idea did appeal. Just the prospect of it brought a sweet tightness to her chest.

Realizing the drift of her thoughts, she hardened her resolve and tipped her chin at Mike.

"Then there's Quinton—"

"Who is getting better by the day, and who is all for us getting together. Next reason?"

"My, uh, my parents are staying at my home. I can't neglect them."

"According to Quinton, they're out on the town almost every night. I don't think they would miss you. So what's your next reason for not going out with me?"

Beginning to feel cornered, Leah blurted out the first thing that entered her mind. "Because your relationships never last."

Mike's eyebrows shot skyward. "That's it? That's why you're so leery of me?"

"Yes," she lied.

Actually, though Mike had dated a lot of women, he did not have a reputation as a womanizer. Quite the opposite. The women he had dated thought he was wonderful and had nothing but good things to say about him. That he had managed to remain friends with them all said a lot about his character.

At the moment, however, that was the best excuse Leah could come up with.

Mike stepped closer. The move and the look in his eyes caused Leah's heart to give a little leap. She took a quick step back and bumped into something solid. Moving nearer still, Mike braced his hands on either side of her, gripping the metal shelving at her back, effectively penning her in.

"Sweetheart, you have nothing to worry about. It's true that I've dated a lot of women. I'm a healthy, normal male, and I don't apologize for that. But I swear to you, none of those relationships was serious. None even came close. You can ask any of the women I dated and they will tell you that I was open with them, that I never made any promises or did anything to lead any one of them to believe that my feelings ran deeper than fondness and friendship."

"I believe you. But I'm just not interested in that sort of casual relationship."

"Neither am I. Not with you. Honey, what I feel for you is anything but casual," he drawled with an ironic half smile. "Haven't you figured that out yet? I'm crazy about you."

"Mike!" His name came out a breathless exclamation. She stared up at him, her heart booming against her rib cage.

"I have been from the moment I met you two years ago."

"Mike, you can't be serious."

"Oh, but I am," he murmured. "Very serious."

His head tipped to one side and began a slow descent toward hers. Beneath half-closed lids, his gaze zeroed in on her mouth, and in those pale-blue eyes burned a sensual fire that instantly set off a matching inferno deep in Leah's belly.

"So you see," he whispered, "you don't have anything to worry about."

Leah tore her gaze away from those mesmerizing eyes, only to encounter that beautifully chiseled mouth, drawing slowly, inexorably, closer.

She trembled and pressed back against the metal shelving, torn between common sense and longing, and a deeper emotion she dared not put a name to.

Don't just stand here. Stop him, she commanded herself. All you have to do is turn your head aside and say no. Mike is not the kind of man to force his attentions where they aren't wanted. This is insane. Put an end to it now, while you still can.

Trembling, Leah looked at his slumberous eyes again, at that handsome face, flushed now with desire, and knew she was lost.

It had been so long since a man had looked at her with that kind of desire, so long since she had experienced this wonderful giddiness in the pit of her stomach, this knee-knocking, heart-pounding, breath-stealing anticipation. Actually, she had never felt quite this way before. The feelings Lyle's kisses and caresses had elicited hadn't even come close to what Mike made her feel with just a look.

With his mouth a mere inch from hers he paused, and his gaze locked with hers. He was giving her one last chance. Though his eyes blazed with hunger and heat, she knew it would take only the smallest gesture—a resisting

hand on his chest, a shake of her head, a whispered no—
and he would stop. The decision was hers.

There was no doubt in her mind what she should do—
what she must do.

But it was already too late. In her heart she had known
that all along. She tried. She tried with all her might to
summon the strength to deny him, to deny them both, but
intellect and conscience were no match for the yearning
that consumed her. Trembling, she stared back into those
crystal-blue eyes, unable to utter a sound.

Then her last chance slipped away.

As his lips settled over hers, her heart leaped with an
almost unbearable excitement that squeezed her chest
painfully. Her breath caught in her throat and her eyes
fluttered shut. When he pulled her into his embrace the
only resistance she offered was a moan.

Throwing caution and common sense to the wind, Leah
melted against him, twining her arms around his neck and
kissing him back with a hunger and passion that matched
his own.

A distant voice of reason warned her that she was playing with fire, but caution was no match for the longing
and the need that pulled at her. No matter what happened,
no matter how ill-advised it was, she simply could not
deny herself this.

It was crazy. Insanity. But she no longer cared. She had
been too long without a man's touch, and her feelings for
Mike had grown too strong to ignore.

The kiss grew deeper, hotter. Leah lost all contact with
reality. The world around her simply ceased to be. Nothing else existed—not Quinton; not Julia; not her father;
not the hospital full of people, any one of whom could
walk through the storeroom door at any moment. Nor did
she spare a thought to how furious her stepmother would
be if she ever found out that Leah was falling in love with

her son. In those heady moments there was only Mike, and the exquisite pleasure of being in his arms.

Mindless with desire, they pressed closer, their bodies straining together, hands desperately roaming and clutching, mouths open and greedy. Insatiable. Their breathing grew labored, and small, urgent sounds issued from their throats.

A fever consumed Leah, burning from the core of her being, setting her on fire, pulsing through her veins. It was both pleasure and pain, a searing need so great she thought she would surely die of it.

Her response drew a low sound from Mike, rough and sensual and deliciously primitive. He widened his stance and pulled her closer still, his hands cupping her bottom, pressing her intimately against him, telling her without words the state of his arousal.

The fire in Leah's belly burst into an inferno. She clung to Mike, lost in a blaze of passion.

"Oh, my! I'm so sorry. I didn't know...that is..."

The feminine voice was a jolt of reality, sending shock zinging through Leah, making her jump. She tore her mouth from Mike's and glanced over her shoulder, and her heart sank.

Standing just inside the doorway was none other than Nurse Hazel Peterson, the biggest gossip in the hospital. The gray-haired woman's mouth was still agape, but her eyes were alight with avid interest.

Leah would have pulled from Mike's embrace had he not held her tight. Cradling the back of her head in his hand, he pressed her hot face against his chest to shield her from Hazel's curious stare. With what Leah thought was astonishing calm, he looked over her head at the nurse and replied, "Don't worry about it, Hazel. No harm done."

"I'm so sorry, Dr. McCall. Truly I am. If I'd known that you and Dr. Albright were in here—"

"It's okay, Hazel. Really. Now, if you'll just give us a minute, we'll be out of your way."

"Of course, Doctor," she agreed pleasantly. But when she made no move to leave he gestured toward the hall.

"A private moment."

"Oh! Yes, of course. How silly of me. I'll, uh, I'll just get the supplies I need—"

"Get them later, Nurse."

"Oh. Certainly. Whatever you say, Doctor."

She agreed readily enough, but the disappointment in her voice was evident. Clearly, Nurse Peterson had hoped to hang around and perhaps pick up more juicy tidbits to relate to her cronies. However, under Mike's steady stare, she had no choice and reluctantly began to back out of the room.

"I'll, uh, I'll leave you two alone then and come back later for the supplies I needed. It's not urgent that I get them now."

Her chatter was a stalling tactic, but Mike wasn't falling for it. "I thought not. Now, if you don't mind..."

At the sound of the door finally clicking shut Leah groaned. "I don't believe this. Hazel Peterson, of all people!"

A rumbling began in Mike chest. It took a few seconds for Leah to identify the sound, but when she did she jerked back as far as his encircling arms would let her and scowled.

"Mike McCall, don't you dare laugh. If you do, so help me, I'll smack you. This *isn't* funny!"

"Sure it is." He chuckled, unfazed by her threat. "C'mon, sweetheart. It isn't the end of the world. Actually, I'm kinda glad it happened." Grinning, he grasped her shoulders and bent and placed his forehead against hers. "Now you have to go out with me. By the end of the day Hazel will have told everyone who'll listen that she caught Dr. McCall and Dr. Albright making out in the storage room."

"We were *not* making out," she protested, blushing scarlet.

"Sure we were. And it was damned exciting, too. Hell, we nearly set the place on fire." His eyes danced with wicked humor. "I'll bet when old Hazel spotted us she was so envious her tongue was hanging out. Hell, she's probably still panting."

"You're terrible." Mike's devilish humor was impossible to resist. Leah did not feel in the least like laughing, but she could not keep a smile from twitching her lips.

"Hey, now. Cheer up," he coaxed, seeing her worried look. "It's not as tragic as all that. Hospital romances go on all the time."

"Maybe. But none of them has ever involved me."

"Well, it's time one did." He cupped her chin and tilted up her face until she was forced to meet his gaze. "I've shot down all your objections, so there's no reason we can't be together. Unless you can look me in the eye and honestly say that you just don't want to be with me. That you don't want to explore these feelings we have for each other."

Leah felt like an insect struggling on a pin. No matter how she twisted and turned, there was no escape. She tried to do the intelligent thing and tell him that wasn't what she wanted at all, but gazing up into those straightforward blue eyes, she could not summon the lie.

The trouble was, she did want to be with him.

After a while, her shoulders slumped. "No, I can't tell you that."

A gusty sigh of relief escaped Mike, and he pulled her back into his arms, holding her close against his chest.

"You won't regret it, sweetheart. I'll never hurt you. You have my solemn promise on that." He waited a beat, then asked, "Do you believe me?"

"Yes."

She did believe him. Mike was the kind of man every woman dreamed of, dependable, caring, a delightful companion, and she had no doubt that he would be a wonderful lover. He was secure enough in his masculinity not to see her as a threat, as Lyle had done. Most important of all, he was a man of integrity.

Knowing that, however, only made Leah feel guiltier. Still, she could not give him up. Not yet.

What they had wouldn't last, no matter how deep their feelings went. It couldn't. No matter what objections Julia had, once Quinton was out of the woods she would have to tell Mike the truth. He deserved that much.

But until then, she simply could not deny herself this little piece of happiness.

Snuggling her cheek against his chest, she closed her eyes and hugged him tight. Oh, Mike. If only I could promise not to hurt you, she thought sadly.

Chapter Seven

The weeks that followed proved to be a period of extreme inner conflict for Leah. Never had she been so happy and so miserable at the same time.

She treasured every moment she spent with Mike. Even when she wasn't with him, she went around with a tightness in her chest, a feeling of expectancy, just knowing that before the day was over she would see him, that he would look at her in that way he had that made her go warm all over, that he would take every opportunity to touch her and that before they parted he would take her in his arms and kiss her.

Mike made Leah feel things she had never experienced—giddiness and excitement, an almost delirious happiness. When they were apart she was filled with a constant, bone-deep longing to be with him, to see him, to touch him, to hear his voice. When they were together she felt more alive than she'd ever felt in her life.

He was a wonderful companion—intelligent, charming, handsome, good-natured. Beneath that affable charm and good looks was a man of substance, a man upon whom a woman could depend.

A man to whom a woman could entrust her heart.

There was also an innate, careless grace and sexuality about Mike that took her breath away. Every move he made seemed sexy to Leah. Just watching him walk down the hospital corridors elicited some very embarrassing fantasies that drove every other thought right out of her head. She was profoundly glad that her co-workers could not read her mind.

Mike was slow to anger, she discovered, but he was no pushover. He was a man of strong opinions and even stronger character, and when roused, his temper was formidable.

Also—perhaps most important of all—he made her laugh with his silly jokes and his devilish personality. Laughing, she had discovered, was something she had not done nearly enough before meeting Mike.

He made her feel special and cherished. And loved. And it was wonderful.

At the same time, however, anxiety and a sense of futility plagued Leah. In the beginning especially, she worried constantly that any day Julia would learn about her and Mike from someone on the hospital staff. Leah knew her stepmother would be livid and would not hesitate to make a scene.

However, as the weeks passed smoothly she realized how unlikely that was; Julia did not engage in conversation with people she thought of as underlings. Leah relaxed somewhat, but the possibility, though more remote, still hung over her like a dark cloud.

The situation had changed since she had promised not to reveal Julia's secret. Mike had to be told the truth, but she didn't want it to come from her stepmother in one of the woman's hysterical rages.

In any case, Leah knew she should be the one to tell him. He deserved that much. And she was going to. But not yet. Not just yet.

The time wasn't right, she told herself day after day, week after week. Quinton was improving, but he wasn't out of the woods yet. When he was released from the hospital, then she would tell Mike everything.

Until then, she was determined to savor this time with him and enjoy every moment to the fullest.

Except when one of Leah's expectant mothers went into labor or she or Mike had an emergency, they were together every evening. Mostly they continued to spend their after-office hours with Quinton, but two or three evenings a week, after visiting for a while with her brother, they went out together.

Invariably on those occasions the air between them vibrated with sexual tension. Every kiss, every touch, every look that passed between them, was rife with hunger and longing. Yet their evenings always stopped short of intimacy. Both their schedules were hectic and they spent the majority of their free time with Quinton. Even so, there had been opportunities. But Mike seemed determined not to rush her.

The sensible part of Leah was glad, even while the romantic in her yearned for more. Day by day she was falling more in love with Mike. She wanted to make love with him, longed to share the special closeness and intimacies that only people in love experience, but she knew it best not to take that step.

A part of her felt guilty even contemplating a physical relationship with Mike. She knew she didn't deserve him. From the first she had deceived him on several levels. One day soon, she was going to have to tell him the truth, and when she did he would surely despise her. How much harder that would be to accept if they were lovers.

So she continued to bide her time and take each day as it came.

Sometimes, if one or both had a tough day, their dates consisted of merely eating dinner in the hospital cafeteria, then saying good-night with a passionate kiss in the parking lot. Other times they took in a movie or baseball game or some other form of entertainment. As often as not, however, they simply enjoyed each other's company, either going for long walks or sitting at their table in a restaurant, talking until the place closed.

They talked about any- and everything—their struggles to get through medical school, their busy practices, particularly interesting or challenging cases they'd had, what they liked and disliked about St. Francis Hospital. They also discussed, and sometimes argued good-naturedly over, movies and books and music.

And, of course, they talked about family.

The last thing that Leah wanted to discuss with Mike was Julia. However, she was afraid it would seem odd if she didn't exhibit at least some curiosity, so one evening over after-dinner coffee she forced herself to broach the subject.

"You never mention your natural mother. I, uh, I assume from that your parents are divorced."

She had expected some sort of reaction to the question—a start, a frown, maybe coolness. But Mike didn't so much as blink.

"Yeah, my mother walked out on Dad and me years ago, when I was five. At the time, Houston's economy was in a real slump, particularly the building industry. New construction had all but come to a standstill, and R&R Construction, the company Dad and my uncle Reilly own, was teetering on the brink of bankruptcy. So my mother bailed and married a rich man.'' Mike shrugged. ''I haven't seen her since.''

''Do you remember her at all?''

''Not really. My memories of her are vague, just little fuzzy snippets really. And I don't recall ever seeing a picture of her. Dad must've destroyed them all when she left. To tell the truth, I doubt that I'd recognize her if I ran into her on the street.''

For Leah, that bit of information was welcome, but at the same time disturbing.

Mike's expression was neutral, showing neither sorrow nor anger, but the very matter-of-factness of his tone wrung Leah's heart. How could Julia have done such a thing? A failed marriage was one matter, but to walk away from your child and sever all contact with him was unforgivable.

Tears stung Leah's eyes as she placed her hand over Mike's. ''I'm so sorry. That must have hurt terribly.''

''If it did, I don't remember it. Hey, don't worry about it, sweetheart. Dad and I got along just fine on our own. He's a super father and a good man. Even today, he's still my best friend.''

''That's nice.'' She gave him a wan smile, but her heart ached for the little boy he had been.

''Yeah, it is. For eight years it was just the two of us, but he saw to it that I had everything I needed, materially and emotionally. Also, there was my uncle Reilly, Dad's identical twin, and all their family, which includes doting grandparents, aunts and uncles and a passel of cousins, so I never felt lonely or neglected.''

''That's good.''

''Hmm.'' Mike fiddled with the handle on his coffee cup, and a tender look came over his face. ''Then Tess came into our lives.'' He shook his head and chuckled at the memory. ''After my mother walked out, Dad became something of a misogynist, but even he couldn't bring himself to be rude to a pregnant woman.''

''You're kidding. Tess was pregnant when your father met her?'' Leah goggled at Mike over the top of her cup.

''Yep. Very pregnant. And a widow. Her husband had died not knowing he was going to be a father.

''At first Dad wanted nothing to do with her and he did his damnedest to avoid her. But he was too much of a gentleman not to give an expectant mother a hand when she needed one. Which turned out to be pretty often. Tess was alone in the world expect for her best friend, Amanda Sutherland. Actually, her name is Amanda McCall now. She's married to my uncle Reilly, but she still uses Sutherland as her professional name.''

''Amanda Sutherland? The news anchorwoman on television? She's married to your uncle?''

''Yep.''

''My goodness,'' Leah murmured with a touch of awe. ''You do have an interesting family.''

''If you think that's something, Aunt Meghan, Dad's baby sister, is married to Rhys Morgan.''

This time, Leah's jaw dropped. A full five seconds ticked by before she could croak out, ''The *singing star?*''

Mike nodded.

''Oh—my—word!'' The drawn-out, breathless exclamation tumbled from Leah's lips. Mike grinned at her astonished expression, but she didn't care. She put her hand over her heart and let out her breath in a long sigh. ''Rhys Morgan is an icon. I can't believe he's married to your aunt.''

''At the family gatherings, Rhys is just one of the guys. We tend to forget that he's a superstar. Someday I'll have to tell you about how he and Aunt Meghan got together. It's a real doozy of a story.

''But then, so is Uncle Reilly and Amanda's.'' A wry

look came over Mike's face. "Come to think of it, none of the courtships of the Blaines and McCalls has been ordinary. Including Dad and Tess's.

"As I was saying, Dad tried hard to resist Tess, but he didn't stand a chance. He ended up being her Lamaze coach."

"You're *kidding!*"

"Nope. He even delivered her baby in the back of his Jeep while they were trying to outrun a hurricane. They were on their way to my grandparents' home in Crockett when Tess went into labor. I wasn't there, but from what I hear, Uncle Reilly was driving like a bat out of hell and cussing a blue streak, trying to get to the hospital, while Dad was in the back with Tess, delivering Molly.

"I think he was halfway in love with Tess before that, but when he put Molly into her arms, he completely lost his heart to both of them. He and Tess were married a few months later."

Mike's grin flashed. "I was thirteen at the time, and I got a terrific new mother and a baby sister all in one fell swoop. Man, I was in heaven."

Moisture glistened in Leah's eyes as she looked across the candlelit table at him. Her chest was so tight she barely choked out, "Oh, Mike, that's such a beautiful story."

"Every word of it's true. Scout's honor." He held up three fingers and gave her a twinkling grin, and Leah chuckled, as she knew he had intended.

"Tess is the best thing that ever happened to Dad and me. Over the years she and Dad have given me a brother and another sister. I was almost Quinton's age when Ethan was born, and in my first year of college when Tess had Katy. It was fun being the big brother and watching them grow up. I guess they're partly the reason I went into pediatrics—they and all the other little ones added to our family over the years.

"Dad has two brothers and a sister, and they grew up with three cousins. Their childhood homes in Crockett are just a few hundred yards apart. As kids, the seven of them kept a path worn through the woods between the two places, and now the next generation of kids is doing the same."

"That sounds like a wonderful way to grow up," Leah said wistfully.

"Yeah. Even today, the McCall and Blaine cousins are all still close, so much so they might as well be siblings. Which isn't so surprising, since my grandmother McCall and Aunt Dorothy, the cousins' mother, are identical twins.

"Now Dad, Uncle Reilly, Uncle Travis and Aunt Meghan, plus all the cousins, have children of their own. At last count, during our annual family get-together at the grandparents' home in Crockett last Christmas, there were twenty-one grandchildren ranging in age from three months to me at thirty. By now, there may be more on the way." His teasing grin flashed again. "We're a prolific bunch."

"Twenty-one?" Leah repeated weakly, staring at him. "Oh my, that is a large family." For the first sixteen years of her life, until Quinton came along, Leah had been an only child. She couldn't imagine a family that size.

"Wait'll you meet them. When we're all together it's bedlam, but it's fun. The grandparents love it."

Leah gave him a wan smile but didn't comment. She doubted very much if she would be around long enough to meet Mike's family.

The thought brought a painful tightness to her chest, and she found herself battling a sudden urge to cry. To change the subject she asked, "Did your father's company survive the recession?"

"Does a goose go barefoot? You bet. They went

through some rough times financially, but they hung on and eventually the company prospered beyond Dad's and Uncle Reilly's wildest dreams.''

He went on to tell her about some of his father and uncle's struggles all those years ago. With his sense of humor, Mike was a born storyteller who could make the most ordinary tale not only fascinating but amusing, as well. He also had a way of drawing out a person. There was some innate something about Mike that fostered trust. Before you knew it, your defenses were down and you were confiding your deepest secrets.

When he'd finished his hilarious stories about his family, without missing a beat he said, ''So there. I've told you all the family secrets. Now it's your turn.''

Leah's instinctive reaction was to dodge the question. She had never discussed her childhood or the loss of her mother with anyone, not even Sandy. Some things were just too painful, too private.

These past few weeks, whenever their conversations had drifted in that direction she had managed to sidestep, either giving him a vague answer or changing the subject. She should have known that he would not let her get by with that forever. The look in his eyes told her evasion would not work this time.

''There's not much to tell really. It's very dull and boring.''

''I doubt that. Nothing about you could bore me. Anyway, turnabout is fair play. So, why don't you start by telling me about your mother?''

Dismayed, Leah looked at him across the table, but she could see the steady resolve in his eyes. Sighing, she studied the coffee in her cup and searched for the right words. Finally she gave up and said baldly, ''My mother died when I was fifteen.''

"Aw, jeez." Mike flinched. "I'm sorry, sweetheart. I didn't realize. Look, if this is too painful—"

"No, it's all right." Leah ran her finger around the rim of her cup. He had given her an out, but oddly, she couldn't take it. Now that she'd started, she felt compelled to finish. "Her name was Elinor. Dr. Elinor Albright. She was a neurosurgeon, a brilliant one. I suppose her love of medicine rubbed off on me. She was bright and skilled, a strong, beautiful, confident, capable woman. I loved and admired her very much."

"Hmm. Sounds like my kinda lady. Which means, she sounds like you."

Leah looked up and met Mike's warm gaze. His smile was affectionate and teasing and made her heart do a funny little skip.

"I've always had a weakness for strong, beautiful women. That's one of the reasons I'm so crazy about you."

Leah stared at him. Mike always seemed to know exactly the right thing to say. Which was what made him so easy to talk to, to confide in. Although she knew it was probably foolish, she could feel the last of her reservations crumbling.

"Yes, well, not all men are like you. I've suspected for years now that Mother's strength was what caused my father to divorce her."

Mike couldn't hide his astonishment, and Leah's mouth twitched with grim humor.

"You mean, he walked out on a great woman like her?"

"Yes. Like you, I was young, only three when it happened, so I don't remember the actual event, but for years I hated my father. For leaving us, but mostly for breaking my mother's heart."

"I take it that means you don't hate him anymore?"

"No, I suppose not. As an adult I've come to realize that Peter Albright is one of those men who truly needs to be needed. It's important to him that his wife be a woman he can pamper and spoil, someone who depends on him emotionally, financially, physically and every other way."

Leah shrugged and her lips quivered in a wry, sad smile. "All my mother needed from him was his love.

"I think, because she was such a strong, self-sufficient woman, he thought she would weather their breakup with hardly a twinge, but he was wrong. Losing him devastated her. After he left, she never even looked at another man."

And that explained a lot, Mike thought, studying the sadness in her eyes. He reached across the table and took her hand, squeezing it lightly. "Is that why you've never married? Because you don't trust a man to cherish you for your strengths as well as your looks?"

"Maybe. I don't know. It's not a groundless fear, you know," she argued, bristling slightly.

"Leah, not all men are like your father."

"That's true, but many are. I was even engaged to one back in med school."

"Really?" That bit of information hit Mike like a kick in the stomach. Which surprised him. He and Leah were both in their thirties. Of course there had been other men in her life before him. He'd known that. Even so, he hated the idea that she had come so close to making a lifetime commitment to someone else. "So, what happened?"

Briefly, she told him how Lyle's family influence had always paved the way for him, and how ill-prepared he'd been for the pressure of med school. "He hated it that I was at the top of our class and he was at the bottom. When he finally flunked out he broke off our engagement. I haven't seen him since."

Though she strove for indifference, Mike heard the hurt

in her voice. He decided on the spot that Lyle What's-his-name was a idiot. However, if the man had been there at that moment Mike would have been hard-pressed to know whether to slug him or kiss him. He hated him for hurting Leah, but he would be forever grateful to him for setting her free.

"The man was a fool. You're better off without him." Mike grimaced. "Sorry. I know that sounds clichéd, but it's the truth."

"I know. Marrying Lyle, under any circumstance, would have been a huge mistake. But an experience like that does tend to make one a bit leery."

Mike put his hand over hers. "Sweetheart, at the risk of repeating myself, not all men are alike. I'll always be there for you, Leah. You can count on that."

She didn't look convinced, but Mike didn't push it.

"After your mother died what happened?"

"I went to live with my father. It was awful at first. I barely knew him. I'd seen him only once a year or so for most of my life. To make it worse, he and Julia had been married only a short time. She wasn't exactly thrilled to be saddled with a teenager."

Leah sighed. "In all fairness, looking back, I really can't blame her. I wasn't exactly what she bargained for when she married my father."

"Your stepmother's name is Julia? What a coincidence, that's my mother's name, too."

"Really?" Leah replied, giving him a weak smile. "Anyway, there I was in a strange house, with people I didn't know, one of whom was a father I thought I hated. I felt abandoned and lost and unwanted, and so grief stricken I wanted to die. Luckily, Cleo took me under her wing."

"Cleo?"

"Dad's housekeeper. Actually, she's my housekeeper

now. Cleo moved from Dallas with Quinton and me when I joined the staff at St. Francis. If it hadn't been for her, I'm not sure I would have survived those first few months after my mother died.

"Then the most wonderful thing happened. My stepmother became pregnant, and everything changed."

Wry amusement touched Leah's mouth. "Well, it was wonderful for me, at any rate. To tell you the truth, I don't think she was exactly thrilled to be having a baby at age thirty-six, but I was over the moon at the prospect of a brother or sister. Quinton filled a void in my life at a time when I desperately needed someone to love, someone who would love me back unconditionally. He gave my life a sense of purpose. For me, his birth was like a gift from heaven."

Leah flashed Mike a chagrined look. "I have to admit, I practically stole Quinton from my stepmother. From the day they brought him home from the hospital, I've looked after him.

"When he was about two months old, Dad and Julia hired a nanny. Boy, did I resent that woman. I used to rush home from school, head straight for the nursery and shoo her out. Looking back, I realize what a possessive little tyrant I was. I was only sixteen then, but I think Miss Grimes was afraid of me. Even though my father paid her salary, she quickly realized who was in charge of Quinton."

Mike laughed. "You were a real little mother hen, weren't you? No wonder you went into obstetrics."

"I suppose you're right." Leah accepted his teasing with a smile. What she hadn't bothered to tell him was how relieved and pleased Julia had been to have someone take over her baby's care. She had loved playing with her infant son when he was clean and fed and in a sunny mood, but the instant he turned cranky or needed changing, she'd given him back to Leah to tend. Nor did she explain that the nanny had been hired so that her father and stepmother could resume their vagabond lifestyle.

"On the plus side, though, my devotion to Quinton pleased Dad and Julia and helped to cement our relationship." Mainly because it freed them of the responsibility.

"Now I understand how you and Quinton got to be so close. And I gotta tell you, your parents were fortunate to have you to look after Quinton while they traveled," he added shrewdly, letting her know that he wasn't fooled by her carefully edited story.

If he found anything odd about parents leaving their infant son in the care of a teenager and a nanny for months on end, he said nothing.

At that moment, both Leah and Mike realized that they were the only diners left in the restaurant, and that all around them the waiters were setting up the tables for the next morning.

Taking the hint, Mike paid the bill and escorted Leah out.

In the car she laid her head back against the seat and closed her eyes. It had felt good, almost cathartic, to finally talk about the past, but she wondered if she had revealed too much. It was so difficult to remember that Mike was Julia's son, and she must be constantly on guard not to let anything slip.

The restaurant was only a few blocks from St. Francis, and neither Leah nor Mike spoke until he brought his car to a halt beside hers in the hospital parking lot. Switching off the engine, he turned toward her and rested his right arm along the top of the seat. The interior of the car was lit only by the amber glow of the halogen lights of the parking lot. Though the dimness, their gazes met and held.

One of the lights buzzed, and a june bug hit the windshield with a thump. Mike's fingers toyed with the ends of her hair, then trailed down the side of her neck. Leah shivered, and he smiled.

"Tomorrow is Sunday," he whispered seductively. "Spend the day with me."

"I...I ca—"

He placed two fingers over her mouth. "I checked with Sandy. She told me you don't have a patient near her due date right now. John Houseman is covering for me, so we're both free. Spend the day with me, Leah."

"I'd like to Mike. Truly, I would. But I can't. Julia and my dad have invited some old friends over tomorrow, and they expect me to be there."

She prayed that he could not see her guilty flush in the dim light. The excuse was a bald-faced lie, as had been all the others she had given him in the past few weeks.

When their romance had begun she had not anticipated how complicated it would be to keep him and his mother apart. It had been so long since she'd dated anyone on a regular basis it had not occurred to her that Mike would want them to spend most of their free weekends together, or that he would expect to pick her up at her home when they went out on those nights.

So far she had managed to come up with excuses to meet him elsewhere, usually at the hospital, but moments like this one were becoming more and more awkward, and she was running out of excuses. She knew that Mike was beginning to wonder why, after dating her for months, he had never been inside her home, and why he'd never met her parents.

Most evenings her father and Julia had an engagement and they rarely returned before two in the morning, so it was probably safe to allow Mike to pick her up at her house, but Leah wasn't taking any chances.

She would like nothing better than to spend all her spare time with him, but with Julia and her father staying at her place, it was just too risky. Her stepmother was a cunning and curious woman. She was sure to get suspicious if Leah were gone every weekend. And with Julia's volatile temper, there was no way of knowing how she would react if she ever discovered the truth.

"I see."

Mike studied her, his expression unreadable. Hooking his hand around the back of her neck, he pulled her to him. His kiss was hard and rough. His lips rocked over hers as though he would devour her, while his tongue stabbed into her mouth, dominating, possessive.

With a sigh, Leah melted against him, understanding the angry passion simmering inside him. Within moments, though, the kiss gentled, softened into quivering awareness. The caress of his lips on hers turned into something just as hungry, just as heated as his anger, something so irresistibly sensual it brought tears to Leah's eyes and made her heart squeeze painfully.

She slid her hands under his suit jacket and clutched Mike's shirt. Her toes curled inside her shoes. She pressed closer and kissed him back with unabashed hunger and yearning. Oh, Mike. Oh, my darling, she thought sadly, as a tear seeped from the corner of her eye. If only…

They were both trembling when Mike broke off the kiss. Breathing hard, he cupped her face with one hand and looked deep into her eyes. "I want to be with you, Leah."

"I want to be with you, too," she replied, trembling under his intense stare.

"Do you? Do you really?"

"Yes. More than anything."

"Then why do I get the feeling that you're trying to shut me out of parts of your life?"

"No! It's not that at all."

For an excruciatingly long time he studied her, his pale

eyes probing for the truth. Leah had to fight the urge to squirm.

"Good," he said at last. "Because I want to be included in your life. In all of it." He rubbed his thumb over the slight cleft in her chin, over her lower lip, and his pupils expanded as he watched it tremble. His gaze lifted to meet hers once again. "I love you, Leah."

He caught her completely off guard. She sucked in her breath and her eyes widened. Her heart pounded against her ribs. At one and the same time, the words filled her with incredible joy and broke her heart. Above all else, she wanted Mike's love, but it could never truly be hers. For love demanded honesty and trust. Openness.

"I love you more than I ever thought it was possible to love anyone," he continued before she could speak.

"Oh, Mike," Leah murmured in a small, aching voice. "You can't be sure of that. It's too soon. There are things about me that you don't know."

Mike chuckled and gave her an adoring look. "Trust me, sweetheart, I'm sure. Maybe on your part it is too soon. I can handle that. We've been seeing each other only a few months, after all. But the truth is, I've loved you almost from the moment I met you."

She stared at him, as pain twisted her heart. "Oh, Mike."

Feeling wretched and undeserving, Leah lowered her head. Her hair swung forward in a shiny curtain on either side of her face. It slid over the back of his hand like warm silk. Mike smiled as a tendril caught in the short, dark hairs there. He loved the silkiness of her hair, its texture, its sweet fragrance. For years he had dreamed of touching it like this, running his fingers through the slippery mass.

"I learned about love from watching my dad and Tess," he went on in a soft voice. "What they have is so beautiful words can't describe it. It's…hell, it's nothing short of magic. Growing up in that house, watching them together, I knew I could never settle for anything less. Throughout my twenties I kept expecting to meet that one someone who would bowl me over, but it didn't happen. I was beginning to think it never would happen for me.'' Tipping her face up, he smoothed the thick curtain of hair back and whispered, ''Then my first day at St. Francis I met you.''

Emotion tightened Leah's chest. The declaration thrilled her, even while she sought the words to refute it. ''Oh, Mike. That's sweet, but you can't expect me to believe you fell in love with me on sight. You have to know someone before you can love her.''

''True. But the moment we were introduced and you gave me that cool look, I started to tumble. As the months and years passed, I fell headlong in love.''

Tears filled Leah's eyes and her chin quivered. His words were so touching, so wonderful, exactly the sort of things she had dreamed of hearing from the right man. That Mike was that man was one of life's cruel ironies. To have to deny him was tearing her heart to shreds. ''Mike, you don't know—''

''Shh. I do know. I've never felt this way about any other woman, never felt this excitement, this urgency, this sweet pain that swells my heart.'' He cupped her face with both hands and looked deep into her eyes. ''I love you, Leah. Everything about you. I love your intelligence, your compassion, your dedication to your brother and your patients, that genteel stubbornness that drives you and makes you strive for perfection. I love your beauty, your classiness.'' A hint of a grin twitched the corners of his mouth. ''The elegant tilt of your chin, the sexy way your hips sway when you walk and those gorgeous legs. I even love that cool look you use to dismiss someone. Lord knows, you turned it on me often enough." He ran his fingertips over the curve of her cheek, and his voice grew deeper, more intense. "Most of all, I love your goodness. Your loyalty. Your integrity."

Leah almost cried out. His gentle words flayed her, each one flicking her conscience like a whip. "No, Mike, please," she protested in a forlorn voice. "Don't confer virtues on me that I don't possess. I'm not what you think. I mean, there is something you don't know about me. Something I've done that—"

"Hush." He placed four fingers over her lips, halting her confession. Tenderness and love marked his expression and glowed from his eyes as he gazed down at her. "There is nothing you could possibly have done that would make me stop loving you. Nothing. Do you understand?"

"Yes, but—"

"No buts. All I want to hear from you now is if you think it's possible that, given time, you could love me as I love you," he said softly. "If the answer is no, then tell me now, and we'll end it here. Tonight."

The storm of emotion that raged inside Leah's chest nearly suffocated her. She stared at him with wide, teary eyes, joy and sorrow, longing and despair, tearing her apart. Could she ever love him? Of course she could. She already did. Mike was all and more that she had ever wanted in a man. How could she not love him? Still, for a moment she considered lying. Wouldn't that be more sensible? Safer? And in the long run kinder, even for Mike?

The debate ended there. Sensible or not, when Mike's eyes clouded with pain at her hesitation, she abandoned any thought of lying.

"Oh, my darling, of course I can. I already love you. Don't you know that?" she managed, her voice quivering with emotion. Turning her head, she pressed a soft kiss into his palm. "I love you so much. So very much."

"Leah." He breathed her name on a heartfelt sigh as he lowered his head and his lips captured hers once again. The kiss was long and deep, rife with feelings too profound for words.

When it was over, Leah laid her cheek against his chest. Her arms went around his waist and held him tightly. Beneath her ear she heard the thunder of his heart, felt the heavy rise and fall of his chest.

Mike nuzzled his cheek against the top of her head.

Hugging him more tightly, she bit down hard on her lower lip. Tears moistened her lashes, and one squeezed out of the corner of her eye to trickle down her cheek. Dear God. How could anything be so right and so wrong at the same time? Loving Mike, having him love her back, was the most wonderful thing that had ever happened to her. But Leah knew with painful certainty that she was going to pay dearly for this glimpse of happiness.

But not now. Not just yet. Please, God, she begged silently as she snuggled closer against Mike's chest. She breathed deeply, savoring his virile-man scent, his reassuring strength, his warmth. *I'll tell him the truth soon. I swear I will. But please, let me have his love for just a little while longer.*

Chapter Eight

"May I help you, Dr. Albright?" the nurse behind the station asked, eyeing Leah with speculation and not a little envy.

Pretending not to notice, Leah kept her expression professional.

The young woman's reaction was typical. Leah would have preferred to keep her relationship with Mike private, but, as he had predicted, Hazel had spread the tale of that embarrassing scene in the supply room quicker than the speed of light. After that, secrecy, at least where the hospital staff was concerned, had been impossible.

For almost three months, Leah and Mike had been the hot topic on the hospital grapevine.

Fortunately, so far, she'd managed to keep her father and Julia in the dark.

"I'm looking for Dr. McCall," Leah informed the young nurse. "I was told he was here in the pediatrics ward."

"Yes, he is. I believe he's in room 412, checking on the Harrison child. Shall I page him for you, Doctor?"

"Thank you, no. I'm sure I can find him."

As Leah walked away down the hall she heard a sigh and felt the young woman's gaze on her back. She rolled her eyes. Another in the legion of women smitten with the handsome Dr. McCall. She had been encountering a lot of them lately.

The door to room 412 stood open. Leah started to knock, but when she caught sight of Mike and his patient she halted in the doorway.

A little girl of about two, dressed in a tiny hospital gown, sat on top of the covers with her legs tucked under her and angled out to each side in that limber way that children have. Her big blue eyes were wide and her cherub face rapt as she listened to Mike. A young blond woman, whom Leah assumed was the child's mother, occupied a chair beside the bed and watched Mike with something close to adoration.

Dressed in a dark suit, Mike sat with one leg hitched up on the side of the mattress as he kept up a string of nonsensical patter that made a game of the examination he was performing.

"Yep, you're definitely better. I can see all the way through and out your other ear, and there's not a bad germ in sight," he said, peering into her ear through an otoscope.

"Really?" the little girl whispered.

"Nary a one. I told you that superduper magic medicine would whup up on 'em. But germs are tricky little devils. Just to be safe, I'd better listen to your lungs and heart and make sure none of the nasty little critters are hiding in there, trying to fool us into thinking that they're all zapped."

He untied the neck of her gown and slipped his stethoscope down under the front. "Now then, Bethany, can you take a deep breath and hold it?"

"Uh-huh," she replied, nodding solemnly.

"Good. If those pesky germs are hiding I'll hear them breathing, but you have to help by holding your breath and staying very still and very quiet. Okay?"

"Okay, Dr. Mac, I will. I promith," the child lisped as though taking a sacred vow.

When Mike finished the examination he scooped the child up in his arms. "Way to go, Bethany! We whupped all those nasty germs and you're good as new again! You know what that means?"

"You'll tell me a joke, like you promithed?"

"You got it, cutie. Okay, how's this? Knock, knock."

Bethany grinned from ear to ear. "Whoth there?"

"Cows."

"Cowth who?"

"Cows go moo, not who, silly."

The child giggled with delight, then wrapped her arms around Mike's neck and gave him a smacking kiss on the cheek. "I wuve you, Dr. Mac."

"I love you, too, sweetie."

Leah sighed. Another female heart lost to Dr. McCall.

Mike looked up and spotted her standing in the doorway. His eyes softened, caressing her without words, and she felt a funny little hitch in the region of her heart.

"Well, look who's here. Bethany, this pretty lady is a doctor, too. Only, she helps babies get born. Say hello to Dr. Albright."

Stepping forward, Leah smiled. "Hello, Bethany."

The little girl's happy expression turned to suspicion. She looked Leah over in a surprisingly adult female fashion. Recognizing a rival, she glared and tightened her arms around Mike's neck to a stranglehold and remained stubbornly silent.

Leah fought back a chuckle. If Bethany had been an adult she would have probably gone for Leah's eyes, claws bared.

"Whoa, sweetheart. Easy there," Mike squawked.

"Here now, Bethany, you're choking Dr. McCall." The child protested loudly as her mother pried her arms loose and took her from Mike. "Now, now. Is that any way to thank him for making you well? Hmm?" she coaxed, bouncing her daughter on her hip.

"I want Dr. Mac!" Bethany sobbed. "I want Dr. Mac!"

The child kept up the litany, wailing and straining toward Mike while he introduced Leah and Thelma Harrison at a shout.

Nothing Mrs. Harrison or Mike could do consoled the child or quieted her. Finally, escape was the only choice. He kissed Bethany's tear-streaked cheek, shouted in her ear that he would come back the next day if she was good, hooked his arm around Leah's waist and hustled her out.

Ah, blessed relief, Leah thought, a little frazzled by the tantrum. Bethany's wails could still be heard in the hallway, but the decibel level had dropped to something a bit below earsplitting. With each step the child's anguished sounds faded into the distance behind them.

Leah glanced at Mike out of the corner of her eye. He seemed relaxed and content, totally unperturbed by his patient's tantrum. When he felt her gaze on him he glanced her way and cocked one eyebrow. "What?"

She gave him a droll look. "Chalk up another conquest for Dr. McCall."

Mike grinned. "What can I say? It's my fatal charm that gets 'em."

He meant it as a joke, but it was true, Leah mused. What woman could resist a man like Mike? Without even trying, he cast a spell on every female he met, from nine months to ninety years. Was it any wonder she loved him? The truly amazing thing was that it had taken her so long.

"Oh, really? And do all your female patients fall in love with you?"

"Yep. Pretty much," he admitted cheerfully, without a trace of modesty.

It occurred to Leah that the mothers of most of his patients were young, nubile women in their twenties. Probably bored with the domestic life and feeling the pressures of motherhood, she thought sourly, experiencing a strange twinge. No doubt, more than one looked forward to her child's checkups.

Leah frowned. Now, where had that come from?

"Why? You jealous?"

She shot him a startled look, for an instant certain that he had somehow read her thoughts.

"Of a two-year-old? Please."

"Why, Dr. Albright, you're blushing. You *are* jealous."

"Don't be ridiculous."

Mike threw back his head and laughed, which drew the attention of the nurses and several others. Embarrassed, Leah tried to shush him, but he surprised her by grabbing her hands and pulling her to a halt in front of him "Honey, trust me, you have absolutely nothing to worry about. My heart belongs to you and only you," he murmured, and there, in the middle of the hallway, heedless of the nurses and visitors walking by, he wrapped his arms around her and kissed her.

Shock held Leah still. Pleasure set her head to spinning. Heat raced through her, turning her knees to mush, until all she could do was clutch at the lapels of his suit jacket and hang on.

The kiss ended as quickly as it had begun. Dazed, Leah gasped for breath and blinked at him. Mike's eyes twinkled back. His face wore a self-satisfied expression that would have raised her hackles had she been able to shake off the miasma of passion still whirling through her.

Vaguely, she was aware of the attention they were drawing, the twitter of chuckles and low voices all around, but she couldn't seem to gather enough strength or presence of mind to do anything about that, either.

Mike grinned. ''What's the matter, sweetheart? Cat got your tongue?''

Leah opened her mouth, closed it, opened it again, but no sound came out.

''Never mind. We'll talk about it later.'' Seeming inordinately pleased, he slid his arm around her waist. ''Now come along. We don't want to keep Quinton waiting.''

They were almost to her brother's room before Leah gathered her scattered senses enough to protest. ''Mike, what on earth were you thinking, kissing me right in front of the staff?''

''Honey, I don't think you're ready to hear that yet.''

''That's not funny, Michael. We're already the hot topic of conversation around here without you pulling a stunt like that.''

''Exactly. So it hardly matters, does it?'' He opened the door to Quinton's room and, with his hand in the small of her back, nudged her inside.

''It does ma—'' Two steps into the room Leah jerked to a halt. ''Dad! What are you doing here?''

Peter Albright took his time rising from his chair. As he did, his gaze swept over them, zeroing in on Mike's hand resting on Leah's waist.

''I came to visit my son. Is there anything wrong with that?''

''No. No, of course not. It's just that I didn't expect to see you. You, um, you and Julia usually visit him in the afternoon.'' Her panicked gaze darted around the room. ''Where is she, by the way?''

''I'm here alone. Julia isn't feeling well.''

''Oh, that's too bad,'' Leah said, but she almost sagged with relief.

''Actually, that's why I'm here now. I was just telling Quinton that his mother had one of her migraines this afternoon and had to take to her bed, which is why we missed our usual afternoon visit. Poor darling. You know how those things devastate her. She's still sleeping off the effects of the medication, so I thought I'd pop in for a quick visit with my son.''

''I see. Well, that's nice. Not that Julia is ill, of course, but that you have some time to spend with Quinton,'' Leah clarified in a flustered rush. Glancing at her brother, she saw that he was chewing his bottom lip, looking worried, his gaze swinging between their father and Mike.

''Aren't you going to introduce me to your friend?'' Peter asked.

Before Leah could find her tongue, Mike stepped forward with his hand outstretched. ''How do you do, Mr. Albright. I'm Mike McCall. It's a pleasure to finally meet you, sir. Leah has told me a lot about you. So has Quinton.'' He glanced at the boy and grinned. ''I've been looking forward to meeting you for months, but somehow our visits never seem to coincide.''

The instant Mike revealed his name Peter gave a start. Throughout the pleasantries he stared at the younger man.

''McCall, you say? You wouldn't happen to be the Dr. Mike McCall who's on staff here, would you?''

''Guilty, I'm afraid.''

''Then you're the one who—'' Peter broke off and cast a worried look at his son. ''That is...''

''You don't have to worry about Quinton, Mr. Albright. He knows that I'm his bone marrow donor.''

"You told him?"

"Don't blame Mike, Dad. I guessed," Quinton explained.

"I see."

Leah held her breath, not sure how her father would react. He looked at a loss himself, but after a moment he recovered his composure. Smiling, he tightened his grip on Mike's hand and shook it harder.

"Well, this is a pleasure. I can't tell you how very pleased I am to have this chance to thank you, Dr. McCall."

"That isn't necessary, sir. I was happy that I could help. In my position, anyone would have done the same."

"Well, now, I'm not at all convinced of that. And you didn't just help. You saved our son's life. For that, his mother and I will be forever indebted to you."

The praise made Mike uncomfortable, and he glanced at Leah with an abashed half smile. "I really can't take too much credit. To tell the absolute truth, there's not much I wouldn't do for your daughter."

Leah's heart sank. She almost groaned. That did it. Any hope she'd had of salvaging the situation flew right out the window with that remark.

"And now that I know Quinton, the same applies for him." Mike went on without the slightest inkling of the damage he was doing. He glanced at Quinton and grinned again, then lowered his voice to a conspiratorial murmur that the boy could not help but hear. "Don't tell him I said so, but you've got yourself a great kid there."

"Aw, Mike," Quinton protested, blushing scarlet, but his grin stretched from ear to ear.

"Thank you, Doctor. We think so."

Peter's reply was pleasant enough, though anyone who knew him well could detect the constraint in his voice.

Leah could almost hear the wheels turning in his head, and she could see in his eyes that he was not pleased.

"So...you have been visiting with my son?"

"Yes, sir, I have. Most evenings I stop by to shoot the breeze with Quinton. I hope you don't have a problem with that."

"No. No. But...isn't it unusual for donor and patient to meet? My wife and I were under the impression that anonymity was the rule."

"Usually, that's true. But in this case it never existed. I knew all along who the patient was."

"Ah, but my son did not know his donor."

"Aw, jeez, Dad!" Quinton groaned. "Why're you making a federal case out of it? Me 'n' Mike are buddies. He knows all about fishing and hunting and building models and a whole bunch of really cool stuff. And he knows a ton of jokes. Anyway, why shouldn't I know the guy who saved my life?"

Why, indeed, Leah thought sadly, as she and her father exchanged a look.

"I appreciate your concern, Mr. Albright," Mike said. "But trust me, you don't have to worry. I'm not some nut case who's going to intrude into your son's life. Added to that, Quinton seems to enjoy our visits, and I know that I do. To tell the truth, I've become quite attached to your son. We seem to have formed a special bond."

Leah and her father exchanged another apprehensive glance. Mike could have no idea how much that revelation had unnerved Peter, but she did. It had rattled her, too, when she had first learned that the brothers had met and formed a friendship.

"However, if you would prefer that I stay away from him, I'll understand and abide by your wishes. You are his father, after all."

"Daa-ad! Please! Mike is my best friend. Don't send him away. Pleeeeeze, Dad!"

Peter pressed his lips together and looked back and forth between his son and Mike. "Well, since it appears to have done Quinton no harm, I don't suppose there's any reason you can't continue to visit."

"Yes! *Yes!*" Quinton cheered.

Leah twisted her hands together. Their father was not pleased. She knew he had given in simply because he couldn't think of a strong enough reason to ban Mike from seeing Quinton. At least, not one that wouldn't make him appear to be a churlish ingrate.

The whole thing was probably moot, anyway. Once he told Julia about this visit, all hell was sure to break loose.

Mike stuck out his hand again, and Peter shook it.

"You won't regret it, sir, I promise you."

"Yes, well, I hope not. Now, if you will all excuse me, I'd better be going."

"Don't cut short your visit on our account."

Mike slipped his arm around Leah's waist again and the warm look in his eyes as he smiled down at her made her heart sink. No one could mistake his expression for anything but adoring.

"Leah and I have dinner plans. We just stopped by to say good-night to Quinton before we left."

Peter said nothing for a moment. He merely gave them a long look. "Then by all means have a nice evening. Now, I really must be going. If Julia wakes and finds me gone she'll be upset." He smiled at Quinton. "Goodnight, Son."

"Dad, wait." Leah caught her father's arm. "Dad, please. Could I talk to you for a moment? In private?"

"I'm sorry, Leah, but I must get back. We'll talk later tonight." He glanced at Mike, then back at her. "After you get home from your date."

Feeling sick, Leah watched him stride away down the hall. She wanted to run after him and beg him not to tell Julia about her and Mike, but she knew she would be wasting her breath. Peter never kept anything from Julia. Leah knew that when she got home later that night her stepmother would be waiting to pounce.

Chapter Nine

Mike's eyes narrowed. Leah looked worried. He also noted the nervous way she twisted her fingers together, the tautness of her body.

Something had upset her—something about her father's visit. Until they had walked into Quinton's room she'd been fine—a little dazed by his kiss, perhaps, but not tense or worried. Yet the instant she'd spotted Peter Albright she had turned into a bundle of nerves. What had happened to upset her so? The visit had seemed amicable enough.

True, Mike had been a bit surprised at their manner. In his large family they greeted one another with hugs and kisses and genuine affection, not that polite restraint that Leah and her father had exhibited toward each other. Hell, he'd seen strangers meet with more enthusiasm than that.

Even so, nothing had been said or done during that brief meeting to cause her concern.

But she was definitely upset about something.

"Is anything wrong?" he asked quietly, moving to stand beside her.

Leah glanced at him, and what he saw in her eyes increased his uneasiness.

"No. No, of course not. Everything's fine," Leah replied brightly.

Too brightly.

He studied her in silence, and she shifted nervously. He wanted to challenge the statement, but he sensed that now wasn't the time. "Well, that's good. Are you ready to go to dinner?"

"I..."

She glanced again in the direction her father had taken. As Mike watched, she seemed to reach a decision that he suspected had more to do with her problem than his question. Squaring her shoulders, she tilted her chin and gave him a determined smile.

"Yes. I'm ready whenever you are."

"Hey, sport, you don't mind if we take off, do you?"

Quinton looked anything but displeased. He lay propped up on a pile of pillows with his hands clasped behind his head, his expression as smug as a cat full of cream. "Nah. There's a John Wayne movie on television that I want to watch tonight anyway. So go ahead."

Though she tried to put up a good front during the walk to the car and the short drive that followed, Mike wasn't fooled. Leah's side of their conversation consisted mostly of one-word replies to his questions and occasional spurts of desperately cheerful chatter, but in between she was quiet and preoccupied.

"Here we are."

At the sound of Mike's voice Leah jumped. "What? Oh, are we there already? I'm sorry. I must have been daydreaming."

Mike watched her as she looked around. The sun was beginning to set, giving the dim light a reddish glow. Through the gloaming, he saw her eyes widen.

"Where are we? This isn't a restaurant."

"No. It's my house."

Her head snapped around. "*Your* house?"

"It's a town house, actually, but I call it home."

"But you said—"

"That I was going to treat you to one of the best meals you've ever had. It will be, I promise."

"But you didn't tell me we were going to your place."

"Yeah, well, I thought it was past time that one of us saw how the other lived." The words blurted out before he could stop them, his voice tinged with resentment he could not hide.

He saw the flash of guilt in her eyes, and immediately regretted the outburst. So she had used one flimsy excuse after another to keep him out of her home and to avoid coming to his. So what? She probably had a good reason for not wanting him there. After that stiff meeting with her father earlier, he suspected that it had something to do with him. Maybe Peter Albright had a drinking problem. Or maybe he and his wife didn't get along, and Leah was embarrassed by their behavior.

"Mike, I—"

"Sorry," he said, cutting her off. "I shouldn't have said that. Just forget it, okay. Shall we go in?" When she simply stared at him, making no move to get out of the car, he cocked one eyebrow. "Do you have a problem with me bringing you here? We've been going out for over three months, Leah. Surely by now you know you can trust me."

Smiling gently, he reached out and stroked her cheek with his fingertips.

The feathery touch sent fire streaking through Leah's

body, making her shiver. She stared at him through the gathering dusk, her heart pounding.

"You have nothing to worry about, sweetheart. This isn't some big seduction scene. I have no intention of rushing you. I promise you, when we make love it will be because that's what you want." He tipped his head to one side and gave her a coaxing smile. "You do believe me, don't you?"

His voice was as soft and warm as velvet, caressing her, filling her with yearning. "Yes, I believe you," she whispered.

The trouble was, she wanted him to seduce her. She wanted desperately to make love with Mike. She had for weeks. Just the thought of doing so made her warm all over.

"Good. You won't regret it."

His mood seemed to change instantly from serious to lighthearted. As he started to open his door, he stopped with his hand on the handle and winked at her. "I'm a great cook."

Mike was irresistible. Even though Leah was worried and filled with dread, a weak smile tugged at her mouth. "Modest, too."

He leaned back across the seat and kissed her on the lips. For all its briefness, the kiss was firm and full of passion, taking Leah's breath away and sending a delicious quiver all the way to her toes, which curled inside her Italian pumps.

When he raised his head his eyes were smoldering, but after giving her a searing look from under those dark eyebrows, he winked. "Hey, what can I say? When you're good, you're good." The gleam in his eyes told her he was talking about more than cooking. Another delicious shiver quaked through her.

As they walked up the brick path to his front door, Leah

looked around and realized that they were in a sort of commons at the end of a cul-de-sac formed by three rows of large, two-story town homes of varying sizes and architectural styles. Each home had a patch of lawn in front that boasted several trees and masses of flower beds. In the center of the parklike commons was a small, lit fountain with benches all around.

"This is lovely. I had no idea these town houses were tucked away back here."

"Thanks. My dad's company built them. I like it here. My place is roomy and comfortable and I don't have to mow the lawn. Best of all, it's just nine minutes from the hospital during peak traffic hours. During a middle-of-the-night emergency, I can make it in three." Mike unlocked the door, reached inside and flipped on the lights, then stepped back to let her precede him.

"I know what you mean. My house on Sunset Boulevard has six bedrooms and Cleo has her own apartment off the kitchen. It's a charming old place with lots of character, but it's way too big for just Quinton and me. The main reason I bought it was its proximity to the hospital."

When she stepped through the doorway, Leah found herself in a spacious foyer with a marble floor, misty-green-and-cream silk wallpaper and a graceful walnut staircase following the curve of the wall to the second floor. Nestled against the stairs was an antique gossip bench, and against the opposite wall stood a majestic grandfather clock, ticking with each ponderous swing of the brass pendulum.

"This is lovely."

Amusement danced in Mike's eyes. "Would you like to look around?"

Without waiting for an answer, he led her into the living room. Leah walked to the middle of the Oriental rug and turned in a slow circle.

She had expected Mike's home to be the typical bachelor dwelling, barren of decoration and containing only a sparse amount of leather-upholstered pieces, perhaps a recliner or two and gooseneck lamps. Definitely there would be a TV-VCR and maybe a coffee table made of a piece of glass on stacked cinder blocks with two or three remote controls lying on top.

What she found, instead, was a warm, cozy home, tastefully decorated with a charming mix of new and antique furnishings, in a color scheme of pale green and cream with touches of deep wine. There was nothing fussy or feminine about it, nor was it overtly masculine; merely homey and inviting.

"I'm impressed, Mike."

"You sound surprised. What kind of home did you think I'd have? A bare bones place to flop? Or maybe a passion pit?"

"No. No, of course not," she denied, but the description was so close to the truth that she blushed. The twinkle in Mike's eyes told her he knew he'd been right.

It occurred to Leah that few men had the taste or the interest to put together a place like this. Nor did it have that sterile look that usually marked a professional decorator's work. She immediately experienced a flare of jealousy at the thought of another woman helping Mike furnish his home.

Unknowingly, he alleviated her fears with his next comment as he led the way to the kitchen at the back of the house.

"I've never been a fan of the bachelor grunge look. I wanted the same kind of hominess that I grew up with after Tess came into our lives, so I got her to help me with the decorating. She has the knack for turning a barren space into an oasis where you want to kick off your shoes and relax."

That was an understatement, Leah thought, still craning her neck to look around as she followed him through a swinging door.

"Just let me wash my hands, and I'll get started. Have a seat." He waved toward the high stools lined up along the bar that separated the kitchen from the breakfast room, and disappeared into a small powder room off the kitchen.

"May I help?"

"Nope. Just relax," he called out over the rush of running water. "I did most of the prep work this morning before I left for the hospital."

Thank goodness. The offer had been made out of politeness. Cooking was not Leah's forte. The most she could manage was to nuke something in a microwave now and then, and even that usually resulted in disaster.

Nerves jittering, Leah clasped her hands and looked around at the kitchen. Done in blue and white with copper accents, the well-lit room was a model of efficient design and equipped with what appeared to be every conceivable modern appliance.

She herself wouldn't know a rotisserie from a wok, but she had a feeling that Cleo would think Mike's kitchen was heaven.

White, glass-fronted cabinets held cobalt-blue glassware and gleaming white-and-blue china. The cook island in the middle of the room was topped with white granite and held a range and a small sink.

Decorative blue-and-white tiles featuring French cooking terms and names of spices dotted the white-tiled backsplash above the countertops, which were also of white granite. Pots of every shape and size, mostly copper, hung from the rack suspended from the ceiling beneath a giant skylight that would flood the space with cheery light in the daytime.

Country scenes in blue and white covered the wallpaper. Baskets, hand-thrown pottery, wooden bowls and mugs and copper containers filled with trailing ivy occupied the shelf that circled the room a foot or so below the nine-foot ceiling.

In the adjoining breakfast room a copper pot filled with dried flowers sat in the middle of the table. Several more containing live plants lined the shelves of the wrought-iron baker's rack against the inside wall. The flooring in both rooms was pegged oak, polished to a high sheen.

Guilt niggled at Leah. She loved her rambling old house, but it had been built around the turn of the century. The kitchen was old-fashioned and inefficient and probably put an undue burden on Cleo. She had asked Leah to have the room remodeled when Leah had bought the place three years ago.

She had meant to, but shortly after moving in, Quinton had been diagnosed with leukemia. After that, domestic projects had fallen far down her list of priorities. Between her busy practice and looking after her brother, she hadn't give the matter another thought.

Actually, though structurally sound, the whole house could use a face-lift, she supposed. Certainly her stepmother had complained often enough about the outdated decor and antiquated bathrooms.

Leah turned in time to see Mike tie a dish towel around his narrow middle. He had taken off his coat and tie and the top three buttons of his shirt were undone; the sleeves were rolled up almost to his elbows. A dusting of short dark hair covered his forearms and more peeked out the open collar. Leah's pulse fluttered. He smelled of soap and looked outrageously relaxed and sexy.

"How about a glass of wine?" Without waiting for an answer, he pulled a bottle from the wine rack and filled two glasses with Bordeaux.

Handing one to her, he raised his own. "To us."

Leah's heart tripped. Us? Would there even be an ''us'' by this time tomorrow?

Somehow she managed a smile for Mike and repeated the toast. Their glasses clinked, and he tipped his head to brush her mouth with his in a lingering kiss.

Fighting back tears, Leah closed her eyes and savored the warm feel of his lips, the exquisite tenderness. She needed this. Oh, how she needed this. She needed Mike.

It wasn't fair. Things had been going so well. Why? *Why* did her father have to visit Quinton tonight?

Why did Mike have to be Julia's son?

Despair shuddered through Leah even as the kiss stirred her soul.

Mike raised his head and smiled, dropped another quick kiss on the tip of her nose, then stepped back and unhooked pans from the rack overhead.

''Make yourself at home. This won't take long.''

Sipping her wine and feeling inept, Leah watched him move around the kitchen with an easy confidence and panache that she could only admire. With a minimum of fuss, he started a pot of rice cooking, then dumped a glug of oil into a heating, odd-shaped pan.

''I hope you like stir-fry.'' He removed several bowls from the refrigerator, took the lid off one, dumped finely cut strips of beef into the pan and stirred expertly as they sizzled and popped. ''It's a favorite of mine. Plus, it's easy to prepare.''

''I love stir-fry.''

''Great.'' He sent her a smile over his shoulder, dumped a bowl of chopped vegetables into the skillet and proceeded to add various seasonings—a pinch of this and a dab of that, a splash of wine and another of soy sauce—with the confidence and flair of a gourmet chef. Soon, a wonderful aroma filled the air.

In a surprisingly short time they were seated at the glass-topped table in the breakfast nook.

"Mmm, this is delicious," Leah said after the first fork-ful. "I had no idea you could cook."

"Honey, you ain't seen nothing yet. I have all kinds of talents you haven't sampled." Smiling, Mike took a sip of wine and gave her a sleepy-eyed look that was pure seduction. "But you will."

A thrill shivered through Leah, even while sadness squeezed her heart. She would give almost anything if only that were true.

To cover her reaction, she reached for her wineglass and took a sip. She was being ridiculous. From the begin-ning she had known that she and Mike had no future to-gether. But somewhere along the way she had let down her guard, and without her realizing it, hope had begun to blossom. Now the thought of losing him brought pain like a knife twisting in her chest.

The practical side of Leah's nature was appalled that things had gotten to this point, that she had allowed her foolish heart to get involved.

Leah tried to relax and enjoy the evening, but in the back of her mind was the frantic awareness that in all likelihood, this would be the last one she would spend with Mike.

Despite her hunger, she was too heartbroken and on edge to eat. Her stomach felt as though it were tied in a knot. The most she could do was toy with her food, mov-ing it around on the plate with her fork and nibbling a bite now and then for appearance's sake. She smiled and kept up her side of the dinner conversation. What she said she had no idea, but at least she managed to keep her misery from Mike.

After dinner, he seemed surprised when Leah insisted on helping with the dishes.

"Have you ever loaded a dishwasher before?" he asked with a teasing grin, filling the sink with soapy water. "Or put those pretty hands into dishwater?"

"Of course I have." Leah tied a towel around her waist and began to fill the dishwasher's cutlery basket. She might not know how to cook, mainly because during the early years her mother had done all the cooking and in her father's home that was Cleo's job, but she'd done her share of dishes. As a teenager, she had felt more comfortable with the housekeeper than her father and step-mother, and you didn't hang out in Cleo's kitchen for long without being put to work. "I'm not useless, you know," she replied huffily, and stuffed a serving bowl into the bottom rack.

Mike scooped up a mound of soapsuds and deposited it on the end of her nose. "Sweetheart, I never thought for a minute that you were."

"Sorry." She wiped the end of her nose and gave him a rueful look. "I guess I'm supersensitive about coming from a monied background."

"Sugar, you may have money, but no one can accuse you of being one of the idle rich." Mike leaned over and gave her a quick kiss. "I think you've more than proven yourself. In fact, your dedication to your patients, and to Quinton, is one of the things I love most about you."

"Thank you." Embarrassed, she ducked her head and busied herself loading glasses into the top rack.

They had barely finished cleaning up when Mike's beeper sounded. While he checked in with his answering service, Leah turned off the lights and wandered over to the two glass walls that formed the outer corner of the breakfast nook, to look out at the moon-drenched court-yard at the back of the town house.

An ancient oak tree dominated the small space, its branches spreading over almost the entire courtyard.

Mike's father had obviously designed the house around the tree, rather than chop it down, as most local builders would have done.

A large bed of hosta and bleeding hearts and various other shade-loving plants circled the base of the tree's enormous trunk. The perimeter stone wall surrounding the courtyard was bordered with rosebushes and petunias in riotous bloom. Between the base of the tree and the flower beds was a postage-stamp lawn.

More of Tess's work, Leah thought. From what she'd seen so far, Mike's stepmother was a woman whom she would like to get to know better.

Unfortunately, that was unlikely to happen.

The night was warm, but a chill rippled over Leah. She folded her arms over her midriff and rubbed her elbows. Closing her eyes, she pressed her lips together to keep them from trembling. She was going to lose Mike. Time had run out. She had to tell him the truth, tonight, before Julia descended on him in a rage.

Dear Lord, how would she bear it? She loved him so.

Hands settled on Leah's shoulders, making her start.

"Hey, take it easy. It's just me." Using his thumbs in a rotating motion, Mike massaged the tense muscles around her shoulder blades. "You want to tell me what's bothering you?"

"Nothing. I'm fine."

"C'mon, Leah. You've been as edgy as a caged cat all evening. You hardly ate a bite of your dinner. What's wrong, sweetheart?"

So much for thinking her bright chatter had fooled him. "Really, nothing's wrong. I'm just a little tired, that's all."

His hands stilled on her shoulders. Several seconds ticked by. The taut quality of the silence told her he didn't believe her. She waited, braced, trembling inside, her body rigid beneath his hands.

After a moment, Mike's arms slipped around her waist and pulled her back against him. At the feel of his lips nibbling the side of her neck, some of the tension seeped out of her. With a sigh, she relaxed against his chest, grateful that he hadn't pressed. Perhaps it was foolish, but she wanted—needed—just a while longer with him before she told him the truth.

She laid her arms over his and gripped his wrists. Smiling, she closed her eyes and reveled in the feel of crisp hair tickling the tender undersides of her arms, the warmth and solidity of his body.

"How was your patient?"

"Fine. It was nothing serious. Just a new mother worried because her infant has colic."

"Did you prescribe something?"

His teeth grazed her neck, then he nuzzled his face in her hair. "Nope. Even better, I gave her my dad's remedy."

A nip on her earlobe sent a delicious shiver rippling down Leah's spine. Her heart took off at a gallop, and she tightened her hold on his wrists. "Wh-which is?"

"The same thing he did whenever any of his children had colic. He'd unbutton his shirt and the baby's sleeper and cuddle him or her, bare tummy to bare chest, and walk the floor."

Mike's tongue explored the swirls in her ear. Leah caught her breath as pleasure speared through her.

"The heat of his body relieved the infant's stomach pain and the cuddling comforted. Worked every time."

Mike's hands flattened against her midriff and began to move in slow circles. When his thumbs grazed the undersides of her breasts, Leah's brain fogged over. Coherent speech required intense concentration. "Y-your father sounds like a wonderful dad."

"He is." Silence returned as Mike's hands explored and his lips feasted on tender skin. "Speaking of fathers," he mumbled, using his nose and mouth to nudge aside the collar of her blouse, "I enjoyed meeting yours tonight."

The reminder was like pouring ice water over Leah's head. The erotic sensations coursing through her body froze instantly, painfully, as the tension came rushing back. Her fingers unconsciously dug into Mike's wrists.

"D-did you?"

"Mmm. You have his eyes."

"Yes. I know."

"But other than that, I can't see any resemblance. You must look like your mother," he murmured against the top of her shoulder an instant before his teeth nipped the smooth skin.

Leah nerves were stretched so tight she didn't feel the tiny pain. "That's right, I do."

She sensed the change in Mike, the sudden stillness, the wary intensity, as though he were trying to pick his way through a minefield. She chewed her bottom lip and waited.

Finally he raised his head. "Is there some problem between the two of you? Something you'd like to talk about?"

"No. Of course not."

"I know you told me you weren't close to your dad, but earlier you actually seemed upset when we walked into Quinton's room and found him there. Did you two have an argument or something?"

"No. My father and I never argue." There wasn't enough emotion between them for that. "I was just surprised to see him there at that time, that's all. He and Julia usually visit in the afternoons."

"I see. Speaking of Quinton's mother, I'm looking forward to meeting her, too, sometime."

For a moment Leah couldn't breathe. She stared blindly out at the tiny courtyard garden, while her heart did an erratic little dance in her chest.

"Perhaps you will soon."

Sooner than you might like. Leah knew if she couldn't somehow head Julia off, tomorrow her stepmother would swoop down on Mike in a rage, uncaring of what she revealed or who she hurt.

She pressed her lips together and closed her eyes. It was time to stop stalling. She had to prepare him. She simply couldn't let him find out the truth that way. She loved him too much.

Drawing a deep breath, Leah screwed up her courage. "Mike…"

He turned her within his embrace, and she found herself looking up into eyes that burned with passion and deep emotion.

"Mike, I…there's something—"

"Shh. Whatever it is, it can wait. This can't."

She had only an instant before his mouth covered hers, possessive, hungry. Despair and longing warred within Leah, but the battle was brief. The need was too great.

A moan rolled from her throat. Later. She would tell him later, she vowed. Right now, she needed this. She needed him.

Going up on tiptoe, Leah locked her arms around Mike's neck and pressed closer, returning the kiss with a raw hunger that matched his.

Her fervor seemed to catch him off guard, but only for an instant. With a growl, Mike tightened his arms around her and widened his stance. With one hand, he cupped her bottom and pressed her hips fully against his arousal. Desire shuddered through Leah, hot, clawing.

The kiss packed a punch that sent them both spinning out of control. They clutched each other, unable to get close enough, to touch enough. Small sounds of frustration and want escaped them.

Without warning, Mike grasped Leah's shoulders and broke off the kiss. "No," he gasped. "No."

Leah moaned and instinctively tried to return to his embrace, but he held her at arm's length.

"Wait. We can't do this."

"Mike, please."

"No. We have to stop. Now, while I still can."

Hurt swelled inside Leah. Her heart beat like a drumroll and her breathing was harsh and ragged. Tears stung her eyes. "You don't...you don't want me?"

"Don't want you! Honey, I want you so much I'm in agony. But I promised you I wasn't going to seduce you. I intend to keep that promise even if it kills me." His mouth twisted. "And believe me, it just might. Look, I'm sorry. This is my fault. I shouldn't have let things go this far."

Hurt gave way to soaring happiness. Leah looked up at him with shining eyes. "Mike, it's all right. Really."

"No, it's not all right. I don't break my word. When I— Leah, you're not helping," he scolded when she tried to wriggle back into his arms. "Stop that."

"Mike, darling, you don't understand." She reached up and framed his face between her palms. "I want you to make love to me. Now. Tonight."

He sucked in a sharp breath, and Leah saw his pupils widen. The decision had not been a conscious one; the words had just come tumbling out, but the instant she spoke she knew that this was what she wanted. She loved Mike, and she wanted to make love with him, if only this once. In all probability, after tonight she would never have another chance.

"Leah, sweetheart, are you sure? I don't want to rush you. I've waited this long. I can wa—"

She placed her fingertips over his mouth. "Shh. Stop worrying." She gave him a warm look, all the love she felt shining in her eyes. If a tender sadness marked her smile he did not seem to notice. "I'm absolutely certain. More certain than I've ever been of anything in my life."

For an instant Mike closed his eyes, as though giving thanks, and Leah felt a tremor ripple through him. When he looked at her again his eyes sizzled with emotion. Placing his hand over hers on his cheek, he turned his head and pressed a warm kiss against her palm.

Heat speared down her arm and through her body, all the way to the core of her womanhood. Leah's knees threatened to buckle. The simple caress was the most erotic thing she had ever experienced. Emotion swamped her. Moisture glittered in her eyes, tears of joy, of love, of need. Of wrenching hopelessness.

"Oh, Mike." Her voice quavered, and a fine tremor shook her hand as her fingertips traced his mouth. "Love me. Love me now. Please, my darling."

Mike needed no more invitation than that. He swung her up into his arms and headed for the stairs. Curling her arms around him, Leah laid her head on his shoulder and pressed her face against the side of his neck.

What she was doing was wrong. She knew that, accepted it. But, dear heaven, she loved him so. If she was going to lose him, surely she deserved this one night. One night of closeness and love to hold in her heart. A memory that, in the lonely years to come, she could take out and relive now and then. It would likely be all she would ever have.

She would tell him the truth afterward, but for now she would take what happiness she could, while she could.

That she would pay for the decision later, and pay

dearly, Leah had no doubt. So be it. For this one, shining night, she would love and be loved by the only man who had every truly captured her heart.

At the top of the stairs Mike turned right on the landing and carried her into his bedroom. A lamp burned low on a bedside table. Without breaking stride, he crossed the navy carpet to the king-size bed. There he stopped and looked into her eyes. His own were blazing in a face that was flushed and dark with passion.

"Are you sure, Leah? If we do this, it's going to change everything between us. You know that, don't you?"

Oh, my dearest darling, everything between us is about to change anyway, whether or not we become lovers, she thought sadly. "Yes, I know," she whispered. She cupped the side of his face with one hand and smiled tenderly. "And I'm sure. I'm very sure."

He searched her eyes, her face. Leah trembled, but she met his gaze squarely, and after a moment he dipped his head and covered her mouth with his.

A low sound purred from her throat—part relief, part joy, part delicious anticipation. Eagerly, sinking her fingertips into his hair, she clasped his head with both hands and abandoned herself to his caress.

This was no gentle kiss, no sweet supplication. It was firm, almost rough, full of hunger and need too long unanswered, emotions too deeply felt for words. Each gave, each took, and still it wasn't enough, would never be enough. With every touch, every soft gasp, every moan, they demanded more.

The mattress depressed under Mike's knee, and a moment later she felt its softness against her back, then the wonderful warmth and hardness of his body settling over her.

His mouth left hers, trailing nibbling kisses over her

cheek, the side of her neck. "I feel as though I've waited forever for you," he murmured.

Leah smiled and slid her palms over his back, exploring the broad muscles that banded it, absorbing the feel and warmth of him through the thin cotton shirt. "I know, my love," she whispered. "I feel the same."

Turning her head, she strung kisses along his jaw, then nipped the firm flesh. Mike grunted. In retaliation he traced the swirls in her ear with the tip of his tongue, filling the shell with the hot moistness of his breath. Leah shivered and felt him smile.

He tried to slip his hand beneath the coat of her trim teal suit, but the garment was too formfitting around the rib cage to allow access. He rolled to one side and raised up on one elbow.

Shaking with eagerness, Leah clumsily started to snatch at the buttons that ran down the front of the jacket, but Mike put his hand over hers and stopped her. "No. Let me." His gazed locked with hers. "I want to see you," he murmured in a voice so hot it raised goose bumps along her spine. "All of you."

Leah felt the same about him, but his words, his sizzling stare, made her so limp with desire she couldn't seem to raise her hands to the buttons on his shirt. Instead, she lay still, trembling with anticipation.

With tormenting slowness, he slipped the top button free, then the second. "Lovely," he whispered as he pushed apart the lapels to reveal a wedge of creamy skin and a lacy teal bra. He bent his head and kissed the swells of pearly flesh that rose above the delicate garment.

Leah made a restive move. "Mike, please."

Smiling, he raised his head. "Please what, my love?"

"I...I..." She groped for an answer, but she couldn't think. She could only twist and pant and struggle to absorb the thrilling sensations that battered her.

The third button slipped free, and Mike spread the lapels wider, gazing his fill. The long stare seemed to sear her skin. He was setting her on fire with just a look. Breathing hard, Leah turned her head from side to side on the pillow.

"Hurry, darling. Please. Hurry."

"Oh, no. I've waited too long for this night to rush things. I want to savor every beautiful inch of you. Kiss every inch of you." To demonstrate, he bent his head and kissed her shoulder, her collarbone, then returned once again to the tops of her breasts, drawing a moan from her.

"Do you like that, love?"

"I..."

"Hmm? Do you?"

"Y-yes."

He traced his tongue along the top edge of her bra, leaving a moist trail of fire on her skin.

"And that?"

"Yes. *Yes.*"

Again he nuzzled his face against the pillowy flesh. She clutched his shoulders, his head, her body shifting restlessly beneath him. When his tongue stabbed into the cleavage between her breasts she cried out. "Mike! Oh. Oh!"

"You like that, too, hmm?"

"Yes. Yes!"

He dipped his head lower and gently blew on her right nipple through the fragile teal lace. She sucked in a sharp breath, and clutched his shoulders tighter, digging her fingers into his flesh, urging him closer.

A wickedly sensual chuckle rumbled from Mike. As he dealt with the fourth and final button he complied with her unspoken desire, closing his mouth over her nipple and suckling her through the lace with a slow, devastating rhythm that seemed to tug at her womb.

Leah's back arched off the mattress and a keening wail tore from her throat. The pleasure was so intense she couldn't think, couldn't speak. She thrashed and moaned and clawed, but Mike showed no mercy, dealing the same sweet torture to her other breast.

Driven by instinct more than conscious thought, Leah worked one hand between them and fumbled at the buttons on Mike's shirt. When one refused to give, in frustration she tore it off, then gave the shirt a yank that popped the others off and sent them flying.

"Easy, love," Mike murmured.

But she didn't hear him. Even if she had, she could not have stopped. Driven by a raging passion she'd never before experienced, she yanked his shirt free of his trousers, spread the front edges and plunged her hands underneath.

Her fingers curled into the rough hair on his chest, raced over warm flesh, testing firm pectoral muscles, broad shoulders, a wide rib cage. With the pad of her forefinger, she rubbed the tiny nipple she found buried in the thatch of hair.

Mike grunted and jerked. "Ah, sweetheart. Sweetheart," he groaned, now as helplessly lost as she.

Leah's arms circled his torso and her fingers danced over shoulder blades, down his spine, exploring each tiny knob. When she encountered the waistband of his trousers she made a frustrated sound very near a growl, jerked her hands back around to his front and began to snatch at the buckle on his belt.

Mike's plans for a slow, leisurely lovemaking vanished, consumed in the raging fire of passion that burned out of control. Caught up in her urgency, he turned his attention to the zipper on her skirt.

After that there was no more teasing foreplay, no more words. They rolled together on the bed, mindless to everything but each other, gasping and kissing, as frantic hands snatched and groped to deal with hooks and buttons and zippers.

The power and intensity overwhelmed Leah. She had expected pleasure. She hadn't known she would drown in it, that it would permeate every cell of her body until it bordered on pain. Until she trembled with it.

Until now she had thought she understood what it was to need, to want. She had been wrong. So wrong. This dark urgency that consumed her drove her to the brink of insanity. Her love for Mike, her desire for him, was so unrelenting and powerful that if it was not fulfilled soon she felt she would surely shatter into a million pieces.

Within moments Leah's suit and bra lay on the floor in a crumpled heap, along with Mike's shirt. When her undergarments became an obstacle, Mike's thin supply of patience ran out. With an oath, he jerked to his knees. Quickly, he hooked his fingers under the waistband of both her panty hose and the tiny teal bikini panties and peeled both down her body. He tossed the items over his shoulder and froze.

"You're beautiful," he said in a gritty voice. Like a man mesmerized, he ran his gaze slowly over her, from the top of her head all the way to her toes. Then he bent over and kissed her belly, slowly, almost reverently.

Leah's heart did a slow roll in her chest.

Without a word, he rose to stand beside the bed and strip out of his remaining clothes, his gaze holding hers all the while.

Leah was a doctor; the male body held no mystery for her. Yet when Mike stepped out of his trousers and Jockey shorts, the sight of him made her mouth go dry. He was magnificent—leanly muscled and rangy, with broad shoulders and narrow hips, his manhood fully aroused.

The sight sent a frisson of fear fluttering through her. Then the bed dipped under his weight. As his body settled onto hers Leah enfolded him in her arms, and the flash of anxiety passed. Now nothing else existed; nothing else mattered but this.

When her legs parted for him, Mike raised up on his arms and looked deep into her eyes. "I love you, Leah," he whispered as he made them one. "I love you."

The declaration jolted Leah, and for an instant she experienced the twin sensations of joy and guilt. Then the loving began, and the feelings faded like smoke in the wind, and there was only pleasure. Exquisite, intense, consuming pleasure.

Thrilling sensations buffeted them like ships on a storm-tossed sea, drove them with merciless insistence as their bodies undulated together to the ancient rhythm. Wrapping her arms and legs around Mike, Leah welcomed each powerful thrust, met it with an intensity that matched his, her body arching like a bow.

The pleasure built and so did the urgency, sending them, panting and straining toward the ultimate pleasure. They clasped each other close, their bodies on fire, quivering and flushed as the need clawed at them.

Together they reached the zenith. Release came in a rush, an explosion of ecstasy that rocked them to their souls and wrung cries of triumph and rapture from them both.

For a long time neither moved. In delicious, boneless lassitude, they clung to each other and basked in the afterglow. But all too soon hearts slowed and breathing returned to normal, and reality, and memory, returned.

Lying beneath Mike, Leah ran her hands absently across his sweat-slicked back and gazed over his shoulder at the fuzzy circle of light cast on the ceiling by the bedside lamp. She pressed her lips together and closed her eyes. Dear Lord, what had she done?

"Mike..."

"Mmm?"

Stirring, he drew a deep breath, then raised up on his forearms. His face had that relaxed, sleepy-eyed look that came from making love, and his hair was mussed, the dark strands sticking up in all directions. That had been her doing, she realized, blushing a bit as she recalled the abandoned way she had stabbed her fingers through his hair and clutched it.

"Hi."

"Hi." Her throat was tight and achy with emotion. A quavery whisper was all she could manage.

He smiled down at her with so much love and tenderness Leah could have wept.

Some of what she was feeling must have shown in her face. Instantly his expression became concerned.

"Are you all right? Did I hurt you?"

"Oh, darling, no. Of course not." When he continued to frown she framed his face with her hands. "Will you stop worrying. I'm fine. Really. I'm not made of glass, you know. Mike, what we just shared was the most beautiful thing I've every experienced. I feel terrific." Physically, at least, she added silently.

His face cleared and his gentle smile returned. "Good. I'm glad. Because I feel the same."

"Mike, I..." She stared up at him, painfully aware of what she had to do. She couldn't have this discussion lying intimately with him like this. She needed to put some space between them, let their heads clear before she dropped her bombshell.

She shifted. "Mike, could I get up, please?"

"Sure," he said in a cautious voice, rolling to one side. "Sorry. I didn't mean to crush you."

"You didn't. I just needed to sit up, that's all." Feeling self-conscious and awkward, she swung her feet to the floor and bent over to retrieve her clothes, painfully aware of his gaze on her back.

"Hey, you're not planning on leaving, are you?"

Leah twisted around on the bed, clutching her clothes to her breasts. "No...not yet." She felt vulnerable, and she had simply wanted the meager protection of clothes when she confessed. "It's just that, well...I think we should talk."

"Okay."

He moved so fast she had no chance to escape. In a blink he reached out and hauled her back into his arms. Leah found herself on her back again, looking up into Mike's jubilant face, which was nose to nose with hers.

"But I don't want to hear any confession or any doubts. We love each other and that's all that's important. Whatever else is bothering you, we'll handle later." A sensual smile tilted his mouth and his eyes darkened as they focused on her mouth. "Right now, I have more interesting things in mind."

"Mike, wait. It's not that simple. You have to listen to me."

"Later," he murmured, and cut off any further protest with a kiss.

Leah tried to resist, but she never stood a chance. Mike's lips were warm and persuasive. With his scent all around her and the feel of his naked body pressing so intimately against hers, her head began to swim, and her defenses crumbled. Sighing, she wrapped her arms around him.

The electronic beeping seemed magnified in the still of the room.

"Nooo. Not now." Groaning, Mike rested his forehead against hers. "If that's Mrs. Norton calling again about her colicky baby, I swear I'll—"

"No. I think it's mine."

Leah scrambled from Mike's arms and pawed through the tousled bedcovers. Propped up on one elbow, he watched her frantic fumbling with equal parts amusement and resignation.

Finally, after hanging naked over the side of the bed in the most undignified manner possible, she found her suit jacket on the floor, halfway underneath. Leah dug the beeper out of the pocket and shut it off. Without a stitch on, she sat up, swung her legs over the side of the bed and reached for the telephone, every trace of modesty and self-consciousness forgotten as the doctor in her took over.

Distantly, as she listened to the message left with her answering service, she was aware of Mike's gaze on her bare back, of the indolent way he lay sprawled on the bed, watching her every move, but she was too busy to think about that.

"I have to go to the hospital." She hung up the telephone, stepped into her panties and started yanking up the rest of her clothes. Her suit was impossibly wrinkled, but it couldn't be helped. "One of my patients has gone into labor."

Mike's appreciative gaze fixed on her breasts. As she leaned forward to slip into her bra, they momentarily yielded to gravity, hanging like luscious ripe pears for an instant before the teal lace cupped around them. "Do you have to go now? How far apart are her contractions?"

"It really doesn't matter. She's barely entered her third trimester."

In one fluid roll, Mike was out of the bed and stepping into his trousers. "I'll drive you back."

"You don't have to do that. It's getting late. Just call a cab."

"It's barely ten. And I'm driving you."

Chapter Ten

"It's about time you got home, young lady. And just where do you think you're going?"

The angry statement brought Leah to a halt with one foot on the bottom step of the stairs. She closed her eyes, her jaw tightening.

She had entered the house quietly through the back door, hoping her father and stepmother had given up and gone to bed. She should have known better.

It was two in the morning. Her heart ached with the knowledge that she was about to lose Mike. Added to that, she had just spent more than three hellacious hours in the OB, and she was too tired and too emotionally wrung out to do battle, but apparently, she had no choice. Drawing a bracing breath, Leah turned to face Julia's wrath.

Her stepmother stood in the arched opening to the living room with her hands on her hips. Venom shot from her eyes and her mouth was compressed into a thin line. She practically vibrated with fury. Leah's father stood just behind his wife, his somber face full of disapproval.

"I was going to bed. Actually, I'm surprised that you're still up. Didn't Nurse Johnson call you to tell you I had an emergency?"

"An emergency." Julia snorted. "Oh, please, did you really think we'd fall for that? You just didn't want to face me, now that I know the truth."

"Julia, whether you believe me or not, I did have an emergency. One of my patients went into labor over two months early. I've spent the last several hours trying to save her baby."

"And did you?" her father, at least, had the grace to ask.

"For the moment. I stopped the bleeding and the contractions, but for how long is anybody's guess."

"Do you mind," Julia snapped. "I didn't wait up for you to discuss some woman's pregnancy. I want to know about you and Mike."

Leah raked her hand through her hair. "Okay, fine. Let's get this over with. But may we have this discussion in the living room, where I can at least sit down? I'm dead on my feet." Without waiting for a reply, she brushed past them and sank onto the sofa.

Julia followed hot on her heels, but instead of sitting she paced in front of the sofa like a prosecuting attorney, shooting glares at Leah. "How could you? How *could* you?"

"How could I what, Julia?"

"Don't play dumb with me. You know exactly what I'm talking about. How could you get involved with Mike? You've been carrying on with him right under my nose and never said a word. How could you *do* that to me?"

"First of all, Julia, not everything is about you. My

relationship with Mike has nothing whatsoever to do with
you. I certainly haven't been seeing him to annoy or hurt
you. It wasn't planned at all. It just happened.''

"How can you say this has nothing to do with me?
After all I've told you about my ex-husband and his family, after all I've done for you, and you betray me like
this. It's…it's as though you've stabbed me in the heart.''

All Julia had done for her? Leah almost laughed out
loud at that. Had the situation not been so sticky, she
would have demanded to know exactly what her stepmother had ever done for her, except allow her to raise
Quinton.

"For heaven's sake, Julia. Must you be so dramatic?
It's not as bad as all that.''

"Don't get smart with me. I want to know how long
this thing between you and Mike has been going on.''

Leah leaned her head against the soft sofa back and
tried to appear unconcerned. Julia was like a shark on the
prowl for prey. It wouldn't do to let her smell blood.
"Since shortly after the transplant surgery, when he
started dropping by to visit Quinton.''

"And that's another thing," Julia declared, throwing up
her hands. "Why, in heaven's name, did you allow that
to get started? You know how dangerous it is for Mike
and Quinton to get together. You said yourself that it
could be very detrimental to Quinton at this point if he
found out that Mike is his half brother. You should have
barred him from visiting right at the very beginning.''

"Oh? And just how was I supposed to do that? Say,
'Thank you very much, Dr. McCall, for your bone marrow, but I don't want you around my brother?''

"If that's what it took, yes!''

"Now, dearest," Peter said in a placating voice, "Leah
does have a point. She was in an awkward position.''

"Don't you dare take up for her. Leah's a smart

woman. She could have come up with a way to put a stop to the visits if she'd tried. She certainly didn't have to get romantically involved with Mike. Ohhhhh! I just don't *believe* this!''

Julia ranted and raved for several more minutes, pacing from one end of the room to the other. She moaned over Leah's disloyalty and lack of consideration, raged at Mike and his father and the entire McCall family, whined about how much Leah had hurt her.

Finally, Leah could take no more. ''Julia, look at it this way. The more time Mike spends with me, the less time he'll have to spend with Quinton.''

Julia came to a sudden stop. She turned around with an arrested expression on her face and slowly a sly smile curved her mouth. ''Why, you clever little devil.''

''What do you mean?'' Leah asked cautiously.

''You're keeping Mike occupied so he won't have much time to be curious about Quinton. You're keeping him distracted.''

''What? No, wait. Good heavens, I didn't me—''

''Why, that's positively brilliant. What man would choose to sit around in a hospital room and visit with a teenage boy when he could be out romancing a lovely young woman? I love it!'' As quickly as her elation had come, it turned into a pout. ''But you really should have told me what you were up to. Surely you knew that I would approve. By keeping quiet, you've caused me needless upset. That was really thoughtless. I'm surprised at you, Leah.''

Leah opened her mouth to set her straight, then closed it again. Her comment had been a flippant one, made out of frustration. She certainly hadn't expected Julia to take it seriously. Still, if believing she could be so devious kept her stepmother from confronting Mike with the awful truth and gave Leah more time with him, why not?

* * *

"Knock, knock."

Except for the nurse and the receptionist seated behind the counter, Leah's waiting room was empty. Both Sandy and Mary Ann stopped what they were doing and looked around as Mike stuck his head in the door. A smile lit the faces of both women, but Sandy's immediately assumed a sardonic expression.

"Well, well, look who's here. If it isn't the hunk of St. Francis."

Mike grinned and stepped inside. "Gee, sugar, I didn't think you'd noticed. Anyway, that's not what you were supposed to say."

"Oh, Lordy. Not another one of your corny jokes."

Mary Ann giggled behind her hand, while Sandy rolled her eyes and faked a long-suffering sigh that didn't fool Mike a bit. He knew the starchy nurse was fond of him. Both women had made it clear that they heartily approved of the romance between him and their boss. He suspected they were getting a vicarious thrill out of the courtship.

And a courtship was exactly what it was, though he doubted that Leah realized it yet. But she would soon. After the previous night, their relationship had reached a new level. Now it was time to pick up the pace.

"Oh, well, I suppose I'll have to play along or you'll pout," Sandy grumbled. "So who's there?"

"Collin."

"Collin who?"

"Collin the doctor, I'm not well."

"Oh, brother. Just remember, you said it, not me."

Not in the least offended, Mike sauntered across to the waist-high counter that separated the waiting room from the office. "Ah, c'mon, Sandy. You know you're crazy about me," he cajoled, and gave the older woman a kiss on the cheek before she could dodge him. "Why, if it wasn't for Leah, you would have probably already seduced me by now.''

Sandy gave him a droll look. "Be glad I haven't. You never would've lived through it. I'm too much woman for you, boy-o.''

Mike threw back his head and laughed. "Now, that I don't doubt for a minute.''

Sandy folded her arms and tipped her head to one side. "You're mighty chipper today. Is there anything Mary Ann and I should know? Anything you want to tell us?''

"Like what?'' He raised his eyebrows and gave the women an innocent look.

"Like maybe you and Leah have gotten engaged. It'd be just like her to keep the news to herself.''

"Sandy, sweetheart, don't worry. When that happens you'll be the first one we tell. Scout's honor.'' He looked around. "Speaking of the lovely Dr. Albright, is she busy?''

"She's in her office, taking a nap. She was up until the wee hours trying to stop a premature labor. Came dragging in here this morning looking like forty miles of bad road. I had Mary Ann reschedule a couple of her appointments, got her to eat a bowl of soup, then threatened her life if she didn't grab a little shut-eye. But…'' Sandy glanced at the clock on the wall "—I'm afraid her next patient is due in about ten minutes. I need to wake her up, but you can do the honors if you want.''

"Thanks, Sandy. You're a sweetheart.'' He headed down the hallway, whistling under his breath.

"And no hanky-panky in there,'' she called after him.

Mike flashed her a grin over his shoulder and winked. "Spoilsport.''

When he eased open the door to Leah's office he found her asleep on the gray-and-rust print sofa. She lay curled on her side, her cheek cradled on her hand, one of Sandy's hand-crocheted afghans draped over her. One stockinged foot peeked out at the bottom.

Her hair had come loose from the clip at her nape, and a honey-colored strand curled across her cheek. Delicate blue veins in her eyelids were visible through the translucent skin, and fatigue had left smudges beneath her eyes.

Mike stopped beside the sofa and gazed down at her with what he knew was a sappy expression, but he couldn't help it. She was so damned beautiful, even exhausted, it made his heart clinch just to look at her.

Sweet heaven, how he loved her. And she loved him.

Still, he didn't kid himself. When she heard what he'd come to tell her, she was going to resist.

For some reason he couldn't quite pin down, from the beginning Leah had been reluctant to allow their relationship to progress along its natural course. She had fought him, subtly, every step of the way, resisting each new intimacy—not just sex, but anything that deepened the bond between them—and even though he knew she loved him, he doubted that had changed.

Mike's jaw set. Well, too bad, sweetheart. Reluctant or not, your fate is sealed. We turned a corner last night, you and I, and there's no going back.

He eased down beside her on the edge of the sofa, bracing one hand against the back. Leah stirred and sighed, but she didn't open her eyes. Smiling, Mike smoothed the lock of hair off her cheek and bent and kissed the corner of her mouth.

Leah made a purring sound in her sleep, and in a move so natural it took his breath away, she turned her head into the kiss.

He caressed hers lips with soft, intimate nibbles and rubs, exploring strokes of his tongue. Keeping his eyes open, he watched her reaction.

Her lips instinctively sought to deepen the kiss, but he

held back, and she moaned and shifted restlessly. Her breathing grew rapid. His hand cupped her throat, and his fingertips felt her pulse begin to pound.

Slowly, her eyelids fluttered, blinked, and he felt her smile.

"Darling," she murmured sleepily against his mouth, and looped her arms around his neck.

In that unguarded moment all her barriers were down, and she responded with a sweet ardor that revealed the depth of her feelings. At once, the tender caress became a kiss of soul-stirring passion.

They luxuriated in the lushness, going slow, savoring the richness and texture, losing themselves in the heat and intensity. Their lips rocked together with leisurely sensuality, drawing out the pleasure to an exquisite level. It was the taste of love, and they gloried in it.

Mike's heart hammered so hard it felt as though it would burst. Desire clawed at him.

Then suddenly, Sandy's warning about no hanky-panky whispered through what was left of his mind, and he recalled where they were. With an effort he pulled back and broke off the kiss.

Leah made a protesting sound and tried to pull him back, but he put his hand on her chest to restrain her.

"Easy, love. Easy." He tweaked her nose and smiled. "Sandy warned me about carrying on in a lascivious manner with her boss. If we're not careful, she's going to come marching in here with a shotgun."

Leah gave him a sultry look from beneath her eyelashes. "You're not afraid of Sandy, are you?"

"Damned right, I am. That woman is hell on wheels when she's got her dander up. So behave yourself."

"*Me?* I was just lying here sleeping, when you came in and started kissing me."

"Are you complaining?"

Her expression softened. She smiled and ran her fingers through his hair. ''Not one bit.''

''Good.''

''So, what are you doing here in the middle of the day?''

''I came by to see how you were and to find out how it went last night with your patient.''

''Hmm, it was touch-and-go for a while, but she seems to be stable now. And I'm fine, despite what Sandy may have told you.''

''I'm glad to hear that. You're going to need all your energy on Sunday.''

''What's happening Sunday?''

''That's the other thing I came to tell you. We're having dinner at my parents' house.''

''What!''

Mike saw the flash of panic in her eyes. She started to sit up, but he grasped her shoulders and pressed her back down.

''Mike, I ca—''

''Shh.'' He placed his hand over her mouth, cutting off whatever excuse she was about to make. ''No arguments, no excuses. We're going.'' Leah made a protesting move and a garbled sound against his palm, which earned her a stern look. ''I mean it, Leah. Look, I love you and you love me. The next logical step is to meet family. I've already told them we would be there, and they're all looking forward to meeting you, including the kids. Oh, and my uncle Reilly and my aunt Amanda will be there, too, to check you out.''

Her eyes widened at that, and he grinned. ''You might as well jump in with both feet. I come from a big family, and they're all going to want to get a look at you. But don't worry, they don't bite.''

He removed his hand from her mouth and gave her a

quick kiss. Before she could react, he stood up and headed for the door. With his hand on the doorknob, he stopped and sent her another commanding look. "And this time I'll pick you up. Maybe I'll even get to meet that elusive stepmother of yours."

Not if I can help it, Leah thought. Sitting up, she ran her hands through her tousled hair and stared after Mike, her heart booming like a kettledrum.

"Don't look so worried, sweetheart. My family's great. You're gonna love 'em."

That was precisely what worried her.

By Sunday, Leah was a wreck. Meeting Mike's family was daunting enough, but the idea of him coming face to face with Julia gave her nightmares.

She did not dare reveal to her father and stepmother that Mike was picking her up, or that they were spending the afternoon with his family. Even if he failed to recognize Julia, she was simply too unpredictable. It would be just like her to suddenly tell all, if for no other reason than to test Mike's reaction.

In addition, even though, for all the wrong reasons she approved of her seeing Mike, Leah knew her stepmother would have a walleyed fit if she knew she was planning to spend the day with the McCall family.

For two days Leah fretted over how she would get Julia and her father out of the house before Mike arrived, only to learn on Sunday morning that they had a lunch and golf date with friends at the country club that day.

Mike seemed disappointed, but that soon faded once they arrived at his parents' place in northwest Houston.

The moment she entered the McCalls' spacious Georgian-style home Leah knew she'd been right to worry. The McCalls were everything Mike had said: friendly, gracious, full of life and good humor, and though they teased one another unmercifully and the children often squabbled, there was a strong current of fierce familial love and loyalty running just beneath the surface that even a stranger like her could detect.

For years, Leah had listened to Julia's complaints about her first husband and his family. According to her, the McCalls and Blaines were cold, domineering, manipulative and selfish. Leah knew Julia well enough not to put much stock in that description, especially after discovering for herself how wrong her stepmother had been about Mike. Even so, the reality took her by surprise.

Far from being the unfeeling tyrants that her stepmother claimed them to be, Mike's family were, in fact, the epitome of what Leah had always thought a family should be, the kind of family she had always dreamed of having.

Everyone greeted her with warmth and openness, with the exception of Mike's father. Though not unfriendly, there was a certain constraint to Ryan McCall's greeting that let her know that, regardless of how his son felt about her, he was reserving judgment. Perhaps it was guilty conscience on her part, but she felt as though those blue eyes of his could see right into her soul. Leah had to resist the urge to squirm under his stare.

Though they had met only briefly at the hospital months before, Tess hugged Leah as if she were an old friend.

"It's so good to see you again, Dr. Albright. Mike tells us your brother is recovering well."

"Please, call me 'Leah.' And yes, Quinton is doing beautifully, thanks to your son. In fact, his doctors say he can come home soon."

"Oh, that's wonderful news. I'm so happy for you both. I'm still amazed at what a stroke of luck it was that Mike turned out to be a match for him. It just proves that miracles do happen."

"Yes, I suppose so." Leah wondered what Tess's reaction would be if she knew the truth, that there had been nothing miraculous or lucky about the match, only deviousness and lies and manipulation.

She wasn't given a chance to dwell on the subject as Tess introduced her to her husband's twin brother and his wife, who, it turned out, had been Tess's best friend since they were toddlers.

Leah was a bundle of nerves, and meeting Amanda Sutherland McCall only increased her jitters. The local TV anchorwoman had been a fixture on the six o'clock news for fifteen years. Though in her midforties, she was one of the most strikingly beautiful women Leah had ever seen.

"Ms. Sutherland, it is such a pleasure to meet you," she began nervously.

"Please, sweetie, it's just plain Amanda. Ms. Sutherland exists only on television. At home I'm just another one of the McCall clan. Just ask my husband and kids."

"That's right," fourteen-year-old Trent and eleven-year-old Margaret Mary agreed in unison, flashing that infectious grin that all the McCalls seemed to share.

When Leah turned her attention to Reilly, her first thought was she'd never be able to tell Mike's father and his twin apart. Both men were tall and lean and ruggedly handsome, with identical vivid blue eyes, chiseled features and black hair that was going gray. It was like looking at two older versions of Mike, she realized with a pleasant sense of shock.

Reilly stepped forward and took Leah's hand in both of his. His twinkling gaze ran over her with obvious appreciation. "My, my, what a winner you are. Brains *and* beauty, all wrapped up in one tiny package. But then, the McCall men always could pick 'em. I tell you, though, if I were single, I swear I'd take you away from that nephew of mine.'' Shooting Mike a taunting grin, he lifted Leah's hand to his mouth and placed a courtly kiss on the back.

''Hey. None of that, now. Let go of my girl,'' Mike commanded, but he grinned at his uncle as he slipped his arm around Leah's waist.

''All right. Come along with you, you big Irish lug,'' Amanda ordered in a long-suffering voice, slipping her arm through her husband's. ''Honestly, Reilly, you are such a flirt. I can't take my eyes off you for a moment.''

''Ah, sugar, I was just jerking Mike's chain. You know you're my one and only love.''

''Idiot. Of course I know. And lucky for you that I do. If I thought for a minute that you'd so much as look at another woman I'd skin you alive.''

Reilly grinned and winked at Leah and Mike as his wife led him away. ''The woman's crazy about me.''

Amused, Leah watched the striking couple walk away. Never again would she confuse Mike's father and his twin. In looks the two might be identical, but Ryan McCall was serious and intense, almost brooding—a legacy from Julia, no doubt. Reilly, on the other hand, had a sunny, mischievous personality and didn't seem to take many things seriously.

''He's right, you know. She is crazy about him,'' Mike murmured in Leah's ear. ''And he's nuts about her, too. Uncle Reilly was a real ladies' man until he met Amanda, but one look at her and he fell hard. He still has an appreciation for feminine beauty, mind you, but Amanda is and always will be the only woman for him.''

''That's wonderful.'' Touched by the story, Leah looked up at Mike with a smile and found he was watching her in that same intense way that his father watched Tess, his gaze devouring, primitive, utterly possessive, as though he would absorb her into his soul if he could.

''That's usually the way it is with all the men in my family.''

His words, the look in his eyes, made her chest tighten painfully. Oh, Mike, my darling. What have I done?

Until that moment, she hadn't known it was possible to feel elation and pangs of conscience at the same time. When this thing between her and Mike had started she had not intended to hurt him. That such a thing was even possible had not occurred to her, given his reputation as a carefree bachelor. Now it seemed inevitable.

For his sake, she should tell him the truth. The longer she waited, the worse his heartbreak would be.

But how could she? Only two days before, when Dr. Sweeney had given her the good news that Quinton could go home soon, there had also been several conditions attached.

''Your brother's blood count looks good and his immune system seems to be functioning well, but we must remain cautious,'' Dr. Sweeney had explained. ''Remember, Quinton has been living in a sterile environment all these months. His immune system has not yet been put to the test, and we don't want to suddenly bombard it with everything that comes down the pike. Therefore, for the first couple of months he is to be exposed to no more than six people, including family and household staff, and they must wear surgical masks in his presence, as will Quinton,'' he had cautioned her with a stern ''I mean business'' look over the top of his glasses. ''After that, if all continues to go well, we will gradually allow more contact with others, until he is fully integrated into the world again. In all likelihood he should be able to resume a normal life by Thanksgiving.

''However, in the meantime, it is most important that he not undergo undue stress of any kind. As a doctor, you know how much a patient's mental attitude and emotional well-being have to do with recovery. I am counting on you, Dr. Albright, to see to it that Quinton remains happy and stress free.''

Leah chewed on her bottom lip, oblivious to the chatter all around her as she and Mike followed the other members of his family into the large den at the back of the house. Even if she somehow found the courage to do so, she couldn't possibly reveal the truth to Mike and Quinton now.

Tears threatened, but she blinked them back. What was she going to do? The deeper she got into this relationship, the more complicated and hopeless it became.

''Well, that was the last one for the day, thank heavens.''

''Mmm. It seems like every pregnant lady on the south side of Houston has been in here today.'' Leah arched her back and rolled her shoulders, then headed down the hallway toward her office. Sandy fell in step beside her.

''So, how did you like Dr. McCall's family? We've been so busy all day I haven't had a chance to ask until now.''

Leah glanced at her nurse. She knew that look; Sandy was so curious she was about to burst. ''I liked them just fine.''

''I see. Then you had a good visit?''

''Yes. It was nice.'' Which was the understatement of the decade. Despite nerves and guilty conscience and all the other things worrying her, she'd had a wonderful time. Mike's family had a way of putting you at ease and making you feel welcome that made you forget your troubles and relax.

Conversation over dinner had been lively and interesting, if a bit on the noisy side, nothing at all like the polite and proper dinners she shared with her father and Julia.

Mike's family had talked freely, and sometimes argued, about everything. And not just the adults. The children were allowed, even encouraged, to join in any discussion.

In her office, Leah shrugged out of her lab coat and hung it on the coatrack, a hint of a smile tugging at her mouth. Somehow she doubted that sixteen-year-old Molly, fourteen-year-old Trent and thirteen-year-old Ethan would appreciate being called children. But especially Molly. The girl was struggling so hard to appear grown-up.

All day the other children had vied for Leah's attention, but Molly had been disdainful of their childish behavior and told them so several times throughout the day. Nevertheless, when they took their seats at the dining-room table, the girl had elbowed her younger sister aside to get the seat beside Leah.

"Now, what's that smile about, I wonder." Sandy stood in the doorway, eyeing Leah with her arms crossed and one shoulder propped against the frame. "You wouldn't be keeping secrets from me, now would you?"

"Of course not. I was just remembering the conversation I had with Mike's little sister. She's sixteen and as pretty as a picture. I think she was suspicious of me at first. During dinner she gave me the third degree. Evidently, my answers satisfied her, because all of a sudden she started chattering away. I'm not kidding, that child talked nonstop throughout the whole meal."

"Mmm. Sounds like you won over the baby sister. That's a big hurdle. So what did she say?"

"What didn't she say is more like it. Let's see…she told me all about her boyfriend, Steven, and how Mike refuses to accept that she's old enough to date, how he's being a bear about the whole thing and totally impossible and rude to the boy, and how she's afraid that her brother is going to drive him away and would I please talk to him for her. All that, mind you, in one breath."

Leah rolled her eyes and made a face, and Sandy chuckled.

"What did you say?"

"I said I would. What else could I do with those soulful eyes looking at me so pleadingly?"

Leah's teenage years had been spent taking care of Quinton, which had left her with little time to socialize with other girls her age. The one-sided conversation with Molly had been her first exposure to "life-or-death" teenage angst, and by the end of the breathless recital, she had been so dazed and overwhelmed she hadn't had the heart to refuse.

"Anyway, now I have to talk to Mike about something that's none of my business, and he's probably going to tell me to butt out, so what good it will do, I have no idea."

"Actually, I think it's kind of sweet that Dr. McCall is so protective of his sister."

Privately, Leah agreed, though his attitude was undoubtedly old-fashioned and probably chauvinistic.

"If you think it's so sweet, then you speak to him."

"Oh, no. This is your party. So go to it, girl."

"I guess I don't have a choice. I promised I'd talk to him the first chance I got." She had meant to after they'd left his parents' home the night before, but they had stopped by Mike's place for a drink and a few moments alone together. Inevitably, the few moments had turned into two hours of lovemaking. At the first touch of Mike's lips on hers, all thought of Molly's problems had flown right out of Leah's head.

"I suppose I might as well get it over with." With a resigned sigh, Leah retrieved her purse from her desk and headed down the hall toward the front exit.

"Give my love to Dr. McCall." Sandy's laughter followed Leah out the door.

As she walked down the hospital corridor Leah silently rehearsed over and over what she would say to Mike. She was so preoccupied she was three steps inside Quinton's room before she noticed that Mike was not her brother's only visitor. But something in her brother's voice got her attention.

"Hi, Sis, look who's here," Quinton said in a rush.

Leah jerked to a halt. *"Julia!"*

Chapter Eleven

"Hello, darling." With a defiant smile, Julia rose from the chair beside Quinton's bed. In a move calculated to show off her size-six figure, she smoothed down the jacket of her suit and patted her close-cropped platinum hair. "I was just having a nice chat with your young man. Really, Leah, you should have brought Mike home long before now so that your father and I could get to know him. It was very naughty of you to keep him to yourself."

"I...I..."

Leah glanced at Mike, but she couldn't tell anything from his closed expression. Surely if Julia had told him the truth he would not be so calm.

Quinton chewed on his lower lip and sent Leah a worried look.

"How long have you been here, Julia?"

"For about an hour, but now I'm afraid that I really must run. Peter and I are having dinner with the Van Demeers tonight and I'll have to rush as it is to be ready on time.

"It was lovely talking to you, Mike. I do hope Peter and I will see you again before we leave town." She sent Leah a false smile and a look filled with defiance. "We won't be home until late, so I shall see you tomorrow, dear. Bye-bye, now."

Paralyzed with shock and fear, Leah stood motionless and stared as Julia sailed past her and out the door. She shot a quick look at Mike. "Excuse me a moment. I have to talk to Julia."

She caught up with her stepmother at the elevator and grabbed her arm, spinning her around. "Julia, have you gone completely *mad?* What do you think you were doing in there?"

"Leah, you're hurting me. Let go of my arm."

"Answer me, dammit. We agreed that you would stay away from Mike."

Julia shrugged. "I changed my mind."

"You changed your *mind?* That's all you have to say?"

"I got curious." Julia pouted. "It's perfectly natural for a mother to want to see her son, you know, especially after all these years. I wanted to see how Mike had turned out. That's all."

Leah wanted to scream at her that she'd had almost twenty-six years to find out how Mike had turned out, but she wisely held her tongue. "And what about your other son? I told you that Quinton can't be subjected to stress right now. How could you endanger him this way just to satisfy your curiosity?"

"Oh, for heaven's sake. I don't know why you're making such a big thing out of this. Mike didn't recognize me."

Relief almost buckled Leah's knees, but she didn't back down. "But what if he had?"

In answer, Julia lifted her chin a notch higher and looked away.

"What if his father hadn't destroyed all your pictures, and Mike had known what you look like? What then?"

Julia snapped her head around. "What makes you think he destroyed my pictures? Ryan would never do that. He was crazy about me." She sniffed. "He probably still is."

"Oh, for—" Leah raked both hands through her hair and clasped her head, pressing her palms hard against her temples. Talking to Julia was like trying to reason with a spoiled child. "Julia, that is not the issue here," she began again through clenched teeth. "The point is, you broke your word and endangered Quinton."

"Oh, pooh. There was no harm done. And I must say, I don't appreciate you criticizing me this way. I intend to speak to your father about this as soon as I get home." She frowned at her wristwatch and made an aggravated sound. "Oh, just look at the time. You've made me late. I really must run."

"But—"

Julia punched the Down button, and immediately the doors of a waiting elevator opened and she stepped inside. As the doors whispered shut she tapped her foot while checking her watch again, pointedly ignoring Leah.

Staring at the closed doors, Leah shook her head and sighed. How typical of her stepmother to create havoc for her own selfish reasons, then blithely walk away. After having met Mike's father, she was amazed that Ryan McCall had put up with Julia for five years. Leah couldn't imagine two people who were more polar opposites. Why her own father was so besotted with the woman, she would never understand.

Quinton was alone when Leah returned to his room. Whatever concerns he'd had over his mother and Mike meeting were apparently gone. He sat cross-legged in the middle of the bed, watching a baseball game, cheering on his favorite team with typical teenage enthusiasm.

"Where did Mike go?" Leah asked, darting a useless look around the room.

Without taking his eyes from the television screen, Quinton shrugged. "I dunno. Yes! Yes! Atta way!" he yelled, and pumped his arm as an Astros player hit a line drive past the Padres' third baseman and sent the runner on second streaking for home plate.

"Oh." Surprise zipped through Leah. Hard on its heels came uneasiness. They didn't have any particular plans for the evening, but it wasn't like Mike to just leave without a word to her. "Uh, did he say anything? I mean, did he give you a message for me or anything?"

Tensing, her brother leaned forward as another Astros batter walked up to the plate. "Okay, Jose, let's go. Let's go. Knock the cover off the ball this time."

"And here's the windup and the pitch," the announcer reported in a mellifluous singsong. "And it's strike one."

"What? Whaddaya mean, strike! Are you *blind?* That was high and outside, you jerk!"

"Quinton, did Mike leave a message for me?"

"Uh, oh, yeah. He said to tell you he forgot to do something and he'd be back in a little while."

"I see." The tenseness in her neck and shoulders eased another notch. She didn't trust Julia. Despite her stepmother's claim otherwise, when she'd realized that Mike had gone she had experienced a flash of fear that he'd recognized her after all, but apparently his departure had nothing to do with Julia. Leah sighed and rotated her fingertips against her temples. This whole fiasco was making her paranoid.

"So how did your mom and Mike—"

Quinton held up his hand to shush her, his gaze glued to the screen. "Just a minute, Sis."

Leah gritted her teeth and waited. The pitcher shook his head at the catcher twice, then nodded. He scratched, spit a stream of tobacco juice over his shoulder and let fly with a pitch. The batter caught a piece of the ball and popped a high foul.

For what seemed an eternity, Leah waited through a string of fouls and balls called by the umpire.

"Bottom of the ninth and tied at three all, ladies and gentlemen. Astros up, two out, one on and a three-two count. Here comes the windup and the pitch...."

The bat cracked against the ball, and Quinton came to his knees, shouting.

"And it's a high popped fly to centerfield... aaannnd...the rookie, Neely, has it to retire the side."

"Shoot!" Quinton sank back down on the mattress and struck his knee with his fist. "If Jose coulda hit one to the outfield and brought Manning in the game would be over. Now we're into extra innings."

"That's too bad. How did it go between your mother and Mike?"

As the Astros came out of their dugout and the Padres retired to theirs, Quinton plopped back against the pile of pillows with his hands clasped behind his head and grinned at his sister. "Hey, it went great. I guess we were worried for nothing. I think Mom really liked Mike. She was real friendly and asked him all kinds of questions an' everything. She didn't seem upset at all that I'd met my donor."

"Good. And how about Mike? How did he seem?"

"Fine, I guess. He got kinda quiet after a while and let Mom do all the talking. Which was just as well, 'cause he could hardly get a word in anyway. Mom was in a really good mood, and you know how she gets all excited and yakky when she's pleased about something."

"Mmm." Leah knew only too well. Julia could be charming and captivating when things were going her way. When they weren't, she reacted with vicious anger and spitefulness out of all proportion to the situation. Leah supposed she should be grateful that at least her stepmother had been in one of her better moods when she'd decided to pull this stunt. Leah only wished she knew what Julia had said to Mike.

While the ball game dragged on through three extra innings Leah fidgeted and checked her watch every few minutes. The Astros finally eked out another run to end the game just as Mike walked in the door. His gaze barely connected with hers, before it skittered away.

"Hey, man, you missed it," Quinton complained. "The Stros won four to three in extra innings. Man, was it exciting."

Exciting? To Leah the game had been about as exciting as watching paint dry on a wall. Normally, she enjoyed baseball, but she'd been rattled by the surprise encounter with Julia and too edgy to settle.

"Hey, sorry I missed it, buddy."

"Well, it's a doubleheader, so you can catch the second game."

Leah nearly groaned.

It quickly became apparent that she was not the only one having trouble settling. Instead of sprawling in one of the chairs as he usually did, throughout the first two innings of the second game Mike remained standing. His gaze followed the action on the screen, but he shifted from one foot to the other and jingled the change in his pocket. Quinton was so intent on the game he didn't notice, but Leah did.

"Look, tiger, would you mind if Leah and I took off?" he asked abruptly.

"You don't wanna see the game?" Quinton looked shocked, as though he couldn't conceive of such a thing.

"It's not that. I've got a lot on my mind tonight is all."

Mike flashed his rascally grin, but for the first time since she'd gotten to know him, the smile seemed forced. She frowned.

"Besides, if I don't feed your sister soon she's gonna get cranky. You know how it is when she misses a meal."

"Yeah, I guess you're right. You guys better go. I'll see you tomorrow." He turned his attention back to the game and was already shouting insults at the umpire before Leah and Mike left the room.

They walked to the parking lot in silence. Mike appeared withdrawn and something about his expression made Leah uneasy.

"You want to ride with me or follow in your car?" he asked when they reached her car.

"I'll take mine." She gave him a tentative smile. "Actually, you seem to have something on your mind. Maybe I should just go home."

"No!" he said quickly, then added softly, "no. Don't do that. I want you with me."

Sliding his hand beneath her hair, he cupped the back of her neck and pulled her close for a kiss. The simple action reassured her as words never could have. Sighing, she relaxed against him.

Though over almost before it had begun, the caress set Leah's pulse to racing and short-circuited her thought processes. When Mike raised his head he smiled at her muddled expression and urged her into her car. "Stick close, okay," he ordered, and gave the top of her car a thump with the flat of his hand when he shut the door.

During the ten-minute drive to Mike's home Leah almost convinced herself that she was imagining things, reading something into his silence simply because she'd had a scare and was on edge. However, when they entered the house his face still had that tight-jawed look and his silence continued. Worse, he seemed to be avoiding her eyes.

"Mike, what's wrong?"

"Nothing. What makes you think something is wrong?" He turned away and walked into the living room. He shed his coat and tie, tossed them onto the sofa and walked over to the French doors. Outside, the roses bobbed in the gentle breeze and soaked up the last rays of sunshine.

Leah entered the living room slowly, her gaze on his broad back. Mike was usually so upbeat. She'd never seen him like this—tense and brooding, as though he were simmering inside.

"Mike, I'm not an idiot. Something is obviously bothering you. Why won't you tell me what it is."

"I'm just worried about a patient is all."

"Is it?"

"Yes," he snapped, and immediately flinched at his sharp tone. Massaging the back of his neck, he looked up at the ceiling. "Damn. It's no use. I can't do this."

"Can't do what?" Leah's pulse began to pound in her temples like a kettledrum. Mike swung around, and his fierce expression made her throat go dry.

"I know why you didn't want me to meet your parents, Leah."

She felt the blood drain out of her face. Her heart seemed to drop all the way to her knees. "Y-you know?"

Tears filled her eyes until Mike was just a blurry image. Unconsciously, she held out her hands and took a step toward him. "Oh, Mike, I'm sorry. I'm so sorry. But I can expla—"

"Stop it!" he barked, and she jerked to a halt, trembling. ''Don't you dare apologize. You're not to blame. It's them.''

She blinked. ''Th-them?''

''How could they do this to their own son? To you?''

''I...I don't understand.''

''I'm talking about your parents. Your stepmother told me that she and your father are leaving for Greece in two days. *Two* days! She was all aflutter about it. Dammit, Quinton is going home next week. This is a huge victory for him, and they don't care enough to be there? What kind of people *are* they?''

Leah stared at him, her heart hammering. A welter of emotions careered inside her—surprise, relief, guilt. Hope. She swallowed around the constriction in her throat and took another step forward. ''They're different from most parents, Mike. They don't mean to hurt us. Truly, they don't. It's just that neither of them has strong parental feelings. It's just not part of their makeup. I know that's difficult for you to understand, coming from the family that you do.''

''It's damned well impossible. When your stepmother told me they were leaving, I was so furious I wanted to slap her. I don't remember ever being so furious with anyone or ever wanting to strike a woman before.

''Ever since she told me of their plans I've been trying to keep a rein on my anger. I didn't want to upset Quinton. Or you. That's why I left Quinton's room earlier—to cool off before I talked to you. But I can't shake off this anger. Dammit, how could they *do* this?''

''Mike, it's probably just as well. Neither one is good in the sickroom.'' Privately, Leah was glad that her father and Julia were leaving. Merely having them in her home for all these months had been a tremendous strain. Added to that, her relationship with Mike would be much easier without having to worry about Julia's interference.

''Oh, I see. So they go traipsing off to play and leave it to you to look after Quinton.''

''Well, I always have. And I am a doctor.''

''Don't.'' He closed the gap between them and pulled her into his arms. Burying his face in her hair, he held her tight. ''Don't make excuses for them. Dammit, you were little more than a child yourself when Quinton was born. You shouldn't have been saddled with that kind of responsibility at that age.''

''I didn't mind.'' She held him tight and rubbed her palms over his back in slow, soothing circles. Memories softened her eyes and brought a wistful smile to her mouth as she gazed over his shoulder. ''Actually, I loved it.''

''Knowing you, I'm sure you did, but that doesn't make it right. When I think about the kind of childhood the two of you had, how lonely and empty it must have been with no family around, no one to love you or support you when things went wrong, it tears my heart out.''

''Oh, Mike, don't upset yourself. Quinton and I had each other. And Cleo. We did all right. Really.''

''All right?'' He made a disparaging sound. ''You deserve a helluva lot more than just all right. From now on I'm going to see to it that you have it.'' He eased his hold and leaned back, tipping up her chin. His blue eyes were stormy with emotion, fierce with love. ''Neither you or Quinton is ever going to be alone again. I swear it.''

''Oh, Mike,'' she quavered. Tears welled in her eyes and her lips trembled. So much emotion swirled inside her she could barely breathe. Before she could say more he lowered his head and touched his lips to hers in a lingering kiss of such infinite gentleness and caring she thought her heart would surely burst.

When he raised his head he looked deep into her eyes for several seconds. Then he scooped her up in his arms and headed for the stairs.

Still holding her gaze, he climbed the steps slowly, purposefully. "You mean everything to me, sweetheart. Everything."

Leah gazed at his beloved face through tear-filled eyes, too touched to speak, too ridden with guilt and regret to do anything but cling to him.

In the bedroom Mike lowered her to her feet with the greatest care, as though she were a piece of fragile crystal. He cupped her shoulders and looked at her in the last golden glow of twilight seeping in through the windows, his eyes lingering over her every feature, as though imprinting her face and the moment in his memory.

His hands slid up her shoulders, the sides of her neck. His fingertips sifted through the hair behind her ears as his thumbs feathered along her jaw. "You're so beautiful," he whispered, and Leah trembled.

Slowly, his hands glided downward. He slid the jacket of her moss-green suit off her shoulders and arms and let it drop to the floor with a soft plop. The backs of his knuckles grazed her collarbone as his fingers released the top button on her bronze-colored silk blouse. "So very beautiful. All of you." One by one, his fingers worked open the remaining buttons. When he encountered the waistband of her skirt he pulled the slippery blouse free, worked open the one remaining button and spread open the edges.

Mike sucked in a sharp breath, and Leah's knees went weak as she watched his pupils expand.

He stared, mesmerized, so long she felt her nipples pucker and harden against the dark-green lace bra. In a move akin to reverence, he raised his hand and touched her through the diaphanous lace.

A low sound—part shock, part ecstasy—tumbled from Leah. Arching her spine, she turned her face up to the ceiling and closed her eyes, trembling. Speech was impossible. So was coherent thought or movement. All she could do was feel while her body quaked and heated and absorbed the delicious sensations.

Mike noted every nuance of emotion in her face, the rosy flush that spread over her skin; felt the tremors that racked her; heard the raggedness of her breathing. He felt his heart thunder in his chest, his loins tighten. Watching her react to his touch was the most erotic experience of his life. She was so responsive, so open and vulnerable, she took his breath away. He was touching her with only the tips of his fingers, but the fragile contact was like setting a match to tinder.

He turned his hand and trailed his knuckles over the creamy flesh that swelled over the top of her bra, and smiled when she shuddered and whispered his name. He bent, and his mouth replaced his fingers, stringing kisses along the same path. The sensuous rub of his open lips, the warmth of his breath, left a trail of fire on the delicate flesh. At the vee of her bra he paused, and when his tongue dipped into her cleavage she swayed and moaned and plunged her fingers into his hair. Whether she clutched his head for support or to bring him closer neither could say. Neither cared.

"Mike, please," she begged incoherently, moving her head from side to side. "Please."

"All right, love." He nibbled the side of her neck, along her shoulder, and reached around to her back to unhook her bra and draw the straps down her arms. The scrap of lace dropped to the floor with barely a sound. He straightened and gazed at her breasts, cupped them in his palms, ran his thumbs over the rosy nipples. Leah made an inarticulate sound and clutched his upper arms for support.

"Beautiful. You're so beautiful."

Mike ran his hands down her body, deftly unfastened

her skirt and let it slide downward and puddle around her ankles. Hooking his thumbs beneath her panty hose and panties, he knelt and stripped the garments down her body.

Leah held on to his shoulder for balance, and at his silent urging stood first on one leg, then the other, as he pulled the two garments over her ankles and feet and tossed them and the skirt aside. Grasping her hips for leverage, he started to rise, but instead he paused and strung a line of kisses from her knee to the apex of her thighs, then nuzzled the triangle of honey-colored curls there.

Her fingers dug into his shoulders. "Oh, Mike. Mike."

"I know, sweetheart. I know." With the tip of his tongue, he traced a wet line along the juncture of her thigh and her body. A violent shudder rippled through Leah, and as she cried out he pressed his face against her abdomen.

The slight scrape of his beard stubble on the tender skin, the brush of his hair against the undersides of her breasts, was a sweet torment that threatened to buckle her knees. She moaned and tugged at his shoulders. Obeying her silent plea, he surged to his feet and swept her up in his arms in one swift motion. His mouth closed over hers as he bent his knee into the mattress and laid her down on the bed as though she were the most precious treasure in the world.

Their lips parted slowly, and he looked deep into her eyes. "I love you."

Tears banked against her lower eyelids, and she touched his cheek with trembling fingers. "I love you, too, my darling. So much more than I can ever say."

Lifting up on his arms, Mike looked at her, his gaze drifting down her naked body. His nostrils flared and his breathing roughened. The pulse at the base of his throat throbbed erratically. With a featherlight touch, she placed her fingertip on the spot, and Mike sucked in his breath.

In a lightning-quick move, he rolled off the bed onto his feet and began to strip off his clothes, his gaze holding hers all the while. Leah gazed back, trembling. She felt self-conscious, but excited beyond words.

Fascinated, she watched him step out of his shoes and at the same time snatch open the buttons on his shirt and strip it off. The sight of his muscular shoulders and broad chest, with its shadowy triangle of dark hair, kicked her pulse rate up another notch. It made her feel almost wanton to watch him, but she could not have looked away if her life had depended on it. He was so utterly masculine, so beautiful, just looking at him made her weak.

Desire flushed his face; urgency gave it a steely hardness. In one motion he yanked his belt free of the loops and tossed it aside. It hit the carpet with a soft thud that seemed loud in the taut silence. He unfastened his trousers and shucked them, along with his underwear and socks, and for a few brief seconds he stood before her, magnificently naked and aroused.

Leah's heart did a roll in her chest, but she had no time to admire his beauty. In only seconds he once more bent his knee into the mattress, and she held out her arms to him.

The solidness of him, the feel of his warm flesh touching hers, was heaven. "Mike. Oh, my love," she murmured on a sigh.

After that, for a long time the only sounds in the room were the rustle of sheets, the gasps of labored breathing, the murmurs and moans and sighs of love. Passions were high; needs, desperate, demanding; and soon they were one, locked together in the ultimate embrace as old as time.

Driven by love and passion, they rocked to the timeless rhythm, striving for the heights. At last, their undulating bodies tensed. An instant later their cries of completion shattered the hush of the room.

They collapsed together, boneless and replete, their entwined bodies slick with sweat, painted golden by the last rays of the setting sun.

Chapter Twelve

Six days later, Quinton was released from the hospital.

That morning, Mike surprised Leah when he showed up unexpectedly at her front door.

"Mike. What are you doing here?"

"I'm taking you to the hospital to get Quinton, then I'm going to drive you both home and help get him settled in. I got Dr. Lawrence to cover for me, so I'm at your disposal all day."

The generous gesture touched Leah, but she felt guilty about taking Mike away from his practice.

"Darling, this is sweet of you, but it really isn't necessary. I'm sure I can manage."

"Ahhhh, spoken like a truly independent woman. Look, my sweet, I admire and respect that self-reliant spirit of yours, and I don't doubt for a minute that you can handle this on your own, but the simple truth is it will be easier if I help."

"Yes, but your practice—"

"Will survive without me for a day. It's no use arguing, Leah. I'm doing this."

He cupped her chin in his hand and gazed deep into her eyes, and a look of such tenderness came over his face that her heart gave a little bump.

"I told you I would always be there for you, sweetheart, and I meant it." He bent and placed a quick kiss on her lips. When he raised his head his old irrepressible grin was back. "Besides, I want to be in on the homecoming, too."

Love and gratitude swelled in Leah's chest, and as she gazed into those twinkling blue eyes she knew the battle was lost. How could she possibly refuse his offer after statements like that?

It turned out that the release took most of the day. Between the numerous tests that Dr. Sweeney and the other physicians associated with Quinton's case insisted upon and the unbelievable red tape involved in checking a patient out of the hospital, Leah's patience was tried to the limit. Without Mike there to calm her ruffled feathers she probably would have blown her top and ruined her reputation at St. Francis for being cool and unflappable.

Though Leah had been at her brother's bedside every day since the surgery, when at last the tests and paperwork were done and he emerged from the protective bubble, she burst into tears and snatched him into her arms.

At first Quinton returned her fierce hug, but as it did most males, the weeping made him uncomfortable, and after a moment he tried to pull away. However, even though he was eight inches taller and fifty pounds heavier than his sister, he could not pry her loose.

"Hey, Sis, take it easy, will ya? This is supposed to be a happy day."

The surgical mask he wore muffled his voice, but still

she heard the chagrin in his tone. Remotely, she experienced the same feeling, but she didn't care. After all these months, it felt so wonderful to touch him again.

Mike squeezed her shoulder. "C'mon now, sweetheart, buck up. I know those are happy tears, but you're embarrassing the kid. Besides, it's time to give someone else a chance."

The gentle teasing helped to calm her and served as a reminder that they were not alone. Dabbing at her wet eyes with the top edge of her gauze mask, Leah released Quinton and shot Dr. Sweeney and the attending nurse a sheepish look as Mike stepped forward.

"Quinton. Welcome back to the real world, buddy."

Her brother grasped Mike's outstretched hand and shook it vigorously. "Thanks, man. For everything."

"Hey, no problem."

The handshake ended, but still their hands remained clasped. For several seconds they simply looked at each other over the surgical masks that hid the lower halves of their faces. Then, overcome with emotion, they both surged forward, pulling each other into a bear hug, each pounding the other's back.

As Leah watched them, her chin wobbled and her precarious composure threatened to crack again.

At seventeen, Quinton, though gangly, was almost as tall as Mike's six foot one, but each favored his own father. In looks no family resemblance marked them as kin, yet the bond between the two was so obvious it amazed Leah that no one had guessed that they were half brothers.

They held tight to each other, and over Mike's shoulder Quinton's face scrunched up, his eyes squeezed shut against threatening tears.

"Hey, pal. Knock, knock."

Quinton sniffed a few times and gave a watery chuckle.

Stepping back from the embrace, he knuckled his eyes and tried to look suitably long-suffering. "Who's there?"

"Freddie."

"Freddie who?"

"Freddie or not, it's time to go."

"Aw, man." Quinton cuffed Mike's shoulder, but all the same, his grin widened.

Fresh tears trickled down Leah's face. If she wasn't already head over heels in love with Mike, she would have tumbled on the spot. The foolish joke struck exactly the right note to lighten the mood and spare her brother the supreme humiliation of losing his cool in public.

"Well, now, how do you feel, Quinton?"

His composure restored, Quinton turned to Dr. Sweeney. Through his gauze mask, Leah could see his lopsided smile.

"Great. A little wobbly, though."

"That's only to be expected, my boy. After all, you've been confined to bed and that small space surrounding it for months. But you'll get your land legs back before long. Don't worry."

Dr. Sweeney had already given both Leah and Quinton detailed instructions regarding medication, activity and visitors at least twice, but he went over them once more, just to be sure they understood. Finally, there was nothing left to cover and it really was time to go.

Quinton balked a bit about having to leave in a wheelchair, until Mike assured him it was hospital policy, no exceptions.

"Shoot, tiger, if all you'd been in here for was a hangnail, you'd still have to ride out in one of these contraptions. Anyway, you don't want to get me in trouble with Nurse Zankowski, do you?" As though concerned someone might overhear, Mike cast a quick look around, then leaned in close to Quinton and whispered, "Trust me, the woman's a first cousin to Attila the Hun. She'd skin me alive if I let you walk outta here."

That produced a chuckle and a reluctant, "Oh, all right. I'll ride in the stupid thing."

"Good."

While Quinton settled into the chair and the nurse stacked all his belongings on a cart, Mike pulled open the door and held it wide. His eyes twinkled with devilment.

"Knock, knock."

A groan went up from Dr. Sweeney and Leah. Quinton rolled his eyes, but he responded.

"Who's there?"

"Armageddon."

"Armageddon who?"

"Armageddon outta here. How about you?"

Rolling his eyes, Quinton looked over his shoulder at Leah. "Jeez, Sis, let's go before he comes up with another one."

Quinton's good nature had made him a favorite at the hospital in the long months he'd been there. With surgical masks in place, almost the entire staff of St. Francis lined the corridor to see him off as Leah wheeled him out, everyone waving and calling out well-wishes and cracking jokes. Quinton beamed.

A short while later, when Mike pulled his car into the driveway of Leah's home, Cleo stood on the front steps, a surgical mask covering the lower half of her face and her arms outstretched.

"Oh, my sweet boy, my baby," she sniffled, enfolding Quinton against her ample bosom the instant he stepped from the car. "Thank the Lord, you're home with us again."

"Thanks, Cleo," he murmured, returning her hug. "It's great to be back."

When the embrace ended, Quinton paused on the top

step and turned to survey the neighborhood, his gaze greedily taking in every inch of the tree-lined boulevard that ran in front of his sister's house, the stately old homes along it. Emotion shimmered in his eyes. "Man, is it ever great," he said again, almost to himself.

As she watched him, Leah's own emotions almost choked her. She could only imagine how he must feel, returning home after all this time and his brush with death.

For the next few months he would be confined to the house and would view the neighborhood only through the windows, so she didn't rush him.

As Quinton continued to drink in the old familiar sights Leah looked at Mike, and she knew by his expression that he, too, was reluctant to end the moment. It was Cleo, with her ever-practical nature, who broke the spell and started them moving again.

"Well, now, you must be tired. Let's get you inside," she said briskly, steering Quinton toward the door. "You're probably hungry, as well, from the look of you. Thin as a rail." Clucking, she shook her head. "It's only to be expected, I suppose, eating hospital food for all these months. Probably deadened your taste buds. I declare, how anyone gets well eating that swill is a mystery to me. But don't you worry, Quinton, love. We'll soon remedy that. I've laid in supplies to cook up all your favorites. You just tell Cleo what you want for dinner and I'll have it ready by the time your sister unpacks your things."

The boy's eyes lit up. "Can I have fried chicken, and mashed potatoes and gravy and biscuits?"

"Of course you can."

"I think I'm going to like your housekeeper," Mike whispered to Leah as they followed the pair inside. "She sounds just like my grandma McCall."

In anticipation of Quinton's return, Cleo had been cleaning and scrubbing for days. From ceiling to floor the old house shone like a new penny and smelled of soap and furniture polish, overlaid with the pungent odor of disinfectant. Leah doubted that even the heartiest germ could have survived the housekeeper's all-out assault.

"We've set a bed up in here for you," Cleo said as she hurried down the central hallway and opened the library door. "Since all the bedrooms except mine are upstairs, we thought this would be best until you've regained your full strength. You should be nice and comfy here, and if you need anything during the night I'll be able to hear you. As you can see, your sister and I wrestled that old armoire down from the attic to hold your clothes and other belongings."

Mike sent Leah an admonishing look. "You should have gotten me to do that."

"Sorry. I didn't think of it." Over the years, she had grown accustomed to doing everything herself. Besides, she knew it wouldn't be wise to get used to depending on Mike.

He sighed and shook his head. "There's that stubborn independence again."

Mike made several trips to the car to retrieve the various things that had accumulated in Quinton's room since the surgery.

"Well, that's the last of—"

"Shh." With one forefinger across her lips, Leah pointed to the bed with the other.

Coming to a halt, Mike looked in that direction and smiled. Quinton lay sprawled on top of the bedspread, out like a light, his lips slightly parted. He was snoring softly.

Mike tiptoed across the room and put the sacks of books and video games down on the desk. He winked at Leah and whispered, "Pooped out on you, did he?"

"I suggested that he take a nap before dinner, but he wouldn't hear of it," she whispered back as she slipped one of her brother's shirts on a hanger and put it in the armoire. "He swore he wasn't tired. He was just going to stretch out and talk to me while I unpacked his things. He fell asleep in the middle of a sentence."

"It's been a big day for him. All that excitement wore him out. It'll do him good to rest for a while. And I sure don't mind having a few minutes alone with my girl." Mike slipped his arms around Leah's waist, and when she darted a surprised look over her shoulder he pressed his lips to hers.

Even through two layers of gauze masks, the kiss was oddly sensual. The moist warmth of his breath seeped through the cloth and feathered over her skin, into her mouth, sending shivers down her spine and making her nipples contract and pucker into hard nubs. The tip of his tongue pushed against the gauze. Hers responded with a like action. The touch was shockingly erotic.

The kiss was a lingering, voluptuous caress; his arms around her, a solid comfort. As the familiar melting sensation overtook her she sighed and surrendered to it.

A tingle rippled through Leah all the way to her toes, and her heart tripped along at double time. Her mind floated free, and for those few moments she became a purely sensual creature, responding to the pleasure and thrumming emotion Mike's touch never failed to evoke.

When the kiss ended, she leaned back against his broad chest. Closing her eyes, Leah savored his warmth, his smell, the solidity of him, and felt her nerves settle, her body loosen. Until that moment she had not realized that the day had taken its toll on her, as well.

While she was delighted to have her brother home again, she realized suddenly that a part of her was terrified at the daunting responsibility. In the hospital there had been specialists and teams of nurses and the latest equipment and technology that medical science had to offer.

She was a doctor, it was true, but cancer treatment was not her field. Most of what she knew about leukemia she had learned since Quinton's diagnosis.

He had made excellent progress, but she knew that the proof of success lay with this last phase of his recovery. He had been cut loose. Without the protection of sterile isolation and constant monitoring, over the next few months his fragile, newly recovered immune system would be put to the test. The thought terrified her.

But in Mike's arms the nerves she hadn't known were strung so tight calmed and the taut muscles in her neck and shoulders relaxed.

Mike was the only person Leah had totally trusted since her mother's death, the only one with whom she felt secure enough to let down her guard. With Mike she didn't have to be the mature, reliable daughter or the cool, superefficient physician; she didn't have to shoulder all the load herself. Somehow, without her knowing quite how it had come about, he had become the tower of strength that she could lean on, the bedrock foundation of her life.

Leah opened her eyes and frowned, disturbed by the stray thought.

Straightening, she turned and gave Mike what she hoped was a playful smile and a push. "Here, here, that's enough of that. I don't need you distracting me right now. So go on, get out."

"Oh, so I distract you, do I?" He reached for her again, but she slapped his hands away.

"Now, cut that out. Mike, will you behave? I have work to do."

"I can help," he offered with a leering waggle of his eyebrows.

"Forget it. I know what kind of help you'd be. Just get out. Go bother Cleo in the kitchen."

"Throwing me at another woman, are you?"

"Yes. Now, go."

"Okay, okay. I'm going. But if Cleo and I elope it'll be your fault."

"I'll take that risk."

Leah pretended to fold one of Quinton's T-shirts, but when Mike turned to leave she watched him saunter out, adoration and sadness shimmering in her eyes.

In the hall, Mike pulled off his mask and followed his nose to the kitchen. He poked his head inside and smiled when he spotted Cleo at the stove. Cookies cooled on wire racks on the counter, and pots and skillets bubbled and popped on the stove, all sending off delicious aromas.

"Mmm, it sure smells good in here."

Cleo shot a startled look over her shoulder. She appeared flustered to find him in her kitchen. "Dr. McCall. Is there something I can do for you?"

Stepping into the room, Mike let the door swing shut behind him and strolled over to the counter beside her. "I thought I might talk you out of some coffee."

"Certainly. I'll get you a cup." She started to step around Mike, but he held up a hand.

"Don't trouble yourself. I can get it. Just point me in the right direction."

"Oh, but—" she began, but he had already opened the cabinet above the coffeemaker and pulled out a ceramic mug.

"Well, then…" Twisting her hands in her apron, Cleo stared at him as he picked up the carafe and poured the mug full.

Mike leaned his hips back against the counter and took a sip of coffee, watching her over the rim of the mug. He lifted his eyebrows. "What? Did I do something wrong? Was I not supposed to help myself?"

"Oh, no, you're more than welcome to. It's just that…well, none of Miss Leah's young men ever has."

"I see. And have there been many young men in Leah's life?" he probed shamelessly, and filched a cookie from one of the wire racks.

"Not at all. Since her engagement to that Lyle Ballinger ended she's hardly had a social life. I can count on the fingers of one hand the times she's dated since then. Until you came along, that is.

"Now, that Lyle, he wouldn't set foot in a kitchen, much less pour his own coffee." Giving a disgusted snort, Cleo went back to the stove and turned the frying chicken pieces.

"I take it you didn't care for the guy."

"Couldn't abide him. You ask me, Miss Leah never would've gotten engaged to him if it hadn't been for her father and his missus."

"What do you mean?" Mike plucked another cookie from the rack and bit off half.

"Just that they kept throwing him at her. And they discouraged all other young men from coming around. Mr. Ballinger's parents were rich and had the right pedigree. I reckon they thought that it was a perfect match. No matter that he was a spoiled, self-centered snob."

"What about Leah? She has a good head on her shoulders. Couldn't she see what he was?" he asked, and popped another cookie into his mouth.

"Oh, he had plenty of surface charm, mind you. And Miss Leah was lonely and starved for love. Has been ever since she lost her mother when she was just a girl. Also, she wanted to please her father. Deep down, though, I think she always knew that Lyle was a louse. And if you don't stop eating those cookies, young man, you're going to spoil your dinner."

"Nah, nothing spoils my appetite." The admonition pleased Mike enormously. He doubted if Cleo realized how much she had loosened up in the last few minutes.

Since Leah's parents had left and he'd been coming to the house regularly he'd been trying to get past the housekeeper's starchy exterior. Ever since he'd met her, she had treated him with cool wariness, as though she were reserving judgment about him.

"So, what made him break the engagement?"

"Humph. *He* didn't break the engagement. She did. Lyle made a fatal mistake. He insisted that Miss Leah choose between him and medicine."

"The guy was not only a jerk, he was stupid."

"That's right. You ask me, he wasn't good enough for her by half." She lifted the golden brown chicken pieces from the skillet and placed them on a platter lined with paper towels, then turned off the burner and faced him. "The question now is, are you?"

"Good enough for Leah? I doubt it. But I love her, Cleo."

She arched one gray eyebrow. "Do you?"

"More than life itself," Mike replied without hesitation. "And I give you my solemn promise, I'll never hurt her. I swear it."

Cleo studied him. Mike returned her unwavering gaze with his own. After an interminable time, the elderly housekeeper nodded.

When Leah entered the room a few minutes later, she was surprised to find Mike setting the kitchen table for three, while Cleo bustled around, putting the finishing touches on a tray for Quinton.

Of necessity, because they could not eat with masks on, Quinton would have to take his meals alone for now.

"Cleo is joining us for dinner. You don't mind if we eat in here instead of in the dining room, do you?" Mike asked easily as he laid out the utensils.

"Uh, no. No, of course not." Before her brother's illness and the arrival of her father and stepmother, Leah and Quinton had always eaten in the kitchen with Cleo. However, whenever anyone else was there, Cleo wouldn't hear of joining them. Leah was amazed that Mike had been able to persuade her.

When the housekeeper returned from delivering Quinton's tray and they were all seated, Mike took a bite of chicken and groaned in ecstasy. "Mmm, I think I'm in love. Cleo, say you'll marry me. Please."

"Humph. It would serve you right if I did."

"Just name the date."

"Oh, go on with you, you rascal."

Leah's mouth fell open. A pink blush covered Cleo's cheeks and she giggled like a schoolgirl.

Leah couldn't believe it. Her starchy, no-nonsense Cleo had fallen under Mike's spell, too. Was no woman safe from that lethal Irish charm?

The day set the pattern for the weeks that followed.

Leah had feared that perhaps Mike's visits with Quinton might become less frequent, now that he was no longer in the hospital, where it was easy to drop by. But she was wrong. Each evening after he made his rounds he dashed home to shower and change, then showed up at Leah's door.

Together, Mike and Quinton watched sports on television or played spirited, furiously competitive video games. Often, from other parts of the house, Leah could hear their muffled cheers and taunts.

Cleo fussed over Mike almost as much as she did over Quinton. She cooked his favorite meals and made him cookies and fudge and clucked and worried about him when he worked long hours. She treated him as though he were a permanent fixture in their lives, which caused Leah concern.

The elderly housekeeper did not give her affection easily or indiscriminately. That she had taken Mike so completely into her heart stirred mixed emotions in Leah. Because she loved Mike, she was glad that Cleo was also fond of him, but she couldn't help but worry about how the dear old lady would take it when he no longer came around.

Most evenings Leah and Mike dined at home, but once or twice a week they stole an evening for themselves, inevitably ending up at Mike's home. Their lovemaking continued to be passionate and deeply satisfying. Mike had brought intimacy and a contented feeling of belonging to Leah's life that she had never before experienced, and it was wonderful.

With her father and Julia gone, she no longer lived with the constant fear of imminent discovery, which allowed her to relax and enjoy each day as it came. Once Quinton was fully recovered she would have to confess everything to Mike, but until then she intended to make the most of their time together.

Things were so perfect between them that a faint hope had taken root in a corner of her heart and refused to let go. She tried to squash it, telling herself she was being foolish and setting herself up for even more hurt, but she couldn't help it. There was a chance—remote, it was true, but still a chance—that by the time she told him the truth their love for each other would be deep enough and strong enough to withstand anything, even her deception.

Day by day, Quinton grew stronger, and as summer slipped into autumn he began to chafe at the restrictions on his life.

"I feel fine—except for being bored to death. I don't see why I can't at least have more visitors."

"What's the matter, tiger? You getting tired of my company?" Mike chided.

Chagrined, Quinton turned a deep shade of red and

scuffed the toe of his sneaker against the carpet. "Aw, man. You know that's not what I meant."

"I know." Mike patted his shoulder. "Look, just be patient a little while longer. I'll see what I can do."

Two days later, Mike showed up at Leah's door with his sister, Molly. Surprise and a host of misgivings streaked through Leah when she saw the girl. She wasn't quick enough to hide her dismay from Mike, but he misread the cause.

"Don't worry, I got Dr. Sweeney's approval. And Molly has broken up with Steven," he added with so much relish Leah almost laughed, in spite of the situation. "I figured she and Quinton could console each other."

"I'm really looking forward to meeting your brother, Leah," the girl said earnestly.

Left with no choice, Leah handed out masks from the box on the hall table. When they were in place she led the way into the living room, where Quinton was sprawled on the sofa, staring glumly at the television.

"Mask up, tiger. You've got company."

At the sound of Mike's voice Quinton glanced up, then did a double take, jerked up his mask and sprang to his feet.

"This is my sister, Molly. She's been wanting to meet you, and since you said you wanted more company, I got Dr. Sweeney to add her to your visitor list."

Molly stepped forward with her hand extended. "Hi, Quinton. I've heard a lot about you from Mike. I'm so glad you're doing better. I wanted to tell you how much I admire you. You're so brave to go through what you did." A smile crinkled her eyes over the top of the mask. They were as big and brown and soft as a doe's.

"Thanks." Quinton shuffled his feet and turned red to his hairline.

Molly's warmth and sweet personality soon overcame

his shyness, however. Within minutes the two were seated together on the sofa, chatting away as though they'd known each other for years. Neither of them even noticed when Mike and Leah left the room.

Frowning, she glanced back at the teenagers as they stepped through the door.

"Hey, will you stop fretting? They'll get along just fine."

"That's what worries me."

"Don't be silly. I've told Quinton how I feel about Molly. He knows I'll break his neck if he steps out of line. The way I see it, he's the ideal male friend for her."

He sounded so pleased with himself it was almost comical. Leah glanced at his smug face and shook her head. Mike had obviously forgotten what it was like to be seventeen. She sighed. Just what she needed, a teenage romance to further complicate the situation.

"Cheer up," Mike murmured as he snagged her waist and drew her to him for a quick kiss. "They're going to be great friends. That's all."

To Leah's surprise, the prediction turned out to be correct. Quinton and Molly developed a close but purely platonic relationship, becoming pals and confidants.

They had similar tastes in music, movies and books. They also shared an appreciation for the ridiculous, although Molly pretended to gag whenever Quinton laughed at Mike's corny jokes.

Molly told Quinton all about her latest crush, and he spilled his frustration and disappointment about being unable to play football during his junior and senior high-school years. As a sophomore, his coach had been grooming him to take over the starting-quarterback slot, before leukemia had sidelined him.

At least three afternoons a week after school, Molly came to see Quinton. Though he had tried to keep up his schooling at home and while in the hospital, the virulence of his illness during the past year had taken its toll, and he was a full grade behind Molly. An honor student with her mother's gift for teaching, she volunteered to tutor him in several subjects to help him catch up.

The girl was like a tonic, and Quinton looked forward to her visits with more enthusiasm than he'd had for anything since his release from the hospital.

As autumn deepened, weekly Dr. Sweeney allowed more visitors. When the added exposure caused no setbacks, after a couple of weeks the surgical masks came off. In late October, Mike was allowed to take Quinton on a fishing trip at an isolated lake. By mid-November it was obvious that Dr. Sweeney's prediction of a full recovery by Thanksgiving would become reality, and the holiday was set for his "return to the real world."

Profound joy and relief filled Leah, along with a terrible dread. They had won the battle to save her brother's life, but the time when she would have to tell Mike the whole truth was fast approaching.

Molly and Mike were also overjoyed that Quinton's long confinement would soon be over.

"Just think, tiger, you'll be able to celebrate Thanksgiving like everyone else," Mike noted.

Quinton shrugged. "Shoot, that's no big deal around here. Mom and Dad never come home for the holiday and Cleo always spends it with her sister in Dallas. Leah usually covers for several other doctors so they can spend the day with their families. If there's no emergency, sometimes we go out to a restaurant, but that's it."

"What?"

"That's terrible!"

Both McCalls looked horrified.

"That settles it. You're both coming to Crockett with us for Thanksgiving," Mike declared.

Chapter Thirteen

"Really?" Quinton's face lit up like a neon sign. "Hey, that'll be great, man!"

"Oh, Mike, what a super idea," Molly squealed.

Panic filled Leah. "No. No, really, we couldn't."

"Don't waste your breath arguing, sweetheart," Mike said with a self-satisfied grin. "It's settled. Thanksgiving is a time for families. Since yours won't be here, we'll share ours with you. Won't we, Moll?"

"Yes! It'll be fun."

"I appreciate the offer—really, I do. But we couldn't impose."

"Ah, Sis, why'd you have to go and spoil it?" Quinton whined in that disgusted tone only a teenager can achieve.

"Quinton—"

"Look, it's no imposition."

"Mike's right. Grandma McCall and Aunt Dorothy will love it if you come. The whole family has heard about you from Dad and Tess and Uncle Reilly and everyone's dying to meet you. And don't worry about crowding us. There's plenty of room. Gran and Aunt Dorothy have turned their attics into dormitories, one for the boys and one for the girls. We have a blast. And between the two houses, there're plenty of bedrooms for the adults.''

Leah's answering smile was wan. That was going to be her next argument.

The thought of being inspected by Mike's large family put a knot in her stomach the size of a fist, but in the end she had no choice. Unable to come up with a valid reason to refuse, and faced with Quinton's pleading eyes and her own desire to spend the holiday with Mike before she had to confess what she'd done, she gave in.

Leah's nerves were wound as tight as an eight-day clock. She tried to hide her anxiety, but Mike knew her too well. He glanced at her as he drove around the old courthouse in the center of Crockett. On the surface she appeared serene, sitting with her fingers laced together looking around at the storefronts facing the square, but her knuckles were white and a pulse at the base of her throat throbbed in double time.

Mike wondered what was behind the attack of nerves. Surely meeting his family wasn't that traumatizing.

On the north side of town he turned off the highway onto the country lane that led to his grandparents' home. Out of the corner of his eye, he saw Leah stiffen and bite her lip.

''Hey, relax, sweetheart.'' Smiling encouragement, he reached over and squeezed her hands. They were icy. ''There's nothing to worry about. They're not going to bite you. They're nice people. Honest. You're going to love them.''

Leah glanced over her shoulder at Quinton in the back

seat, but he was immersed in a book and seemed oblivious to their conversation. A wan smile wavered on her lips when she looked back at Mike. "I'm sure that's true. But will they like me?"

"Is that what's bothering you?" He laughed and turned into the driveway leading to an ornate Victorian house set far off the road in a grove of trees. "Honey, take it from me, they're going to love you. Now, stop worrying."

Mike had barely brought his car to a stop when the front door of the rambling old house opened. Someone yelled, "Mike's here!" and almost instantly a horde of shouting children burst out onto the porch and came loping down the steps. By the time they climbed from the car, Mike's young relatives were swarming around him, all talking at once, demanding his attention.

Laughing, he hugged all the teenagers, kissing the girls and thumping the boys on their backs, and tossed the younger ones up in the air and twirled them around, which produced squeals of delight and earned him smacking kisses.

As he set the last child on her feet Mike noticed Leah and Quinton standing close together off to one side, observing the greetings. The identical wistful smiles on their faces wrung his heart.

His gaze dropped to their clasped hands, and his throat tightened. In that moment he realized that growing up as he had in a large, close-knit family, he had taken for granted the love and support that had always been a part of his life.

Leah and Quinton had only each other. Since Quinton's birth it had been the two of them against the world, and instinctively they clung together, drawing strength from each other. But the unconscious yearning in their eyes was so raw and poignant it was painful to see. Mike's chest felt as though it were being squeezed in a vise and he couldn't swallow around the lump in his throat.

"Here now, you kids, where're your manners?"

The shout broke the spell, and Mike looked around in time to see his grandparents, Maggie and Colin McCall, hurrying down the front steps.

"Mike has brought guests with him, and here you all are, behaving like a bunch of little heathens. Some impression you're giving of this family," the spry woman scolded as she bustled down the walkway. "Now, stand back and behave yourselves and let him introduce you properly."

Heeding the voice of authority, the youngsters began to step aside, but before Mike could do his part, his grandmother cleared a path through the children and approached him with her arms outstretched and a beaming smile on her face. "First, though, let me give my grandson a hug."

She didn't get a chance. The instant she came within reach, Mike scooped her up in a bear hug and swung her around.

Hoots and laughter erupted from the children. Maggie McCall squealed and slapped at Mike's shoulders.

"Michael Patrick McCall, you rascal! Put me down this instant!" she yelped, but the laughter in her voice robbed the command of any sting.

"You'd better do as she says, Mike," his grandfather advised with a chuckle. "Your grandma isn't as young as she used to be, you know."

"Okay, Granddad," Mike agreed, but he took his time about obeying. When he finally set her on her feet he gave her a kiss, then smiled into her eyes. "Hiya, gorgeous. Miss me?"

"Not a bit," she countered saucily, even as her face softened with love. Going up on tiptoe, she patted his cheek tenderly.

Then, in a blink, her demeanor changed. "And as for you, Colin McCall, I'll have you know I can outlast any of these youngsters and still have energy left to take you on, so watch it."

"Ah, Maggie, love, don't I know it," the elderly man replied with a twinkle in his eyes.

"As you've probably guessed by now, these are my grandparents, Maggie and Colin McCall," Mike drawled with a teasing grin for the elderly pair. Putting an arm around each of their shoulders, Mike drew Leah and Quinton close to him. "And this is Leah Albright and her brother, Quinton."

"My dears, we're so happy you both could join us," Maggie said sincerely, squeezing Leah's hands as she looked her over. "Oh, my, but you are a pretty thing. Reilly told us you were."

"That figures," Mike muttered. "Did he also tell you that she's a doctor and as smart as a whip?"

"Of course he did. But then, I would expect no less. The McCall and Blaine men have impeccable taste in women, after all."

"Amen to that," his grandfather said, stepping forward to take Leah's hand.

When his grandparents finished welcoming Leah and Quinton it was Mike's turn to introduce the children. The instant the last name left his mouth his young cousins would have whisked Quinton away had their grandmother not stopped them.

"You'll just have to wait a bit. Quinton and his sister have others to meet before you kids go dragging him off. Now, come along, my dear," she said, looping her arm through Leah's. "The family is anxious to meet Mike's sweetheart."

Leah cast a panicked look over her shoulder at Mike. He merely grinned and gave her a thumbs-up sign and sauntered along behind the two women, confident that his gregarious family's openness and warmth would quickly cure her jitters.

Bedlam. Mike's long-ago description of his family's gatherings came back to Leah the instant she walked through the front door.

The huge old house teemed with people and rang with the sounds of boisterous conversations and laughter, the happy squeals and giggles of children. Adding to the din, from somewhere upstairs, presumably the teenagers' attic dormitory, came the throbbing beat of rock music. The noise level was horrendous; nevertheless, there was a joyfulness about it that lifted the spirits.

A few of the people milling through the house Leah had already met—Mike's father and Tess; his brother, Ethan and youngest sister, Katy; and, of course, Molly. Reilly and Amanda were there, as well, along with their two offspring, but they made up only a small part of the crowd.

Mike stayed by Leah's side, but his grandmother took charge of the introductions. As she led them around from one group to another, Maggie laughed and exchanged quips with her kin, her eyes sparkling all the while. Though in her seventies, Mike's grandmother had a lively personality, a sharp mind and the Irish gift of gab. It was easy to see where Mike and his uncle Reilly got their devilish natures.

First, she introduced Leah and Quinton to her identical twin sister, Dorothy, and her brother-in-law, Joseph Blaine. Then she led them to the Blaines' offspring, their son, David; his wife, Abbey; and their twin daughters, Erin Delany and Elise Lawford, and their husbands, Max and Sam. Maggie's youngest son, Travis, was a charmer and a flirt like his elder brother, Reilly, but it was clear that he adored his wife, Rebecca.

When Maggie introduced her youngest child and only daughter, Meghan, and her famous husband, Leah was so bowled over she could barely talk. Rhys Morgan was edging toward fifty, but age had only intensified his stunning good looks, and his talent as one of the world's greatest singers was undisputable. Meeting him here, in such a homey setting, seemed almost surreal.

When, at last, they had been introduced to everyone the other teenagers swept Quinton away, and Maggie excused herself and disappeared into the kitchen.

"See. That wasn't so bad, was it?" Mike teased, giving Leah's waist a squeeze.

She darted him an ironic look. "No, not really. Except I feel as though I've been through a tornado. My mind is swirling. I'll never be able to keep all their names straight or remember which children belong to which set of parents."

A red-haired woman standing nearby heard the remark and laughed. "Some big family, huh? But don't worry about it. You'll sort us all out eventually." With a wry glance for Mike, she added, "From what I've heard, I expect you'll be around a good while."

Not in the least shy, the woman boldly looked her over from head to toe. In spite of her frazzled nerves, a smile twitched Leah's mouth. This was one of Mike's relatives she knew she would never confuse with anyone else. She could be none other than the irrepressible Erin Delany about whom Leah had heard so much.

As though satisfied with what she saw, Erin nodded. "Yes. I think you'll do just fine."

"Gee, what a relief to know she meets with your approval," Mike drawled.

Unfazed by his sarcasm, Erin smiled and patted his cheek. "The little ones have been waiting all morning for you to arrive and tell them those silly jokes of yours. Why don't you be a good boy and run along and entertain them while Leah and I get acquainted.''

''At least someone appreciates me.'' He winked at Leah and started backing away. ''See you later, sweetheart.''

Leah shot him a frantic glance, but he merely grinned and mouthed, ''Sorry, you're on your own,'' as he disappeared through the arched doorway.

''So tell me, how are your cooking skills?'' Erin asked, taking Leah's arm and nudging her toward the back of the house.

Leah shot her a panicked look. ''Uh, horrible. I'm afraid I can't cook at all.''

To her surprise, Erin laughed. ''Ah, another soul mate. I knew I was going to like you. With the exception of me and Amanda, the women in this family are so damned domestic it's disgusting.'' She gave Leah's arm a pat. ''We're going to get along just fine. But I warn you, Mom and Aunt Maggie insist that everyone, guests included, pitch in on holidays. The men haul in the tables and chairs and look after the kids while the women do the cooking.''

She laughed again at Leah's look of horror. ''Don't worry, Doc. They'll assign something foolproof like stuffing celery to us domestically challenged types.''

To Leah's surprise, despite her nerves and misgivings about being there at all, the day turned out to be the most deeply satisfying of her life.

The women worked together with an easiness that spoke of long practice, and Leah found the affection and camaraderie between them delightful. They treated her as though she were one of them, and soon she found herself joining in their banter and actually enjoying herself.

Leah filled relish trays with olives, pickles, deviled eggs and the celery that Erin stuffed. She chopped onions, peppers and pecans and took her turn at the sink, washing the seemingly endless supply of pots and pans and mixing bowls the other women used.

Between them, she, Erin and Amanda set the staggeringly long table. Travis and Rebecca also lived in Crockett, and Meghan and Rhys had built a huge house there, which they used when he wasn't on the road. The long dining tables from their homes, and from Dorothy Blaine's, plus another from her kitchen, were butted up against Maggie's, creating a table that stretched from one end of her enormous dining room, through the double sliding doors, all the way to the far end of the parlor. The five tablecloths it took to cover them didn't match, nor did the napkins or the china, silver or glassware—a circumstance that would have horrified Julia. No one in Mike's family cared one whit. There was a place for everyone at the table, and that was all that mattered.

In the Blaine-McCall clan the children were not relegated to a separate table in the kitchen but took their places with the adults. In all, there were forty-one place settings around the long, makeshift dining table, which groaned under the weight of the feast.

The meal was a noisy, confusing, joyous occasion. Everyone talked at once; bowls and platters were passed up and down the length of the table; glasses pinged and silverware clinked against china. Halfway through the meal, Meghan and Rhys's one-year-old twins started crying, which set off Travis and Rebecca's two-year-old toddler. The younger children giggled and tormented one another when their parents and grandparents weren't looking. The teenagers were full of boisterous energy and their own brand of silliness, though disdainful of their younger cousins' antics. All up and down the long table, the adults carried on shouted conversations while they feasted on the delicious meal.

It was chaos—and Leah loved it.

From the look on Quinton's face, she knew that he felt the same. He was having a ball hanging out with Mike's young cousins and experiencing a true family Thanksgiving for the first time in his life.

After the meal was eaten and the dishes were done and everyone was feeling pleasantly stuffed and lethargic the tumult finally subsided. The teenagers disappeared upstairs to their lair and the adults settled down in the parlor to watch football games. The younger children sprawled on the floor at their feet, some playing games, others drifting off to sleep.

Taking advantage of the lull, Mike snagged Leah's wrist before she could join the others and hauled her into the kitchen. The instant the door swung shut behind them he pulled her into his arms and buried his face in the cloud of hair that billowed about her shoulders and down her back. "Ahhh, alone at last."

"Mmm." Circling his waist with her arms, Leah nestled her cheek against his chest and closed her eyes, contented and happy and pleasantly tired. She couldn't remember ever enjoying a day as much.

Mike rested his chin against the top of her head and swayed slowly with her. Leah sighed and snuggled closer.

"Did you have a good time today?"

"Mmm. I had a wonderful time."

"So, does that mean you like my family?"

"Mmm. I love them. They're great."

"Good. I was hoping you'd say that. Because I'd like for you to become one of them—one of us."

In her drowsy state, it took a moment for his meaning to sink in, and even then she wasn't sure she'd heard him right. Pulling back within his embrace, Leah stared up at him, wide-eyed. "Wh-what?"

"Will you marry me, Leah?"

Her heart missed a beat, then took off again with a sickening lurch. She gaped at him, speechless.

"M-marry you?" she finally managed.

A frown creased between his eyebrows. "Surely that can't come as a surprise. You know that I love you. And you love me. Those kind of feelings usually lead to marriage."

"I know, but..."

"Is there a problem? You do want to marry me, don't you, Leah?"

The hurt in his voice stabbed at her heart, and momentarily, she forgot the awesome problem that lay between them. All that mattered was erasing that look from his face. "Oh, my darling, of course I do. I want that more than anything in the world."

Instantly, his eyes went from wary to heated. His slow smile beamed happiness. "I'll take that as a yes."

"Oh, but—"

Cutting off her protest with his mouth, he pulled her close and kissed her with all the passion and love that she had longed for most of her life.

It was a kiss of celebration, of triumph, of blatant possession. He was a man staking his claim, and Leah was powerless to resist him.

Neither heard the door swing open, nor the footsteps cross to the sink, the water gush from the faucet. "You two ought to get a room."

The sardonic remark hit Leah like a bucket of cold water, but when she would have sprung away Mike tightened his hold and grinned at the intruder over the top of her head. "Get lost, David."

His cousin shrugged. "Okay, suit yourself. But if Mom or Aunt Maggie finds you making out in the kitchen you'll catch hell." As calm as a judge, he retraced his steps and sauntered out.

"C'mon, let's go." Mike bent and gave Leah a quick kiss, then snagged her wrist again and tugged her after him, heading for the door.

"W-wait! Mike there's something I have to tell you."

"It can hold. Right now I want to tell the family our news."

"But it's important. No! Wait, Mike, you don't understand!" She tried to dig in her heels, and at the same time plucked at the fingers encircling her wrist, but neither worked.

"Hey, everybody, Leah and I have an announcement to make."

"Now, I wonder what that could be." Sam's dry comment brought chuckles from the others and they looked at Leah and Mike with knowing expressions.

"I've just asked Leah to marry me."

"Surprise, surprise."

"And not a minute too soon," David drawled. "I thought I was going to have to throw cold water on them a minute ago."

Leah felt her color deepen, but before either she or Mike could respond, the front doorbell rang.

"I'll get it!" ten-year-old Bridget Morgan yelled, jumping to her feet and racing toward the door.

"Who in the world could that be?" Curious, Maggie went to the window and looked out. "Oh, my goodness. There's a big black limo in the driveway."

"What!" Her sister hurried over to get a look, too, just as Bridget returned with a small blond woman.

The instant Mike's father saw her, he shot to his feet. "Julia! What the hell are you doing here?"

Leah felt the blood drain from her face.

"Ryan! Where are your manners!" Tess gasped, but he paid no attention.

The older members of his family watched the woman

with wary dislike and uncharacteristic coldness, and for the first time that day, complete silence descended over the room. The only sounds were the distant throbbing of rock music and the chatter of young voices floating down from the attic.

Lifting her chin, Julia ignored the others and met her ex-husband's rage with defiance. "I've come for my son."

Ryan bristled like a junkyard dog. His eyes narrowed and his voice lowered and roughened to something near a growl. "Over my dead body. You've got one helluva nerve. He's not going anywhere with you."

Shock dropped Tess's jaw. "*Ryan!* What on earth has come over you? She has a perfect right to take her son if she wants."

"She has no rights where he's concerned. No rights at all. She forfeited those years ago."

Julia glanced at Mike. Before returning her attention to her ex-husband, she let her gaze flicker over Leah's white face. Even in that fleeting moment the look in her eyes promised retribution. "I'm not talking about Mike. I've come for Quinton."

Mike frowned at his father. "What's going on here? How do you know Mrs. Albright? And why would you think she'd come here to see me?"

"Mrs. Albright?" Ryan's fierce gaze shot from his son back to his ex-wife. "Quinton is *your* son?"

"That's right. And I've come to take him home."

As though the statement had conjured him up, Quinton and Molly and two of the McCall twins came clattering down the stairs. Quinton halted when he spotted his mother, surprise and delight widening his eyes.

"Mom! What're you doing here?" Without waiting for a reply, he surged forward and hugged her. Julia suffered the embrace for only a moment before extricating herself.

"Hello, darling. It's nice to see you, too." She straightened her coat and gave her hair a pat. "Now, go get your things. Your father is waiting in the car. We've come to take you home."

"But, Mo-om," he wailed. "I'm having a great time. Why do I have to go?"

"Don't argue, Quinton. You're coming home with me. You, too, Leah," she snapped. "Go upstairs at once and pack your bags. And hurry up about it. I want you both out of here and away from these people as soon as possible."

"Hey! Wait just a minute, lady," Mike challenged, stepping forward. "'These people,' as you put it, happen to be my family. I don't know what you're implying, but I don't like your tone. And Leah is a grown woman. She doesn't have to go anywhere with you."

Becoming suddenly aware of the tension in the room, Quinton looked from one adult to another, his expression wary. "Hey, is something wrong?" he asked, but no one answered him.

"How did you find us?" Leah finally managed to ask.

"I called home yesterday to wish you and Quinton a happy Thanksgiving, but no one answered. No one answered at Cleo's sister's, either, so I tracked down that rude nurse of yours. She told me you and Quinton were spending the holiday with Mike and his family. Your father and I caught the first plane home. We came straight here from the airport. As you can imagine, I'm exhausted and in no mood to argue, so please get your things."

"Don't listen to her, Leah," Mike urged.

Ryan stared at his son's angry face. Then his gaze narrowed on Leah's guilty one. She shivered under that cold stare.

"You haven't told him, have you? He doesn't know."

"Know what?" Mike demanded.

"That Mrs. Albright is your mother."

Like a bomb exploding, the statement seemed to suck all the air out of the room. Tess gasped, and Quinton looked as though he'd been poleaxed. No one else moved, not even Mike. As though turned to stone, he stared at Julia. The silence became so thick it was suffocating.

"You?" he said finally in a deathly quiet voice. "You're my mother?"

Julia lifted her chin another notch and tightened her mouth but didn't deign to answer the question.

"Mom, tell him it's not true. It can't be true."

The raw hurt and panic in Quinton's voice shredded Leah's heart like sharp talons. Julia slanted a look at her youngest son, her expression softening only slightly. "It's true."

"But th-that means that...that Mike is my brother. Why didn't you tell me? How could you keep something like that from me?"

"I had my reasons. I don't wish to discuss them."

He stared at her, his young face working with emotions. At his sides, his hands repeatedly fisted and unfisted.

Slowly, Mike turned and looked at Leah. "You knew, didn't you? You've known all along."

"Y-yes."

"Leah!"

The one word held a wealth of accusation and pain. There was so much anguish in Quinton's face Leah's eyes filled with tears. "Quinton, please. Let me explain. I couldn't tell you. I had promised Julia that I wouldn't. Please, sweetie, try to understand." She held out her hand to him and pleaded with her eyes, but he turned his head and refused to look at her.

"That was why you were so insistent I be tested as a possible bone marrow donor, wasn't it?"

Quinton whipped his head around. His shocked expression revealed that he hadn't thought of that. When he looked at Leah the condemnation in his eyes made her feel lower that scum.

"I asked that everyone at the hospital be tested."

"Nice try, but we both know that was just a smoke screen. It was me you were really after, wasn't it? Because you knew that there was a chance I'd be a match."

"We hoped you would be," she whispered.

"You must have been over the moon when the test results came back," he said with biting anger.

"Mike, you have to understand. You were our only hope. I had to save Quinton. I couldn't let him die."

"Why didn't you just tell me the truth and ask for my help?"

"W-we couldn't be sure you would help. Julia was afraid that you might refuse in order to get even with her for leaving you all those years ago."

"Dammit, you know me well enough to realize I wouldn't do that. I'd help anyone in that situation if I could."

"I understand that now. But at the time I didn't."

"You would have if you'd taken the time to get to know me."

"I didn't *have* the time, Mike. Quinton was critical. I had to act fast.

"So you manipulated and connived. You used me and lied to me. You even pretended to love me. What's the matter? Were you afraid 'our' brother might need a second transplant? So you decided to string me along for a while? Or were you just having a little fun at my expense?"

"No! No, you mustn't think that! It's not true. I wasn't pretending, Mike—I swear it. I do love you. I love you more than life itself. I was going to tell you the truth. You have to believe me."

"Sure you were."

"I was!" she cried. "It's just that…it was so hard to

do that, well, I kept finding reasons to wait. But I was trying to tell you a few minutes ago,'' she added in a rush when his mouth twisted with disbelief. ''When you asked me to marry you, I knew I couldn't put it off any longer. I had to explain before I gave you my answer.''

''He asked you to *marry* him?'' Julia exclaimed. ''Honestly, Leah, that really was bad of you to let things go that far. You know you were only seeing him to distract his attention from Quinton.''

Mike stiffened.

''No! No, that's not true! Don't listen to her, Mike!'' Leah pleaded, but she could see the ice in his eyes. She took a step toward him with her hands outstretched. ''Please, darling, you have to believe me. I do love you.''

''I think you'd better do as you were told and pack your things,'' he said in a voice as cold and unyielding as granite. ''I want you out of this house. Out of my sight. Out of my life. The sooner, the better.''

Each word struck like a knife stabbing her heart. Gazing at Mike's unforgiving face, Leah barely managed to hold back the cry that rose from the depth of her soul. She glanced around at his family but found no ally there. Most refused to meet her gaze, and the few who did looked at her as though she were vermin.

Tears filled her eyes, but she refused to let them fall. Mustering what was left of her wounded pride, her movements wooden, she forced her pain-racked body to move and walked from the room.

Mike watched her leave, his gaze fixed on her rigid spine, and refused to be swayed by her fragile dignity. She had deceived him. Used him. Dammit, his heart felt as though it had been cleaved with an ax.

''What about me? You want me to get out of your life, too?''

The quivering hurt and insecurity in Quinton's voice

cut through his pain. Mike sighed and shook his head. "No. No, of course not. But look, tiger, you're gonna have to give me a few days, okay? For now, you go on home with your sister. I'll be in touch soon. I promise."

"You most certainly will not," Julia snapped. "You stay away from Quinton. I don't want him to have anything to do with the McCalls, and that includes you."

"Just shut up!" Mike advanced on her and stabbed his forefinger in the air at the end of her nose. His expression was so fierce Julia gasped and took a step back. "This is between Quinton and me. What you want doesn't enter into it. You got that?"

Julia blinked and swallowed hard, speechless for the first time in her life.

Chapter Fourteen

"Why don't you give him a call?"

Leah looked up from the patient file she was reading to find Sandy standing in the doorway of her office. "What?"

"You heard me. Give Dr. McCall a ring. It's been three weeks. He's probably cooled down by now. Everyone knows he can't stay angry for long."

"Wanna bet? I passed him in the hall this morning. He looked right through me." Ignoring the stab of pain in the region of her heart, Leah resolutely returned her gaze to the file and made a notation in the margin of the top page.

"Well, you've got to do something. I can't stand to see you so unhappy."

"Really? I got the impression you thought I was getting what I deserved. You and Mary Ann have made it clear that you disapprove of what I did."

Leah abhorred being the subject of gossip, but there was

nothing she could do about it. Her breakup with Mike was the hot topic on the hospital grapevine. She was deeply ashamed of her part in deceiving him and prayed that the story would not leak out, and so far, it had not. Nevertheless, she had felt a moral obligation to reveal the truth to Sandy, Mary Ann and Cleo, the three people, other than Mike and Quinton, who meant the most to her.

All three women had been shocked and had made no secret of their disapproval. Cleo had been the most offended by her actions. For the past three weeks the elderly woman had gone about her duties with a stony face, barely speaking to Leah. It was no more than she deserved, Leah knew. Still, it hurt.

"Look, I may think you were wrong, but I understand why you did what you did, knowing how devoted you are to Quinton."

"Hmm. It's too bad he doesn't see it that way." Since their ignominious departure from Mike's grandparents' home, Quinton had barely been civil to her. These days, he didn't even speak to her if he could avoid doing so. He was so angry she supposed she should be grateful that he had chosen to remain in her home at all.

During that awful drive back to Houston three weeks earlier, Julia had ranted and raved and accused Leah of stabbing her in the back. "How could you do this to me, Leah? How? You know how I feel about those people. I've lost one son to them. I will not lose another."

Leah had remained quiet, but she knew all Julia's complaints were false. Privately, she was certain the reason Julia hated Mike's family was that in that large, boisterous group she had not constantly been the center of attention—a state of affairs her stepmother would have found intolerable.

Leah's heart had almost stopped when Julia had angrily announced her intention to take Quinton back with them to Europe, where she could be sure he would have no contact with Mike or any of the McCalls.

To everyone's surprise, most of all Julia's, Quinton had rebelled. He informed his parents that if they forced him to go with them, in two months' time, when he turned eighteen, he would return on his own and never speak to either of them again.

Julia and Peter had argued and pleaded—they'd even tried to bribe him with the promise of a sports car—but Quinton had refused to budge. Leah had been almost sick with relief.

Even now, merely remembering the scene gave Leah the shakes. She had lost the only man she had ever loved. She could not have borne it had she lost her brother, as well.

Sandy walked into her office and bent over Leah's desk, bracing her palms flat on the top. "Look, you can't go on this way. You go through each day by rote, you've got circles under your eyes and you've lost weight you couldn't afford to lose. In short, you look like hell."

"Thanks a lot."

"It's the truth, and you know it. For heaven's sake, Leah, you have to do someth—"

"Uh, excuse me."

Leah shot up out of her chair like an uncoiling spring. "Tess!"

Her reaction sent Sandy's eyebrows skyward, and she straightened and studied the woman curiously.

"I hope I'm not interrupting something important, but the young woman at the front desk was leaving just as I walked in. She said I should come on back."

"No, it's all right. We were just chatting. I don't believe you've met my nurse, Sandy Johnson. Sandy, this is Tess McCall. Dr. McCall's stepmother."

"Really?" Interest and speculation glittered in Sandy's

eyes. Leah could almost see the wheels turning in her head. "I'm pleased to meet you, ma'am. Dr. McCall is one of my favorite people."

"Thank you. His father and I are very proud of him."

"Well, look, I'll just get out of your way. I need to run anyhow. See you in the morning, Doc."

Sandy scooted out of the room, leaving an awkward silence behind. Neither Leah nor Tess spoke until they heard the outer door close.

"Won't you have a seat," Leah offered.

"Thank you. Leah, I hope this isn't too uncomfortable for you. Neither Ryan nor Mike know that I'm here. In fact, I'm sure they would both have a fit if they did, but I had to see you. I wonder if you would answer a question for me."

Leah sat back in her chair and picked up a pen from the desk. Rolling it between her thumb and forefinger, she eyed Tess warily. "That depends on the question."

"Is Mike right? Were you just using him? Or were you telling the truth when you said you loved him?"

"I was telling the truth. I love him with all my heart," she replied without hesitation. "I always will."

Tess sighed and closed her eyes. "I knew it. I just knew it. I watched the two of you together, saw the way you looked at each other. Those kind of feelings can't be faked. And I'm positive that Mike loves you, Leah. Otherwise, he wouldn't be so miserable. He hasn't smiled or told one of those foolish jokes he's so fond of in weeks."

"I'm sorry. I know this is all my fault. I wish there were something I could do to make it right, but I can't."

"Have you heard from Mike at all?"

"No, though I believe he has contacted Quinton and the two of them have gotten together. When and where, I couldn't say. At the moment, my brother isn't speaking to me."

"Oh, dear. I'm so sorry."

"Don't be. I have no one to blame but myself."

"You know, Leah, Mike is easygoing and good-natured, but he does have his father's pride. Perhaps if you made the first move and contacted him you two could work this out."

Leah met Tess's hopeful look and shook her head sadly. "I can't do that, Tess. Mike has every right to hate me. The truth is, I did set out to use him. Falling in love was never part of the plan. I won't lie to you. What I did was neither right nor ethical, but if I had it to do over again, given the same set of circumstances, I would probably do the same thing. My brother was dying. I would have done anything to save him. Anything."

Leah shrugged. "That being the case, how can I ask Mike to forgive me?"

"You went to see her? Behind my back? Dammit, Tess, how could you do that? I thought you were on my side."

"Oh, Mike, dearest, of course I am. I love you—you know that. But I can't stand to see you so unhappy. And Leah is as unhappy as you are. Whether or not you believe it, she does love you, Mike."

He snorted and sent her a derisive look. "Yeah, right."

"It's true."

Tess sat down on the sofa and watched Mike pace the length of his living room like a caged lion. His broad shoulders were tense and his jaw set. His anger and hurt were almost palpable, and her heart ached for him. For the first time in all the years that she'd known him, he reminded her of the wounded, bitter man his father had been when she had first met him.

"Mike, I'm not saying what Leah did was right. Even she admits that it wasn't. But she was desperate to save her brother. Your brother," Tess added softly, earning herself an angry glance from those icy blue eyes so like Ryan's. "Surely you can understand that."

"Dammit, she could have trusted me with the truth."

"She didn't know you then, darling. She was afraid to take the chance. In her place, would you have?"

He paced the length of the room one more time, then sank onto the sofa beside Tess, propped his forearms on his spread knees and stared at the carpet. "I don't know. I like to think so, but...hell, I'm not sure of anything anymore." He raked both hands through his hair. "Dammit, why, of all the women in the world, did I have to fall in love with Julia's stepdaughter?"

His use of his mother's first name did not escape Tess. She herself could not abide the woman. Still, she found it sad that Mike could not bring himself to refer to Julia Albright as his mother.

Tenderly, Tess rubbed her hand over his bowed back. If she had given birth to Mike, she couldn't love him any more than she did. It tore her apart to see him in such pain.

"No doubt Leah has the same lament. But, dearest, none of us has any control over whom we love. If we did do you think I would have chosen to fall in love with the bitter, hard man your father was seventeen years ago? Never in a million years. But I had no choice. None of us does. We have to follow our hearts, and where the heart leads isn't always the easiest of paths."

She smoothed the dark hair at his nape in silence for several minutes before asking gently, "Won't you at least talk to Leah and try to work this out? Love like the two of you share doesn't come along that often. It's a shame to let it slip away."

Tess felt his back muscles tense under her palm. He shook his head, his gaze still fixed on the carpet. "I can't.

I'd like to, but I keep coming back to the fact that she deliberately deceived me, and no matter what her excuse was, I can't forgive that.''

Leah stepped from the curtained cubicle in the ER, peeled the rubber gloves from her hands with a snap and tossed them into the bin for contaminated trash. Sighing, she arched her back and rotated her shoulders. Christmas Eve. A night for peace on earth and goodwill toward men. So far, in addition to the usual sprained ankles, sore throats and infants with ear infections, she'd treated an addict who had ODed on heroin, two stab wounds, a gunshot wound and eleven patients with cuts and contusions resulting from a brawl in a bar. And it wasn't even midnight yet.

She certainly hoped that Tony Barella, the intern who was supposed to be working the ER tonight, was enjoying himself at the party he was attending. Working the ER on any night was hectic, but on Christmas Eve it was the pits. Still, she had nothing better to do.

As always on this night, Cleo was curled up with an eggnog in front of the TV in her room, watching *It's a Wonderful Life,* and Quinton was out who knows where.

When she had approached him about doing something together to celebrate the holiday he had curtly informed her that he already had plans. So she had signed up to cover for any doctor who wanted the night off. Anything to pass the time and keep her mind occupied. It had been just her luck, though, that Tony Barella had been the first to see her name on the volunteer list.

Leah had just poured herself a cup of coffee and taken a sip when the double doors of the emergency entrance burst open and an ambulance paramedic crew raced in with a patient on a gurney. Following on their heels came three more crews pushing gurneys.

''We need a doctor, stat! Four injured, and we got one critical here!''

Instantly, Leah forgot her coffee, forgot Mike and her problems with Quinton, forgot the fact that her life was so empty she was voluntarily spending Christmas Eve in the ER.

''Nurse! Get me some help down here!'' she shouted over her shoulder as she hurried over to the incoming patients.

The first thing she noticed was they were all teenagers and all were dressed in formal evening wear. The two boys and one of the girls appeared pretty banged up. They were hooked to IVs and sported temporary bandages applied by the paramedics, but they were conscious and moaning. The other girl lay motionless. Blood from a cut on her head matted her auburn hair and covered her face, obliterating her features. What Leah could see of her skin was pale.

Trotting alongside the gurney, she helped the paramedics guide it into a treatment cubicle. ''What've we got?'' she asked, already examining the victim's obvious wounds.

''Auto accident. Two teenage couples on their way home from a party, broadsided by a drunk driver. The other three are hurt but they'll live. This one...I don't know, Doc. She's in a bad way. Broken pelvis, broken right leg, possible brain and internal injuries.''

Sleepy-eyed interns, rousted out of their cots by the nurses, began arriving. All around, the ER became a blur of frenzied activity as teams of doctors and nurses surrounded each patient. Orders were barked; questions were shouted at the semiconscious teenagers; blood pressures and pulse rates were hastily taken; clothes were cut away from wounds amid groans and cries; and monitors were hooked up. Competent nurses with stoic faces calmly carried out each command the doctors issued. To an outsider the scene could only appear chaotic, but the doctors and nurses worked together like a well-oiled team.

Leaving the less critically injured patients to the interns, Leah snapped on rubber gloves and began a hurried examination of the first girl. As a nurse began to clean the blood from the teenager's face, Leah bent over her and listened to her heart and lungs, examined the bloody bruise on her side and abdomen that was already turning a hideous black, checked her pulse and noted that it was reedy.

Straightening, she pulled a penlight from her surgical coat and moved to the head of the gurney to peel back the girl's eyelids. The nurse had cleaned most of the blood from the girl's face, and for the first time Leah got a good look at the victim. She froze.

"Oh, my Lord!"

"You know her, Dr. Albright?"

"What? Oh. Yes. Yes." She shook her head, clearing away the haze of shock, and snapped, "Somebody get X ray up here! And get her ready for surgery. Stat!"

She whirled away and hurried to the nurses' station. "Get a surgeon here. Find Dr. Ballard if you can."

"I can't call Dr. Ballard, Doctor. He's at a party at Mr. and Mrs. Dunkirk's. You know, the people who're donating the funds for the new wing."

"I don't care if he's having dinner with the president of the United States. Get him here! Now!"

"Yes, Doctor."

As the woman put in the call, Leah snatched up the phone on the counter and punched out Mike's home number. She fidgeted as the phone rang on the other end of the line. "Be there. Please be there," she muttered, glancing back at the curtained cubicle.

She let the phone ring ten times, but there was no answer. Leah slammed the receiver down and ran a hand through her hair. She considered calling his pager, but she couldn't stand by the telephone waiting for him to return the call; she had to get back to her patient. Playing a hunch, she snatched up the receiver again and punched his parents' number.

Ethan answered, but she didn't identify herself, afraid he might hang up on her. "I'm trying to locate Dr. McCall. Is he there, please?"

"Yeah, hang on," he said, then yelled, "yo, Mike! Call for you!"

It seemed to take forever, but finally Mike was on the line.

"Hello."

"Mike! Thank God."

Silence hummed in her ear. "Leah?"

"Yes, it's me. Mike, this isn't easy, but I have something to tell you."

"I don't think we have anything to say to each other."

"Mike, don't hang up! Please, listen. It's Molly. She's here at St. Francis. She's been in an auto accident."

"What!" She could feel his tension coiling. "How bad?"

"Bad."

"I'm on my way."

"Hurry, Mike."

"You keep her alive, Leah. You hear me? You keep her alive!"

"I'll do my best," she whispered.

Heart pounding with fear like nothing he'd ever known, Mike drove from his parents' home on Houston's northwest side to the medical center like a bat out of hell, pedal to the floor and horn blaring. Behind him in their minivan, his family and Quinton stayed on his bumper the whole way. The drive usually took close to an hour. Exactly thirty-two minutes after receiving Leah's call, Mike and the others burst through the double doors of the emergency room at a dead run.

The first person Mike saw was Leah. She was pacing in front of the entrance, waiting for them. The look on her face made his heart contract.

"Where is she?" he demanded.

Before she could answer, everyone started talking at once.

"I want to see my daughter," his father barked.

"Is she going to be all right?" Tess asked tearfully.

"Is she awake? Can we talk to her?"

"I wanna see my sister," Katy wailed.

"Sis, you have to save her," Quinton urged. "You have to."

Momentarily, Leah appeared surprised to see Quinton, but she wasted no time with questions. "Please, calm down, all of you. Please. Now, one at a time, and I'll do my best to answer your questions."

"Where is she?" Mike repeated.

"She's being prepped for surgery. Dr. Ballard is looking at her X rays now."

That brought a cry of distress from Tess, and immediately Ryan pulled her against his chest. The children turned pale and huddled around their parents. His eyes filling with tears, Quinton turned away sharply.

"What are her injuries?"

"You'll have to ask Dr. Ballard, Mike. He's making the evaluation."

Mike started to argue, when he spotted the surgeon, still dressed in a tuxedo, striding down the hall toward them.

Before Mike could say a word the older man held up his hand and stopped him. "There's not a minute to spare, so just listen, all of you. Molly is critical. I won't know until I go in the extent of her injuries or her chances. What

I do know at this point is, without surgery she won't last out the hour, so I need for the parents to sign a consent form at once.'' He looked at Leah. ''There's been another bad accident and all the other doctors are busy, so you'll have to assist me, Dr. Albright.''

''I'll assist,'' Mike declared aggressively.

''No, I'm afraid I can't allow that.'' Dr. Ballard was known equally for his skill and his brusque manner, but his eyes softened as he met Mike's frantic gaze.

''I have a right to be there, dammit. She's my sister.''

''Which is precisely why it would be a mistake. Anyway, you're a pediatrician, my boy, not a surgeon. Dr. Albright is a better choice.''

''Dr. Ballard, I'm not a surgeon, either. I'm an obstetrician,'' Leah protested, darting an uncomfortable glance at Mike and the other McCalls. She knew that she was the last person they wanted operating on Molly.

''I know that,'' he snapped. ''You do C-sections, don't you?''

''Yes. Of course.''

''Then you're a surgeon. Go scrub.''

The surgery took almost four hours. By the time they had finished, Leah was so weary she could barely stand. All she wanted was to fall into bed and sleep the clock around, but she had one more duty to perform. Though an excellent surgeon, Dr. Ballard was notoriously bad at dealing with worried family members in crisis situations, so he had left it to her to handle the post-op briefing of the McCall family.

Though it was almost dawn, everyone but Katy was awake. When Leah walked into the waiting room they all sprang to their feet. Their faces haggard and anxious, they stared at her in silence, their eyes full of questions they were too fearful to voice.

Leah pulled off her surgical cap and shook out her hair. "Molly's still in serious condition, but she's stable," she announced with a tired smile.

"Oh, thank God," Tess exclaimed, and burst into tears. Instantly, Ryan pulled her and Ethan tight against his chest. Over the tops of their heads, his intense blue eyes fixed on Leah. "When can we see her?"

"Not for a while yet. They're taking her to recovery now. After that, she'll go to the ICU. I suggest you all go home and get some rest, and come back this afternoon."

"What were the damages?" Mike asked.

"We had to remove her spleen and repair a ruptured kidney, and her pelvis and right leg are broken, so she'll be in a cast for a few months. Also, she suffered a concussion. Actually, she was lucky there. We were worried about her head injury, but there doesn't appear to be any permanent brain damage."

"So what are you saying, Doctor?" Ryan demanded.

"I'm saying that barring any unforeseen complications, she's going to recover."

With cries of relief and joy, Mike and his family— Quinton included—surged together and hugged one another tight. Tearful and happy, they kissed and hugged and kissed again, everyone talking at once.

Leah watched them with a lump in her throat and her vision blurring with tears. They were so caught up in their elation no one noticed when she turned and walked away.

Mike felt as though a ton of wet cement had been lifted off his heart. Gratitude swelled his chest to bursting as he released his family and swung around. "Leah, I can't thank you enough for—" He stopped, frowning. "Where's Leah?"

"She must have left." Tess pulled away from her husband's embrace and placed her hand on Mike's arm. "Go after her, Mike."

* * *

Dawn was breaking when Leah unlocked the back door and tiptoed into the kitchen. She looked around and smiled. Cleo might be angry with her, but as always when Leah worked late, she had left lights burning.

Leah turned off the dim light over the stove and stepped into the central hallway. She was heading for the stairs just as the front doorbell rang.

"Who in the world?" she muttered, and hurried to the door before whoever it was woke up Cleo. A look through the peephole made her lean her forehead against the door and groan. How could she have forgotten to bring Quinton home with her?

"Sorry, Sis. I forgot my key," he said sheepishly when she opened the door.

"That's all right. I hadn't gone to bed yet." Mike stood beside Quinton on the front porch, and she sent him a hesitant smile. "Thank you for driving him home."

"No problem."

"Man, am I pooped. I'm going to bed," Quinton announced. "'Night Mike."

"Good-night, tiger. See you tomorrow."

Quinton loped up the stairs, and an awkward silence descended. Leah shifted from one foot to the other, and waited for Mike to say goodbye and leave. Instead, he watched her, his gaze strangely intense.

"May I come in?"

"What?" Surprise shot through her, followed closely by dread. She wanted to refuse. She hadn't the energy or the desire to go another round with Mike right now. "I... Yes, of course."

She supposed it was inevitable that he'd want to rehash what had happened, once he'd calmed down. She led the way into the living room, determined to quietly hear him out, but when she reached the center of the room she turned abruptly. "Mike, why are you here? I'm really very tired and I would prefer not to go through all this again right now.''

He stopped a few feet away and stood with his hands in his trouser pockets, watching her. ''I came to thank you.''

Was that all? ''Oh, Mike, please. You don't have to—''

''And to tell you that I love you.''

She stared, certain she had heard him wrong. ''Wh-what?''

''I love you, Leah.''

Hope swelled inside her, but she refused to set it free. She gazed at him sadly and shook her head. ''Mike, don't do this. Your...your emotions are strung out right now and you're feeling gratitude because of Molly.''

''There is that. I'll always be grateful to you for everything you did tonight. But it's more than that. Actually, I've been thinking about this—about us—for several days, ever since Tess told me she'd paid you a visit. What happened tonight with Molly just helped to open my eyes.

''When I thought we might lose her I realized that, given the chance, I would do anything to save her, no matter who it hurt, no matter what I had to do. How could I blame you for feeling the same about Quinton?''

''Oh, Mike.'' Leah didn't trust herself to say more, and when her chin began to wobble she pressed her lips tightly together and gazed back at him through tear-filled eyes.

''Did you mean what you told Tess? Do you love me, Leah?''

Too choked to speak, she nodded as first one tear, then another, spilled over onto her cheeks.

It was all the answer Mike needed. In two long strides he crossed the distance between them and snatched her into his arms.

She clung to him, pressing her face against his chest. It felt so wonderful to be back in his arms. ''I'm sorry. I'm so sorry for tricking you. I wanted to tell you the truth from the start, but…''

''It's okay, sweetheart. I understand. Now.''

''But what I did was terrible.''

''Hey, don't be so hard on yourself,'' he murmured, rubbing a soothing hand over her back. He held her snug against him, his cheek resting against her crown, and she felt him smile.

''Knock, knock.''

Leah made a sound somewhere between a laugh and a sob. Nothing he could have said or done would have convinced her more thoroughly that he was sincere. ''Who's there?'' she mumbled against his chest.

''Hollis.''

She sniffed. ''Hollis who?''

''Hollis forgiven,'' he said in a deep, emotion-filled voice. He tightened his arms around her. ''Come back to me, sweetheart. I love you.''

She leaned back in his arms and looked into his beloved face. It was dark and intense, his blue eyes glittering with love. For her. ''Oh, Mike, I love you, too. So much it hurts.''

He kissed her then, a long, slow kiss from the heart. With lips and tongues and seeking hands they sought to assuage the hurt they had endured, to make up for the long, lonely weeks apart and to block from their memories how frightfully close they had come to losing each other.

The kiss was both carnal and heart-wrenchingly emotional. It was passion and need and raging desire. It was a pledge of love and trust restored, made stronger by trial of fire. It was a storm of hot, raw emotions. It was a solemn commitment for eternity and beyond.

Most of all, it was an exquisite blending of souls.

They were oblivious to the distant sounds of the outside world beginning to stir, to the early-morning light seeping through the windows, to the whisper and slap of house slippers on the hall floor or the discreet cough a moment later.

"Oh, for goodness' sake. Are you two going to come up for air and tell an old woman what's going on, or do I have to get out the garden hose?"

Leah jumped at the querulous comment and would have broken off the kiss, but Mike wouldn't let her. He continued to kiss her with leisurely thoroughness for several more seconds. When their lips finally parted he raised his head and grinned at Cleo over Leah's head.

"Hi, gorgeous. You miss me?"

"Have you been gone?" the old woman sassed back, and Mike's grin grew wider.

"Yeah. But I'm back now."

"Humph. It's about time." She eyed Leah's radiant face and nodded, then tightened the belt on her chenille robe. "I guess I'd better go start breakfast. All that making up is bound to have made you hungry. Lord knows, everything else does. The man's a walking appetite," she grumbled, heading toward the kitchen, slippers slapping against her heels.

Mike laughed and hugged Leah close. "I'm so happy I'm about to burst. Damn, it's good to have everything settled."

Leah snuggled her cheek against his chest. "Actually, we don't have everything completely settled yet."

Mike tensed. "What do you mean?"

"Knock, knock."

She felt his surprise and saw it in his eyes when he grasped her shoulders and held her away from him, but his expression remained guarded. "Who's there?" he asked warily.

"Willa Murray."

"Willa Murray who?"

"Willa Murray me, of course!" she replied, feigning indignation. "Who'd you think I meant?"

Stunned, Mike gaped at her. Then he threw his head back and laughed, a deep, rich sound of masculine delight that filled the room and sent a tingle down Leah's spine. He swooped her up in his arms and whirled her around.

"That's my girl!"

*   *   *   *   *

The titles in *The Blaines and the McCalls of Crockett, Texas* series form a poem:

FOOLS RUSH IN (SE #416)
WHERE ANGELS FEAR (SE #468)
but
ONCE IN A LIFETIME (SE #661)
A GOOD MAN WALKS IN (SE #722)
BUILDING DREAMS (SE #792)
to last
FOREVER (SE #854)
and
ALWAYS (SE #891)
when two people are
MEANT FOR EACH OTHER (SE #1221)

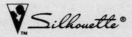

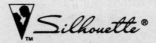

Don't miss these poignant stories coming to
THAT'S MY BABY!—*only from*
Silhouette Special Edition!

December 1998 THEIR CHILD
by Penny Richards (SE# 1213)
Drew McShane married Kim Campion to give her baby a name. Could their daughter unite them in love?

February 1999 BABY, OUR BABY!
by Patricia Thayer (SE# 1225)
Her baby girl would always remind Ali Pierce of her night of love with Jake Hawkins. Now he was back—and proposing marriage!

April 1999 A FATHER FOR HER BABY
by Celeste Hamilton (SE #1237)
When Jarrett McMullen located his long-lost runaway bride, could he convince the amnesiac, expectant mother-to-be he wanted her for always?

THAT'S MY BABY!
Sometimes bringing up baby can bring surprises...
and showers of love.

Available at your favorite retail outlet.

Silhouette Romance proudly presents an all-new, original series...

Six friends dream of marrying their bosses in this delightful new series

Come see how each month, office romances lead to happily-ever-after for six friends.

In January 1999—
THE BOSS AND THE BEAUTY by Donna Clayton

In February 1999—
THE NIGHT BEFORE BABY by Karen Rose Smith

In March 1999—
HUSBAND FROM 9 to 5 by Susan Meier

In April 1999—
THE EXECUTIVE'S BABY by Robin Wells

In May 1999—
THE MARRIAGE MERGER by Vivian Leiber

In June 1999—
I MARRIED THE BOSS by Laura Anthony

Only from

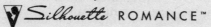

Available wherever Silhouette books are sold.

THE MacGREGORS ARE BACK!

#1 *New York Times* bestselling author

NORA ROBERTS

Presents...

THE MacGREGORS:
Alan—Grant
February 1999

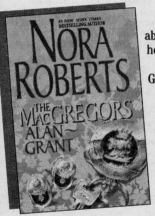

Will Senator Alan MacGregor be able to help Shelby Campbell conquer her fear of his high-profile life-style? And will Grant Campbell and Gennie Grandeau find that their love is too strong to keep them apart? Find out by reading the exciting and touching *The MacGregors: Alan—Grant* by Nora Roberts.

Coming soon in
Silhouette Special Edition:

March 1999: THE PERFECT NEIGHBOR (SE#1232)

Also, watch for the MacGregor stories where it all began in the next exciting 2-in-1 volume!

April 1999: THE MacGREGORS: Daniel—Ian

Available at your favorite retail outlet, only from

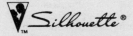

Silhouette®

SPECIAL EDITION™®

COMING NEXT MONTH

#1225 BABY, OUR BABY!—Patricia Thayer
That's My Baby!
When Jake Hawkins returned to town, he discovered that one unforgettable night of passion with Ali Pierce had made him a daddy. He'd never forgotten about shy, sweetly insecure Ali—or how she touched his heart. Now that they shared a child, he vowed to be there for his family—forever!

#1226 THE PRESIDENT'S DAUGHTER—Annette Broadrick
Formidable Special Agent Nick Logan was bound to protect the president's daughter, but he was on the verge of losing his steely self-control when Ashley Sullivan drove him to distraction with her feisty spirit and beguiling innocence. Dare he risk getting close to the one woman he couldn't have?

#1227 ANYTHING, ANY TIME, ANY PLACE—Lucy Gordon
Just as Kaye Devenham was about to wed another, Jack Masefield whisked her off to marry him instead, insisting he had a prior claim on her! A love-smitten Kaye dreamt that one day this mesmerizing man would ask her to be more than his strictly *convenient* bride....

#1228 THE MAJOR AND THE LIBRARIAN—Nikki Benjamin
When dashing pilot Sam Griffin came face-to-face with Emma Dalton again, he realized his aching, impossible desire for the lovely librarian was more powerful than ever. He couldn't resist her before—and he certainly couldn't deny her now. Were they destined to be together after all this time?

#1229 HOMETOWN GIRL—Robin Lee Hatcher
Way back when, Monica Fletcher thought it was right to let her baby's father go. But now she knew better. Her daughter deserved to know her daddy—and Monica longed for a second chance with her true love. Finally the time had come for this man, woman and child to build a home together!

#1230 UNEXPECTED FAMILY—Laurie Campbell
Meg McConnell's world changed forever when her husband, Joe, introduced her...to his nine-year-old son! Meg never imagined she'd be asked to mother another woman's child. But she loved Joe, and his little boy was slowly capturing her heart. Could this unexpected family live happily ever after?